The
HOTEL RIVIERA

Also by Elizabeth Adler

Private Desires
Peach
The Rich Shall Inherit
The Property of a Lady
Fortune is a Woman
Present of the Past
The Secret of the Villa Mimosa
The Heiress
Now or Never
All or Nothing
In a Heartbeat
The Last Time I Saw Paris
Summer in Tuscany

Writing as Ariana Scott
Indiscretions
Fleeting Images

The HOTEL RIVIERA

Elizabeth Adler

Hodder & Stoughton

First published in Great Britain in 2003 by Hodder and Stoughton
A division of Hodder Headline

1 3 5 7 9 10 8 6 4 2

A CIP catalogue record for this title is available from the British Library

ISBN 0 340 83034 4

Printed and bound in Great Britain by
Mackays of Chatham Ltd, Chatham, Kent

Hodder and Stoughton
A division of Hodder Headline
338 Euston Road
London NW1 3BH

For my sisters, Dorothy and Irene

ACKNOWLEDGMENTS

My thanks to those who matter in my life: first, my agent and friend, Anne Sibbald, and her cohorts at Janklow & Nesbit Associates, who look after me so well. To my editor, Jen Enderlin, who always has exactly the right comments to make—and in the nicest possible way! And to Richard, my husband, friend, and traveling companion, without whom none of this miracle of book-writing would have happened. Oh, and to Sunny, my new rescued cat-friend, who keeps me company on the long haul of writing.

The HOTEL RIVIERA

CHAPTER 1

Lola

IT WAS LATE SEPTEMBER WHEN I FIRST MET JACK FARRAR, ON one of those balmy, soft-breezed south-of-France evenings that hinted summer was finally over. And though I didn't yet know it, it was a meeting that would effect great changes in my life.

My name is Lola Laforêt—and yes, I know you're thinking I must be a stripper. Everybody thinks that. Actually, what I am is chef and *patronne* of the Hotel Riviera, and I used to be the much more normal Lola March from California before I married "the Frenchman." But that's a long story.

It's been six years since I welcomed my first guests to the Hotel Riviera, though "hotel" is far too grand a title for this old villa. It's a casual sand-between-the-toes, cool-tile-floors kind of place. There are just eight rooms, each with tall French windows opening onto a terrace spilling over with bougainvillea and night-scented jasmine. You'll find it on a spit of pine-covered land off the Ramatuelle road near Saint-Tropez, down a long sandy lane shaded with umbrella pines and alive with the chirruping of *cigales*. We have our own little private beach here with sand as pale as platinum and soft as sugar, and in summer it's dotted with marine-blue umbrellas and sunny-yellow loungers, and the golden-tan bodies of our guests. Small children run in and out of the lacy wavelets while grown-ups sip iced drinks in the shade. And in the heat of the afternoon they retreat to their shuttered rooms to nap, or to make love on a cool white bed.

Imagine a sunny sea-lapped cove, gift-wrapped in blue and tied with a bow like a Tiffany box, and you'll get the feel of my little hotel. It's a place made for Romance with a capital *R*. Except for me, its creator.

Somewhere in the process my own Romance withered on the vine. Somehow it was never my "Frenchman," Patrick, and I dining alone on the candlelit terrace with the moon throwing a silver path across the dark water, and champagne fizzing in tall glasses. It was never Patrick holding my hand across the table and gazing into my eyes. Oh no. I was always in the kitchen cooking delicious feasts for lovers who had the romance in their lives I so badly wanted, while my own "lover" took in the delights of summer in Saint-Tropez nightlife.

When I met and married Patrick six years ago, I thought I had found "true love." Now, I don't believe that such a thing exists. Yes, I admit I'm wounded, and I know I have always had a penchant for rogues, and that those straight-and-true guys, strong-jawed, steady, the good providers, are definitely not drawn to me. I seemed to attract riffraff like summer flies to a glass of wine.

Which brings me back to Jack Farrar again.

So, there I was, alone on the terrace, taking a breather

before the first dinner guests arrived. It was my favorite time of the year, the end of the long hot summer season when the crowds are gone and life drifts back into a more leisurely pace. The sky was still a flawless blue and the breeze soft against my bare arms, as I sipped a glass of chilled rosé, gazing blankly out over the pretty bay, brooding over my problems.

I'm a woman in limbo. And here's the reason why. Six months ago my husband, Patrick, climbed into his silver Porsche, en route, he said, to buy me a birthday gift. As usual, he'd forgotten my birthday, but I guess someone must have reminded him. He was wearing dark glasses and I couldn't read the expression in his eyes as he lifted his hand in a careless goodbye. He wasn't smiling, though, I do remember that.

I haven't heard a word from him since. Nobody has. And nobody seems to care, though I went *crazy* trying to find him. Of course, the police tried to trace him, his picture as a "missing person" was posted everywhere, and they followed clues leading as far as Marseilles and Las Vegas, without any luck. Now the case is on the back burner and Patrick is just another missing person. "Missing husband" is what they mean. It's not unknown around here, when the summer beaches are crowded with gorgeous girls and the yachts filled with rich women, for a husband to go missing.

You might have thought Patrick's friends would know, but they swore they didn't, and anyhow they were always Patrick's friends, not mine. In fact, I hardly knew the guys he hung out with, or the women. I was far too busy working at making our little hotel perfect. And Patrick had no family; he'd told me he was the last of the Laforêts who had lived and worked their fishing boats in Marseilles for decades.

Speaking of boats, I'm back to Jack Farrar again.

A small black sloop had drifted across my line of vision. Now I don't like *my* cove to be disturbed by vacationers partying all night, with disco music pounding across the water and shrieks and screams as they push each other into the water. I took a long hard look at the sloop. At least this wasn't one of those megayachts; in fact, I didn't believe they would allow such small fry into the Saint-Tropez marina, even if its owner could have afforded it, which, from the look of his shabby boat, I doubted. And which was probably why he'd chosen to anchor in *my* protected little cove with a free view of *my* pretty little hotel instead.

The black sloop cut across the horizon, sails slackening in the tiny breeze, then tacked into the cove where, as I had guessed, it dropped anchor.

I grabbed the telescope at the end of the terrace and got the boat in focus; the name *Bad Dog* was inscribed in brass letters on her bow. I moved over an inch and got a man in my sights. Muscular, broad in the shoulders, powerful chest tapering to narrow hips . . . *And oh my God, he was totally naked!*

I knew I shouldn't but okay, I admit it, I took a peek—actually a long look. What woman wouldn't? After all, he was just standing there, poised for a dive, almost flaunting his nakedness. And I want to tell you the view was *good.* I'm talking about his face of course, which was attractive in an odd sort of way. Actually, I thought he looked like his boat: tough, workmanlike, rather battered.

I watched the Naked Man make his dive, then cut cleanly out to sea in a powerful crawl until all I could make out was a faint froth in his wake. From the corner of my eye, I caught a movement on the sloop; a young woman, all long legs and long blond hair and wearing only a bright red thong, was stretched out on a towel in the stern, catching the final rays. Not that she needed them; like him she was perfectly toasted. Spread her with butter and jam, I thought enviously, and she'd be perfect for his breakfast.

The Naked Man was swimming back to the sloop and I got him in my sights again. And that, you might say, was my big mistake.

He climbed back onto the boat, shook himself like a wet dog in a cloud of rainbow-colored droplets, then flung out his arms and lifted his head to the sun. He stood for a moment, beautiful, hard-bodied, golden from the sun and the sea winds, a man at one with the elements. There was something so free about the gesture, it took my breath away.

I followed as he padded aft, saw him reach for something. A pair of binoculars. *And then he had me in his sights, caught in the act of peeking at him.*

For a long moment our eyes met, linked by powerful lenses. His were blue, darker than the sea, and I could swear there was laughter in them.

I jumped back, hot all over with embarrassment. His mocking laughter drifted across the water, then he gave me a jaunty wave and, still laughing, stepped into a pair of shorts and began unhurriedly to clean his deck.

So. That was my first meeting with Jack Farrar. The next one would prove even more interesting.

CHAPTER 2

I RETREATED INTO THE DINING ROOM IN BACK OF THE TERrace, and began hurriedly to check the tables, polishing a knife here, adjusting a glass there. I checked that the wines were cooling, checked that the linen napkins were properly folded, checked my long ginger hair in the mirror behind the bar, wishing I could call it copper or even red, but ginger it was. I wished one more time that I had exotic almond-shaped eyes instead of my too-round ones, wished I knew a recipe to get rid of freckles, that I was taller and leaner and maybe ten years younger. I was thirty-nine years old and after the events of the past six months, I decided gloomily, I looked every year of it.

I wasn't exactly into a glamorous mode either, in my baggy houndstooth chef's pants and shrunken white tee, with no lipstick and, even worse, no mascara on my ginger-cat lashes.

Horrified, I realized I was looking at exactly what the Naked Man had seen through the binoculars. I thought worriedly I really must make more effort but that anyhow he certainly wasn't interested in me; then I forgot about him and headed for my true domain.

The jewel-colored bead door curtain jangled behind me and I was in my favorite place in the whole world, my big tile-floored kitchen with ancient beams and a row of open windows overhung with blossoming vines.

I'd known the first day I saw it, this had to be *my* kitchen. It had stolen my chef's heart even more than the magical view from the terrace and the sandy winding paths, the shady pines and the wild overgrown gardens. More than the cool upstairs rooms with their tall windows and lopsided shutters, and the downstairs "salon" with its imposing limestone fireplace that was far too grand for such a humble seaside villa. More than any of that, this kitchen was *home*.

It was the place where I could put all thoughts of sophisticated city restaurants behind me and get back to my true foodie roots, back to the simple pleasures of local produce and seasonally grown fruits and vegetables. Here, I would grill fish that swam almost at the bottom of my garden and pick the herbs that grew almost wild to flavor my dishes. I knew I could relax and be myself in this place.

It all seemed so perfect. But first "true love" disappeared; then Patrick had disappeared, and now my only love left was my little hotel. Oh, and Scramble, whom I'll tell you about later.

My private life might be a mess, but all was well in my culinary world. Sauces simmered on the stove; fishes shone silver and bright-eyed in the glass-fronted refrigerated drawer; perfect little racks of Sisteron lamb awaited a hot oven, and individual *tians* of eggplant and tomatoes were drizzled with succulent olive oil from Nice, ready to be popped into the oven.

A fifteen-foot pine table stood under the windows. On it a couple of tartes Tatin cooled alongside a big blue bowl of sliced ripe peaches marinating in vermouth. Next to them were the spun-sugar cage confections, a remnant of my old "grand" restaurant days and with which I liked to top my desserts, because I enjoy the delighted oohs and aahs they evoke from my guests. Oh, and as always, a tray of my signature nut-topped brownies, my American specialty that I like to serve with the coffee.

You'll find no huge white plates centered with tiny "culinary arrangements" here. Our food is simple but lavish, our plates are locally made stoneware, the color of good honey, and we garnish them with only fresh flowers and a sprig of herbs.

I dropped a kiss on my assistant Nadine's cheek in passing. She's been with me since the beginning, all traumatic six years, and I love her to pieces. She's a local woman, dark-haired, dark-eyed, olive-skinned, with a raucous laugh and a sense of humor that's gotten us through many a kitchen disaster. Along with her sister, she takes care of the housekeeping as well as helping in the kitchen, while I deal with the food, the marketing, the menus, and the cooking; and Patrick supposedly took care of the business end, though from our meager bank account, I'm not sure how good a job he had been doing.

Petite dark-haired Marit, straight out of culinary school and a new recruit this season, was chopping vegetables, and Jean-Paul, the seventeen-year-old "youth-of-all-work" was busy cleaning up. The real season was over; it would be an easy night with just the remaining hotel guests and perhaps a couple of last-minute strays who might wander our way.

I slid a Barry White album, my current favorite sexy man, into the CD player, grabbed a brownie, pushed my way back through the jangling beads, and came across Scramble. Okay, so Scramble's not a dog, she's not a cat, or even a hamster. Scramble is a hen. I know it's crazy, but ever since she emerged from the shell, a soft fluffy yellow chicken cradled trustingly in the palm of my hand, I've adored her, and I'd like to believe she loves me too, though with a hen it's hard to tell. Anyhow, the fact is I'm the only woman who cried the whole way through *Chicken Run*. And though you might think it's a sad state of affairs, giving all my love to a hen instead of a husband, Scramble deserves it more. She's never unfaithful, she never even glances at anybody else, and she sleeps in *my* bed every night.

She's quite big now, soft and white with yellow legs, ruby crest and wattles, and beady dark eyes. She's scratching energetically in the big terra-cotta pot with the red hibiscus outside the kitchen door that she's claimed as home, preparing to settle down for the night, or at least until I go to bed when she'll join me on my pillow.

I gave her an affectionate little pat as I passed by, which she returned with a hearty peck. "Ungrateful bird," I said. "I remember when you were just an egg."

I cast a cautious glance at the black sloop as I walked back along the terrace. Lights twinkled and banners fluttered festively. I wondered what the Naked Man was up to, and whether he might row the boat's little dinghy into my cove and join us for dinner on the terrace.

I sighed. I wasn't betting on it.

CHAPTER 3

"THAT'S A PRETTY LITTLE SLOOP," MISS NIGHTINGALE CALLED. "Rather different for these waters, don't you think?"

"It is, and I hope they're not going to play loud music and interrupt your peaceful dinner," I said.

"Oh, I shouldn't think so, my dear, it doesn't look the right boat for that sort of thing. It's more of a proper sailor's boat, if you know what I mean."

I smiled at my favorite guest. Mollie Nightingale was a retired British schoolmarm, and by way of being my friend. Nothing had ever been said, but it was just there between us, that warm feeling, a kind of recognition I suppose you might call it. She had certain qualities I admired: integrity; an offbeat sense of humor; and a personal reticence that matched my own. Miss Nightingale kept her own counsel and I knew little about her private life; just the woman she was here at the Riviera. A woman I liked.

She had been my first guest, the week the Hotel Riviera opened for business, and she had been back every year since, coming late in the season when prices were lower and she could afford to stay for a month, before heading home to her cottage in the Cotswolds and her miniature Yorkie, Little Nell, and another long English winter. Meanwhile, she lived out her annual dream here, alone at a table for one, with a small carafe of local wine and book to hand, and always with a pleasant word and a smile for everyone.

Miss Nightingale was, I would guess, somewhere in her late seventies, short, square, and sturdy, and tonight she wore a pink flower-print dress. A white cardigan was thrown over her shoulders, though it was still warm out, and as always she had on her double row of pearls. Like the Queen of England, she always carried a large handbag, which, besides a clean linen handkerchief and her money, also contained her knitting. Now, I'm not sure if the Queen of England knits, but Miss Nightingale, with her determinedly gray hair set in stiff waves and curls, and her piercing blue eyes behind large pale spectacles, was a dead ringer for Her Majesty.

She was usually first down for dinner, showing up about this time for a glass of pastis, a little self-indulgence to which I knew she looked forward. She'd mix the anise liqueur with water in a tall glass then sip it slowly, making it last until dinner, which I also knew was the social highlight of her day.

I sat with her while she told me about her outing to the Villa Ephrussi, the old Rothschild house with its spectacular gardens up the coast near Cap-Ferrat. She always liked to tell me about the gardens she had discovered; she was a keen gardener herself and her own roses had won many local prizes. In fact, she was often to be found pottering about the gardens here, straw sunhat slammed firmly over her eyes, pulling up a naughty weed or two, or snipping back a recalcitrant branch of honeysuckle that threatened to overwhelm the already out-of-hand bougainvillea.

Settled at her usual table, the one at the end of the terrace nearest the kitchen, glass of pastis to hand, she gazed at the spectacular view and heaved a satisfied sigh.

It was that special time in the evening on the Côte d'Azur, when the sky seems to meld with the sea and all the world turns a shimmering silver-plated midnight-blue. In the sudden breathless silence that always comes when day turns into night, the chatter of high-pitched French voices floated from the kitchen, and a tiny lizard swished by, pausing to stare at us with jeweled yellow eyes.

"Divine," Miss Nightingale murmured. "How you must love it here, my dear. How could you ever bear to leave it?"

Without realizing it Miss Nightingale had struck right at the heart of my dilemma.

I do love it here. The trouble is I do not love my husband. All I feel for him right this minute is anger, because I believe that when Patrick left that morning he knew he was not coming back. He simply left me without a word, left me not knowing where he was, what had happened to him, or even if he were safe. If he'd run off with another woman, or decided just to wander the world the way he used to, at least he should have told me. And if he was in some kind of trouble, then he should have shared that with me too, and not just left me alone like this. Not knowing.

"The Hotel Riviera is my home," I said to Miss Nightingale. "It's my own little piece of paradise. I'll still be here when I'm an old, old lady, still looking after my guests, still cooking, still drinking rosé wine and not believing how blue the late evening sky can be just before night falls. Oh no,

Miss Nightingale, I'll never leave here, even if Patrick never . . ."

"If Patrick never comes back." She eyed me sympathetically from behind her large glasses. "My dear, do you think he's run off with another woman?"

I'd thought of that possibility so many times, lying in bed, tossing and turning, and I'd decided it was the only answer.

"Miss Nightingale," I said, genuinely lost, "what do I do now?"

"There's only one path for you to take, Lola, and that's to move on with your life."

"But how can I? Until I find out the truth?"

She patted my hand, gently, the way she might an upset schoolgirl. I almost expected her to say, "There, there . . . ," but instead she said, "The answer to that, my dear, is you must find Patrick."

I wanted to ask her how, where do I start? But my other guests were showing up for predinner drinks and a chat with the *patronne*, so I pulled myself together, dropped a kiss on her powder-scented cheek, and with a whispered "thanks for being so understanding," went to greet them.

CHAPTER 4

Miss Nightingale

MOLLIE NIGHTINGALE HAD FALLEN FOR THE HOTEL RIVIERA the first day she saw it. She'd fallen for its simplicity: "like a country house by the sea," she'd said, amazed by her luck. And she'd fallen for Lola, who always had a welcoming smile, even though she was so busy. Of course Patrick had never bothered to waste his charm on his guests, he'd saved that for other women, and in fact for the past couple of years, he'd hardly been around. And now he was gone. If it were not for Lola's obvious pain, Miss Nightingale would have said "good riddance to bad rubbish," but she hated to see Lola hurting like this.

She hadn't wanted to bring up the matter of Patrick's infidelity, because she knew if a woman chose to close her eyes to that sort of thing, there was nothing anyone could do about it. But now Patrick had gone missing, and she for one was not surprised. What she was surprised about, though, was that he'd simply left his hotel without making any claims on it. As husband and wife, Lola and Patrick must own the place together, which seemed unfair to Miss Nightingale, who believed that Lola had created the Hotel Riviera, as surely as she believed that God had created man.

Lola always treated her like a favorite aunt, well, great-aunt was more like it, she supposed, because though she hated to admit it, she was getting on in years. Seventy-eight was the exact number, though Lola was too polite to ask and Miss Nightingale was too vain to tell. And if you thought that meant she was old, then you didn't know that inside she still felt like a spring chicken. Her brain was still as sharp as it had been when she was headmistress of Queen Wilhelmina's Day School for Girls, in London.

She and Lola rarely exchanged much personal information, so today's confidences had come as a surprise. Usually, they just talked about the weather, a subject about which there could be no controversy, or about food and wine, or the places Miss Nightingale had discovered on her travels up and down the coast on her rented silver Vespa.

She had found many out-of-the-way places that even Lola had never visited, such as the tumbledown villa near Cap-Ferrat that had once been a hotel, owned by an exotic turn-of-the-century French singer and beauty by the name of Leonie Bhari. Now, Lola was nothing like the famed Leonie in looks, but with her "villa hotel" on the Côte d'Azur and her disastrous relationships with men, Miss Nightingale thought there were distinct similarities.

By now too, Miss Nightingale thought of the Hotel Riviera as her home away from home, though in fact she had started out as the "daughter of the manor" in the village of Blakelys, in the very heart of the English Cotswolds.

Times and circumstances had changed, and now she lived

alone in what had once been the head gardener's cottage in the village her family had once owned, with just her yappy Yorkie, Little Nell, for company on the long winter evenings, and her memories of her beloved husband, Tom, to make her smile, and her monthlong stay at the Hotel Riviera to look forward to at the end of summer.

It was enough, she thought, taking another sip of pastis, smiling as the other guests began to show up for dinner. Though it didn't exercise her brain very much, and she missed that the way she missed her Tom.

CHAPTER 5

Jack

JACK FARRAR, WITH ONLY HIS FAITHFUL DOG FOR COMPANY, was enjoying a drink on the deck of his sloop, his current crew member having taken off for a bout of shopping in Saint-Tropez.

Jack met a lot of women on his travels, like for instance Sugar, the blonde currently crewing his boat: good-looking girls ready for fun and with no demands because Jack certainly wasn't the marrying kind. And anyhow what woman in her right mind would want to spend a year in a boat circumnavigating the globe, battling storms and eating out of cans and having to wash her hair in salt water for weeks on end? None, so far as he knew. And certainly not one he could have spent that kind of time alone with.

In fact, the times spent alone on this little sloop with only his dog for company were quite simply the best. Nothing could compare with those quiet moments, with just the stars overhead and the wind tugging the sails. Just him and the dog, the ink-blue water, and solitude. They were the highlights of his life. As, in another sense, were the storms he battled on the longer voyages, steering the bigger sloop he owned, the *In a Minute,* through towering waves that threatened to capsize them while the wind tossed them around like dandelion fluff. His crew tackled the elements along with him while the mutt cowered in the tiny salon, whining and strapped to a flotation device, just in case. And Jack also strapped himself to the wheel, just in case. Then the adrenaline would shoot through his veins, powerful as hot rum, and his triumph when they overcame the elements was, he thought, the peak of a man's experience.

For Jack, there was nothing to touch that feeling, not even sex, though he was a sensual man. Or perhaps it was just that he hadn't allowed any women into his life to share that deeper, all-consuming emotion that happens when love is added to the sexual equation. He had yet to find a woman who could give him the ultimate sensation he got from battling the elements alone on the sloop.

He was a loner, a nomad, a roamer, at home in the fishing ports of the world. He loved that life and he wasn't about to give it up for any woman.

Of course, on the long-haul trips on the fifty-footer, Jack wasn't accompanied by any flighty women. Then his crew consisted of six men, one of whom was his good friend, the Mexican Carlos Ablantes.

He'd first made Carlos's acquaintance in Cabo San Lucas, a little town on the Baja Peninsula, where he'd gone fishing for marlin and dorado. It was November and the weather had turned rough, with water too cold for the big fish. But Carlos had been born and raised in Cabo and he knew his stuff. He was a true man of the sea, just the way Jack was. Carlos had taken him out on his boat; they'd spent a couple of nights out there together on the Sea of Cortez, reeling in only a lone dorado and getting to know one another, the way men do: few words spoke volumes; they knew who they were and that they liked each other.

Later, Carlos had come north for a spell, and he'd just stayed on. He worked at the boatyard, sailed with Jack on weekends, and crewed for him on his long trips, but every few months Carlos would return to Cabo, lured back like the marlin.

Carlos was pretty good in the galley too. He cooked up a mean shrimp dish, *fajitas de camarones,* and mixed the best margarita in the world, with Hornitos tequila, *limones,* ice, and salt. Soon he and the rest of the crew would be joining Jack, here in the Med, and they'd set off in the *In a Minute* on another of their long voyages, to South Africa this time, heading for Capetown where the surfing was good, the women beautiful, and the wine just fine.

Baja was where Jack had also met Luisa, the one woman he'd really loved. Lovely Luisa—hair like black satin, eyes like green jewels, and skin like bronze velvet. She'd loved him for all of three months, and he'd loved her about the same length of time. But passion can play havoc with a sailor's schedule if he lets it, and Jack wasn't about to do so. He was tough when it came to women. He valued his friendships and his sailing, in that order. Give him his boat, his friends, and his dog and he was a happy man.

Life was pretty good. He had made enough money to keep him in the style he enjoyed, plus a little extra. When he wasn't roaming the seas, he had a boatyard in Newport and that kept him pretty busy. He built racing yachts there, far sleeker and more expensive than his own. But this little old sloop was his favorite.

He thought about the woman who'd caught him naked in the telescope earlier tonight. There was something interesting about her. Something about the long untidy sweep of taffy-colored hair, the lift of her cheekbones, the soft, full mouth, and the stunned look in her big brown eyes when they had met his in the binoculars. He grinned, just thinking about her shock at being caught peeking at him naked, and the way she looked in her too-tight T-shirt and odd pants.

He also liked the look of the small pink hotel, perched above the rocks amid a bower of tamarind and silvery olives. Even without binoculars, he could see the luxurious purple-pink tumble of bougainvillea and the candlelight flickering on the dining terrace. Lamps lit in the rooms behind cast an inviting amber glow, and the crackle of the still-lively *cigales* floated across the water, along with some music. Could that really be *Barry White*? He grinned, thinking about the shocked taffy-haired woman. Maybe there was more to her than had met his eyes.

Either way, he was getting hungry and she was obviously running a restaurant. He might as well kill two birds with one stone, meet the woman and find out if she was as sexy as her mouth and the Barry White implied, and at the same time have a decent meal.

He didn't bother to change, just raked his hands through his disheveled brown hair, hitched up his baggy shorts, pulled on a white T-shirt and his old Tod's driving shoes, the most comfortable shoes he'd ever owned and with which he would never part, despite their age and shabbiness. The shaggy black dog he'd rescued from the pound and certain death some years ago pranced at his side, eager to go wherever Jack led him. He'd named the unruly mutt Bad Dog, because he had never learned how to behave in civilized company. And then, because he loved Bad Dog as much as his boat, he'd named the sloop after the mutt.

"Sorry, old buddy," he said, stooping to caress Bad Dog's head, "but the other diners wouldn't appreciate your finer qualities, especially when you attempt to steal the food from their plates." He grinned. Bad Dog was a street hound, a scavenger of the highest order. Fancy joints with candlelight and good wine were definitely not for him.

He put food into Bad Dog's bowl, made sure he had fresh water, gave him a new chew bone, then climbed into the dinghy, unhitched the line and started up the small outboard. Bad Dog hung his head over the side, gazing piteously down at him. He hated being left behind.

"Back soon, old buddy," Jack called, as he slid over the smooth dark blue water toward the tiny wooden jetty sticking out into the Hotel Riviera's cove. But what he was really thinking about was the look on Miss Taffy Hair's face when she saw him again. In the flesh.

CHAPTER 6

Lola

RED AND JERRY SHOUP WERE NEXT DOWN FOR DINNER. THE Showgirl and the Diplomat, I called them, though in fact they were nothing of the sort, they just looked the roles. She had flaming red hair that I envied, and legs that went on forever, and he was silver-haired, sun-bronzed, and charming. They live in a beautiful country house in the Dordogne and were here taking a month's intensive French course.

We greeted each other with kisses, and Red proclaimed she was brain-dead in French and was speaking only English tonight, even if it was against the school rules, and could they please have their usual Domaine Ott rosé before they passed out from sheer exhaustion.

I smiled and my spirits began to lift, as they always did when I was around my guests. Taking care of people, making them happy, was my chosen role in life.

Jean-Paul, my youth-of-all-work, appeared. He was pale as a lily because he never saw the sun, only the inside of the Saint-Tropez nightclubs, thin as a rail with a shaved head and six earrings. Wearing the Hotel Riviera white and gold tee, black pants and sneakers, he was pretending to be a waiter, bringing dishes of olives and tapenade, baskets of freshly baked breads, and crocks of pale sweet butter stamped with the image of a bewildered-looking cow.

I heard children's voices and the even higher-pitched English voice of young Camilla Lampson, whose nickname for some odd reason was Budgie.

Budgie was nanny to the two small boys who'd been sent to lodge here while their mother, an American actress, spent the summer in a smart villa in Cannes with her much younger boyfriend. Budgie, who's a terrible gossip, had told us indignantly that the actress believed having the boys around made her look older, but in fact they were cute normal kids, and in my opinion any woman who shut them out of her life needed her head examined. I watched them racing around the corner thinking I would give anything for a pair just like them, but acting sensibly for once, I decided not to allow myself to go there right now.

I said hello to the boys, made sure they were set up with Orangina, and commiserated with Budgie, who'd had to endure an entire afternoon of shopping in Monte Carlo with the movie star. I told Jean-Paul to bring her usual kir, a mix of white wine and *crème de cassis,* the delicious black currant liqueur made in the little town of Hyères, just along the coast—I thought she looked as though she needed it—then took everybody's orders and dashed back to the kitchen.

By the time I emerged again my last guests had arrived, my English honeymoon couple, both so young and fuzzily blond they reminded me endearingly of Scramble as a little yellow chick. They were so dopey with love for each other it was enough to make even my newly hardened heart melt. They were to leave the following morning and looked so despondent that I sent them glasses of champagne compliments of the house. From their beaming faces you might have thought I'd given them the keys to my kingdom, so I sent Jean-Paul back with the rest of the bottle in an ice bucket, making them even happier, if possible.

So, there we were, the entire cast of the Hotel Riviera: my eight guests and my staff, just like one happy little family. And then I heard the bell ring in the front hall.

Now if you were wondering, as I was, whether it was the Naked Man, aka Jack Farrar, coming for dinner—and to compliment me on my cooking while I complimented him on his body—you were wrong.

This was somebody quite different.

I wiped my hands on my apron and hurried to answer it.

CHAPTER 7

THE MAN STANDING BY THE OLD ROSEWOOD TABLE THAT served as a reception desk was short, wide, and aggressively jut-jawed, with pumped-up biceps and a marine-cropped haircut, though I knew instantly he was no marine. He was too sleek in his expensively casual clothes and flashy diamond-studded watch, plus he was wearing sunglasses even though he was indoors. He'd parked his motorcycle, an impressive scarlet and chrome Harley right outside the front door, and parked his expensive Louis Vuitton travel bag on my chintz sofa. Now he was pacing the hall and smoking a cigar.

He turned as I came in, smiling my hostess smile of welcome. His eyes flicked over me, taking me in from the top of my ginger head to the toes of my white kitchen clogs, then back again. "You the desk clerk?" he said.

I stiffened. "I am Madame Laforêt, the *patronne*."

He grunted an acknowledgment, flicking cigar ash onto the old but beautiful silk rug I'd bought at a Paris auction and which had cost more than I could afford and necessitated a loan from the bank. I pushed an ashtray across the table.

"Good evening," I said, remembering my manners and my smile, though he had neither. "How can I help you?"

He gave me a long look through his dark shades, bringing back a memory of Patrick driving away, and the sunglasses hiding his expression. I folded my arms defensively across my chest.

"I need a room," he said abruptly.

"Of course. How many nights?" I pretended to check my reservations book though I knew perfectly well we had two rooms free.

"Your best room. Three or four nights, maybe more. I'm not sure."

"Mistral has the best sea view, I'm sure you'll like it. All our rooms are named after famous French artistes and writers," I explained. Not that he cared. I told him the price, and saw the corner of his mouth curve contemptuously and I wondered why, since he obviously thought he was above the Hotel Riviera—he wasn't at the Carlton in Cannes, instead.

I asked for his passport—Dutch in the name of Jeb Falcon, and his credit card—Amex Platinum—then hooked the key to Mistral from the board behind me and said, "This way, Mr. Falcon, please."

Finally, he took off the sunglasses. He gave me another long inspection and I stared back, waiting. His eyes were a dull black in the lamplight and I decided I definitely didn't like him, nor did I like his cold expression. He glanced at his bag on the sofa, then back at me. My lips tightened; if he thought I was going to carry his bag then he was sadly mistaken.

I swear I could feel his eyes burning into my back as he followed me up the creaking wooden stairs, and I quickly showed him his room, handed him the key, and told him curtly that dinner was being served on the terrace, if he wished.

I thought of the sign that said: "Our Welcome Is Bigger Than Our Hotel." Never before had I failed to make a guest feel "welcome," but now I stalked back downstairs wishing this guest had gone somewhere else.

CHAPTER 8

Jack

THE DINGHY GLIDED ALONGSIDE THE RICKETY WOODEN jetty and Jack secured the line around the slab of tree trunk that served as a bollard. He climbed the steps over the rocks and wound his way up a meandering sandy path, passing a small pink house with an old-fashioned front porch. Through the windows he caught a sideways glimpse of an untidy sitting room with squashy sofas upholstered in the local fabrics, and, as he rounded the corner, a bedroom dominated by a massive four-poster, stunningly draped in gold lamé.

"Jesus," he muttered, wondering about the owner's taste, as he strode past the oleander hedge and up to the path that led to the front of the hotel. A red and chrome Harley parked outside took his eye, and he paused to admire it. He wondered if it was Miss Voyeur's, then thought, nah, anyone who was shocked by the sight of a naked man probably drove a sedate little Renault.

The front doors of the hotel stood invitingly open. He walked in and looked around. If the cottage belonged to the owner, and she was also responsible for the décor in here, then he forgave her for the gold lamé bed. *Comfortable* was the word that sprang to mind, and he was a man who appreciated comfort, on land though not at sea, where he never even thought about it. He could smell lavender and beeswax and flowers; jasmine perhaps, though he was not a man who knew much about flowers. And the aroma of something wonderful wafting from the direction of the kitchen.

Without bothering to ring the bell, he strolled through the pretty hall into the salon and through the French windows onto the terrace, where he stood, hands in the pockets of his shorts, looking around.

He thought this was exactly what the south of France on a summer night was about: the flowery terrace overlooking the bay and the strings of lights looped around the peninsula; the scent of flowers; the hum of conversation and a woman's laughter; the tinkle of ice in glasses and the pop of a cork as someone opened a bottle of the local pink wine. He decided this just might be perfection; it all depended on the taffy-haired woman. He was curious about her now, wondered what nationality she was, and whether she tended bar here, or if she was just the hostess. And here she came now, heading his way.

"Bonsoir, monsieur," Lola said, with a deep look from her long-lashed brown eyes that sent a tingle through his spine. She'd pulled back her hair in a ponytail, but the long soft bangs almost touched her lashes, framing her heart-shaped face like a Victorian cameo. Jack realized from her accent she was American, and taller than he'd thought: long legs in wedgie espadrilles that tied in little bows around her skinny ankles, tight white Capris, and a Hotel Riviera tee. No jewelry, save

for a gold wedding band. Hah! So she was married.

He realized she hadn't recognized him, and he grinned back, that lopsided kind of grin that had been known to knock a woman's socks off. But not this one; she was all hostess/business. "Good evening," he said.

"A table for two?" Lola asked, peering behind him, as though expecting to see a female companion, though he guessed from her up-and-down look at him she was hoping the woman might be wearing something other than shorts and a T-shirt and old shoes.

"I'm alone," he said, following her as she threaded her way through the tables and pulled back a chair for him. "Thanks," he said again.

She was looking at him now, really looking, and he saw, amused, that she was blushing. "Oh," she said, "Oh, my . . ."

"I think we've already met." He held out his hand. "I'm Jack Farrar, the guy from the sloop moored opposite the hotel."

"I know who you are," Lola said, stiff with embarrassment, "and I want you to know I didn't mean to spy on you. I was just curious to see who was mooring in my cove."

"Excuse me? *Your* cove? I thought the waters were free to everyone."

"Well, of course they are. But I always think of this as *my* cove, and I'm not fond of rowdy vacationers having wild parties on their boats and disturbing my guests."

"Okay, I promise I'm not going to be rowdy. Now, will you shake my hand and call a truce, and tell me who you are?"

Lola pulled herself together. She gave him her best hostess smile as well as her hand; after all, he was her dinner guest.

"I'm Lola Laforêt. Welcome to my little auberge. Now, can I get you a drink, some wine, perhaps? We have excellent local wines, and if you prefer rosé, I can recommend the Cuvée Paul Signac."

She stood, pencil poised over her notepad, looking haughtily down at him, thinking he was too full of himself and too smug about catching her peeking at him, and anyhow, he'd peeked right back, hadn't he?

"I'll take a bottle of the artist's wine," he said and caught her sharp glance. She probably hadn't thought a scruffy sailor like himself would know about Signac, a painter who'd frequented Saint-Tropez in its early incarnation as a small fishing port.

"A good choice," she said, all professionalism.

"You didn't give me any."

She glanced up. "Didn't give you any what?"

"Choice. You recommended only one wine and I took it."

She glared at him now. "In that case I'll send Jean-Paul over with the wine list and the menu. He'll take care of you." And with that she whisked away.

Well, you blew that one, Jack told himself. Or was it Miss Prickly Taffy Hair Brown Eyes who'd blown it? He thought about her eyes, how her long lashes swept onto her cheeks, the way Bambi's had in the Disney cartoon, and how very appealing that was. But boy, did she have attitude!

A thin French kid, pale as a bleached moth in black pants and a black Hotel Riviera tee, sporting half a dozen gold hoops in his ear, strolled over with the wine list, the menu, and a basket of rosemary-olive bread that smelled freshly made.

"You must be Jean-Paul," Jack said, friendly as always.

"Yes, monsieur, that is me," the French kid said. "Madame said I should take your order."

"I'll have a bottle of the Cuvée Paul Signac," Jack said, glancing down at the hand-lettered umber-colored card that was the menu.

"Right away, monsieur." Jean-Paul moved as though he had lead in his shoes and Jack wasn't betting on any fast service around here.

He glanced round at his fellow diners: a flamboyant couple; a pair of young lovebirds; a girl in charge of two well-behaved little boys; a spinster lady of "a certain age"—actually, probably a little older than that—who looked remarkably queenlike in her pearls and who flashed him a discreet ladylike smile of welcome; and another guy dining alone, like himself.

There were several empty tables on the terrace and a very empty small dining room in the back. He wondered if the food was bad, then thought it was not busy because it was the end of the season. The French *rentrée,* when the whole of France returned to work, had already taken place, kids were back in school, students were back in college, and tourists were back in their home countries. Few people were able, as he was, to wander the world at will.

Jean-Paul returned with the wine in a frosty silver bucket. It was remarkably good: cold, fruity, light. Madame Lola Laforêt had good taste in wine as well as décor. He glanced around approvingly. Everything here was in harmony, gentle and appealing. Except for the nervous-looking guy at the table next to him.

The man was downing a good red Domaine Tempier as

though it were Coca-Cola and looking as though he couldn't wait to leave. Jack thought there was something familiar about him. You didn't easily forget a face like his: that hard impassive look that allowed for no expression. Nor the way he bounced on his toes as he got up, fists clenched, biceps pumped, ready to take on anyone who crossed him; the flashy gold watch, the diamond pinky ring, the expensive loafers and designer sportswear. This was obviously a man-about-town in the south of France. So what the hell he was doing, dining at this little hostelry?

Trouble was, he couldn't place him. Was it at Les Caves du Roy, where Jack had been with Sugar one night? Actually, he'd escorted Sugar there and left her to her own devices after the first half hour, when he could no longer take the decibel level, and anyhow Sugar had found her own company. Or was it on the terrace of the Carlton in Cannes, where he'd been talking business with a man whose boat he was building and who loved boats as much as he did himself?

Ah, what the hell, the guy had probably just been part of the passing parade at the Café Sénéquier, where everybody in Saint-Tropez ended up at some time or other.

He took another long assessing glance as the man passed him on his way out. He didn't like the guy, that was for sure. A minute later he heard the familiar Harley roar and the sound of gravel spurting from tires. He might have guessed the Harley was his.

He turned his attention back to the menu, ordered lobster salad with ginger, and the rack of lamb with eggplant *tian* and sat back to enjoy the wine and the view, hoping for another glimpse of Madame Laforêt—the hostess-without-the-mostest and the eyes like Bambi.

CHAPTER 9

Lola

WHY HADN'T I RECOGNIZED HIM IMMEDIATELY? DAMMIT, I'd seen more of him than most people, but somehow he looked different with clothes on. Was I destined always to behave like a blushing teen, when here I was, a mature grown woman? And a *married* woman, at that, I reminded myself sternly, shaking the cast-iron pan over the heat, browning the rack of lamb before putting it in a hot oven for the prescribed amount of time it would take to cook to perfection.

That task accomplished, I sent the honeymooners a basket of brownies and fresh almond cookies to accompany their coffee, made sure Marit had the vegetable *tians* under control, checked that Red Shoup had her John Dory with red wine sauce, and that her husband had his bourride, the good fish soup that was almost a stew and which was always served with baguette croutons and rouille, a spicy mix of garlic, chili peppers, and mayonnaise. Heaven from the sea, I called it. Not like my sailor, whose attitude I thought had not been exactly heavenly.

I lurked in the kitchen, attending to my duties, reluctant to go back out there and face Jack Farrar again. Then I heard a squawk as Scramble pushed her way through the bead curtain over the kitchen door.

"Out!" I waved my arms at her. She was never allowed in the kitchen, or anywhere else in the hotel, only on the terrace and in the garden, and of course, in my cottage. She gave me the runaround for a few minutes, darting under the table, pecking at the floor, gleaning anything that might taste good to a chicken, which was pretty much everything, until I finally caught her and carried her outside.

I stood at the corner, looking at my contented guests, something that always made me feel good, as though through their satisfaction and happiness I could achieve my own. Miss Nightingale had finished dinner and was reading a book. The honeymooners were nibbling on my brownies and each other's lips. Budgie and the boys had already left, as had Mr. Falcon, whose Harley I'd heard roaring off a while ago. The Shoups were holding hands across the table, which meant they could eat with only one hand, but they seemed to like it that way. That's the effect my magical little terrace has on people. And Jack Farrar had finished his lobster salad and was sipping a glass of wine, gazing out over the water where his sloop rode the miniwaves, red and green mooring lights gleaming through the darkness.

He turned and caught me looking at him. I blushed again; he must have thought I was some crazy kind of voyeur. Pretending I had meant to catch his eye anyhow, I walked over and with my most polished hostess smile said, "Everything all right, Mr. Farrar?"

He folded his arms as he looked up at me. "Everything is

wonderful. And I think we know each other well enough that you could call me Jack."

"So . . . Jack," I said. "Your lamb will be here in just a couple of minutes."

"No problem, I'm enjoying myself. There's something very special about this place, Madame Laforêt."

"Lola."

"Lola. Of course."

"Well, thank you for the compliment. This *is* a special place and I'm glad you're enjoying it."

"The lobster salad was delicious."

I nodded, smiling.

"And the artist's wine you recommended . . . just perfect."

"I'm glad. Well, I'll check on your dinner. Excuse me, Jack."

"Just one more thing." I turned and met his eyes, denim-blue and narrowed into a smile. "Do you always carry a chicken around?"

I'd forgotten all about Scramble, who was giving Jack Farrar her beady-eyed sideways glare and who now began fluttering in my arms. "Not always," I said, as haughtily as I could with a struggling chicken in my arms.

I hurried back to the kitchen, depositing Scramble in the hibiscus pot en route, grabbed Jack Farrar's rack of lamb from the oven; managed to burn my fingers, and uttered a word I felt sure Miss Nightingale would not have been pleased to hear coming from my mouth. I plated the lamb, adding tiny fingerling potatoes, freshly chopped parsley, and a pool of a creamy herby green sauce that made my own mouth water. I wiped the edge of the plate with a cloth, added an orange nasturtium flower, put the plate on a tray with the sizzling vegetable *tian,* straight from the oven, and sent Jean-Paul out with it.

"*Bon appétit,* Jack Farrar," I murmured.

CHAPTER 10

IT WAS LATE WHEN I EMERGED FROM THE KITCHEN AGAIN, and I confess I had deliberately lingered, unwilling to engage Mr. Farrar—Jack—in conversation again. By the time I came back to the terrace he had gone. He'd left a note though, scrawled on the back of the bill—which he had paid in cash.

Chère Madame le chef,
Your lobster was lovely,
Your lamb luscious,
Your clafoutis de-lectable,
And your "artist's" wine de-licious.
But your brownies made me
Homesick and I took the liberty
Of doggie-bagging a few.
My compliments to the chef.

JF

I laughed out loud. Maybe Jack Farrar was okay after all.

By now, everyone except Miss Nightingale had gone up to bed, so I took off my apron, poured a couple of glasses of cognac and carried them out onto the terrace. I put one in front of Miss N and slumped wearily into the chair opposite.

"Oh, my dear," she said, putting down her book, as pleased to have the company as she was with the cognac. "How very nice. Thank you, and *santé*."

We clinked glasses, sipping the brandy reflectively, both enjoying the quiet time after the rush.

After a little while I said, "I see you met our new guest, Mr. Falcon."

Miss N gave a derisive little snort. "Well, hardly. He's not very friendly."

"Not civilized is more like it."

She gave me a long look. "Be careful," she said. "He's dangerous."

I looked at her, surprised. "And what would you know about dangerous men, Miss N?"

"Quite a lot, my dear." Her blue eyes behind the pale plastic spectacles met mine. "I was married to one." And with that she turned and gazed placidly out across the bay.

Now I don't know much about Miss N's private life, but a husband? And a dangerous one? She couldn't have told me anything more surprising.

"I didn't know you'd been married," I said, dying of curiosity.

"Very few people do. He was a Scotland Yard detective, quite a famous one. I kept my own name because that's who I was at my school, you see. I suppose I was a bit ahead of the feminists, but I alway felt I had earned my way in the world without the help of a man, and that I was entitled to be recognized in my own right. I was Miss Mollie Nightingale, headmistress of Queen Wilhelmina's School for Girls, and Mollie Nightingale was who I intended to stay."

"Well, good golly, Miss Mollie," I said with a grin, making her laugh. Impulsively, I reached out and took her hand. "I'm so glad you're here, Miss N," I said.

"Thank you, my dear." She gave me that long piercing stare again. "It's always good to have a friend."

I nodded; there was a good feeling in my heart again. "So, did you notice the other stranger in our midst tonight?" I asked casually. Too casually apparently, because Miss N caught my tone and raised her brows.

"The handsome one? Who could miss him?"

"He's not *that* handsome."

She thought about it. "Perhaps not, but very *fanciable* as the girls at my school would have said. Actually, *sex appeal* is what my generation would have said he had, and that's not a bad thing."

I was a little stunned to hear Miss N talking about husbands and Scotland Yard detectives and fanciable men with sex appeal, but was forced to admit that was exactly what Jack Farrar had. "Not for me, though," I said. "Remember, I'm the abandoned wife, the one still married but without a husband."

"Don't close your eyes to romance because of Patrick," Miss N said sternly. "Live your own life, Lola."

I sighed. "It's hard. Sometimes I don't know what I am anymore, or where I am in my life."

"So exactly *who* do you *think* you are, my dear?" she said.

I looked at her, puzzled. "What do you mean?"

"Tell me, *who* are you? *Who is Lola March Laforêt?*"

I hesitated, thinking about what she meant. "Well . . . I'm a woman. I'm thirty-nine looking at forty. I'm a chef. I'm den mother to my guests. I want to make all their vacation wishes come true, spin a little magic for them, here at the Hotel Riviera." I looked at her. "I guess that's about it."

"Think about what you've just told me. You are *all* those wonderful things, Lola; you do spin a magic spell for your guests. We love it here and it's all because of you. Never forget who you are, Lola, because you are someone special. You touch our lives and leave us feeling better for knowing you. And that is no small feat, my dear."

And then she drained her glass, picked up her book, and with a last, lingering look at the midnight-dark sea, where *Bad Dog* still rode at anchor, she said good night.

CHAPTER 11

YOU KNOW, IT'S NOT EASY DEALING WITH A BROKEN HEART, even though mine was broken long ago, long before Patrick left me. Sometimes I'm so sad at the loss of my dream love affair, I spend entire days in my kitchen trying out new recipes. Hence the extra pounds that have floated onto my once-slender frame, sticking to my bones like marshmallows to hot twigs.

Sometimes, I allow myself to be angry and resentful, stomping around acting mean to everybody; I know it's unfair but I just can't help it, and I'm always sorry afterwards. And then there are the long, long lonely nights when I cry into my pillow, wondering where he's gone, hugging my little hen to my chest while she clucks sympathetically. But then, no one ever said it was easy being a woman.

It had all started out so beautifully with Patrick, so glamorously, so romantically over champagne and caviar and locked glances.

I was working in Las Vegas as dessert chef at a grand restaurant in one of the grandest hotels, with the freedom to create whatever dishes I wished and a fabulous kitchen to do it in. I loved my job, I was happy there, even though there was little time for a personal life, Anyhow I'd decided to take a breather from men, since I wasn't having much luck with them.

It was my thirty-third birthday and I'd made my own cake, chocolate of course with a praline *ganache* filling. After the last diners had departed I shared it with my fellow workers, then I cast off those baggy chef's pants and got into my skinny black jeans and—very daring for me—a black chiffon blouse, the kind that's ruched at the top and hangs sexily off one shoulder. I'd bought it as an impulse birthday gift for myself from one of Vegas's smart boutiques. I was astonished at the astronomical cost, but then I'd told myself firmly that it was my day and no one else was buying me extravagant, romantic gifts.

I inspected myself anxiously in the mirror, adjusting the slipping shoulder and tugging at the low neckline, realizing how foolish I'd been to spend so much, because there was no one at all to look sexily romantic for. Still, it was my day and I was determined to go out. I wafted mascara onto my ginger lashes and brushed my long, straight hair. I shoved my aching feet into black suede heels, grabbed my purse, and headed for the Bellagio casino.

I lingered near the tables of high rollers playing blackjack and *pai gow,* cocooned from the real world in their own sumptuous softly lit area, marveling at the coolness of the dealers and the tense silence of the players. I wondered if they were betting their futures and entire fortunes on one last chance. Poor fools, I thought, little knowing that my own gamble with fate was about to take place.

Fatigue swept over me. I'd been on my feet for hours and my shoes were killing me. This had been a mistake. I didn't want to be here alone, all dressed up with nowhere really to go. I wanted to go home and get into bed with a good book. *Right now!* I spun round and literally fell over him.

"Pardon, mademoiselle, pardon . . . ," he said, and "Excuse me, I'm so sorry . . . ," I said. Then his arms were around me, steadying me, and I was staring into his eyes.

He was without doubt the best-looking man ever to hold me in his arms. In fact, he was all the clichés: tall, dark, handsome, and added to that he was French. What chance did I stand?

"Are you all right?" he asked in a devastatingly romantic French accent. "You look a little shaken."

Befuddled, I was unable to think of anything to say. My shoe had come off in the scuffle and now he retrieved it. "Cinderella?" he said, looking at me. Then kneeling at my feet, he took hold of my ankle and gently slid my shoe back on.

It was just so *sexy,* I almost couldn't breathe, "Oh! Oh! Thank you," I said, groaning inwardly because this was not exactly scintillating dialogue. "I'm sorry," I added, still sounding breathless.

"I am the one who should be sorry, I wasn't looking where I was going. Please, won't you allow me to buy you a drink? Just to make sure you're all right?"

I hesitated, though God knows why—maybe it was a premonition of disaster to come—but then I said yes anyway.

His hand was cool under my chiffon elbow as he guided me to the softly lit bar off the lobby.

"Champagne?" he said.

I smiled back. "Why not? After all, it's my birthday."

One dark brow rose, and I felt foolish and naïve and wished I hadn't shared that with him.

He signaled the waiter. "In that case, *chérie,* we must also have caviar."

I perched on the edge of my chair trying to look 'cool,' while he discussed caviar with the waiter. He was even better at second look, in an impeccably cut dark suit, a shirt of fine cotton in that wonderful marine-blue, and an expensive silk tie. There was a spattering of dark hair on the backs of his bronzed hand and a fashionable bluish stubble on his firm jaw. I felt that familiar clenching in the pit of my stomach.

He turned and gave me a searching look. "Hello," he said, "I'm Patrick Laforêt, from France."

"And I'm Lola March, from Los Angeles. Well, from Encino to be precise, in the San Fernando Valley."

"Enchanté de faire votre connaissance, Lola March," he said and we clinked glasses and toasted my birthday with Dom Pérignon, very pleased with ourselves. Then he leaned forward, looked deeply into my eyes, and said, "But who are you *really,* Lola March? Tell me about yourself."

Now, it's not often a woman gets this sort of opportunity, so of course I took it. I told him how I'd dropped out of college (not my best move but then, as you will see, I'm prone to moves like that) and instead had opted for culinary school, where somehow I knew I would show more talent. I told him how I had worked in lowly positions at great restaurants, and boasted of how I had progressed until now my dessert confections were considered by those in the know to be an edible art form.

"But I still make the best brownies in Vegas," I added finally, not wanting him to think I was all spun-sugar flash and no content. And he laughed and said he adored brownies.

"Not as much as I adore this caviar," I said, spooning more beluga onto wafer-thin toast points, and I saw he was amused by my round-eyed enjoyment.

Then it was Patrick's turn. He leaned closer, elbows on his knees, hands clasped in front of him, as he told me that for generations his family had been fishermen in Marseilles. Now they were gone and he was the last in the line of Laforêts. His father had left him some land outside of Saint-Tropez with a small hotel. He said he was sentimental about it, that he would never sell it "for family reasons," and that he always spent his summers there. The rest of the year he lived like a nomad, roaming the world.

Later, when I thought about it, I realized he never did get around to telling me exactly how he could afford this rich nomadic lifestyle, but it didn't seem to matter then, and I just assumed his family had left him money.

He told me about the Côte d'Azur and about the many different colors of blue in the sea; about the scent of jasmine on crystal air, and how he loved the long, languorous summer nights when the moon flooded the sea with silver light. He told me about the small vineyard he owned on a sandy hill, and about how it felt to be there in the early autumn mornings when the grapes hung, moon-dusted and heavy on the vines, ready for picking. He told me about the long hot afternoons of summer "best spent in a cool bed with the shutters closed, and of course, not alone." And I just sat there silently, eyes wide, like a child listening to a fairy tale, totally enthralled.

He was a dream-weaver, Patrick, and that night he wove my perfect dream of the Côte d'Azur, of a small hotel; of sunshine and flowers; of cool wine and a warm, passionate man.

I was head over heels, no question about it. And although it was not my usual cautious style, we ended up in bed that night, crazy for each other. And on an even crazier impulse one month later we were married and I became Lola Laforêt. I still remember how embarrassed I was when I heard my new name for the first time, and how I had wished I'd been named plain Jane, because Jane Laforêt would have sounded somehow less like a stripper.

It was hot the day we became husband and wife in the chambers of a silver-haired Las Vegas judge. Patrick was almost *too* handsome in a cream linen suit that looked far more bridal than the inexpensive beige silk shift I'd grabbed from my closet—because this was a spur-of-the-moment marriage and there'd been no time for bridal shopping. As usual my shoes were killing me, and my bridal bouquet was a bunch of drooping hot-pink roses, a color I hated, picked up hurriedly from a gas station and already half-dead in the heat.

Despite everything, like any bride, I still have my inexpensive "wedding dress," sentimentally preserved between sheets of special acid-free tissue. And I still have that sad bouquet, pressed between the pages of an album that contains a single wedding photograph, taken by our only witness, the judge's secretary. In it Patrick looks solemn, while I look vaguely alarmed, brows raised, eyes wide, as if aware of what was to come.

Of course, *now* I realize it was more than just Patrick I had wanted. I'd wanted the romance of southern France, the wines, the food, the lovemaking under summer stars, and I realized, too late, that the stars were in my eyes and not in those summer skies.

So you see, the truth is I'm as fragile as every other woman when it comes to love and relationships and men.

CHAPTER 12

THE NIGHT WAS TOO HOT TO GO INDOORS YET, AND I DEcided to take a stroll through the gardens before bed. The scent of jasmine hung on the air, reminding me of those early days when the hotel had just opened; when we had no guests, and were still gluing it all together with spit and hope and no money.

Up the lane at the entrance to the hotel, a small blue sign tacked to a pine tree said, in bright yellow letters, "The Hotel Riviera." Next to it another, bigger sign said, BIENVENUE/WELCOME in what I thought were justifiably extra-large letters, and under that yet another sign said in French: "Our Welcome Is Bigger Than Our Hotel," which was, of course, the truth.

Twin rows of parasol pines yearned toward each other over the lane, providing a welcome avenue of shade in the heat of the day. Wander down that lane, turn a corner, and there it is; square and solid and the color of faded-pink roses, with a row of French windows above and a matching row beneath, flanked by old shutters that have always been somehow askew, no matter how I've tried to fix them. Their green paint has weathered to a silvery patina, and each morning they're thrown open to greet the sun, then closed again in the afternoon to keep out the heat.

Although it's the end of summer, vivid pink and purple bougainvillea still tumbles over the trellises flanking the doors, and the white-pointed petals of jasmine gleam in the darkness. The door stands open, as it always does until midnight, after which guests need to use their own keys, and on a chunk of pink granite set above those doors is carved the name Villa Riviera, and the year it was built, 1920.

Walk up the low stone steps and into the hall and you'll be met by the faint familiar scent of beeswax and lavender. Each piece of furniture, each lamp and rug, each object in this house has a history; a memory of where I had bought it; of how much I'd had to borrow; of who I had been with. All my *good* memories are here.

I ran my hand over the round rosewood hall table that serves as the reception desk, its dents and chips camouflaged under layers of beeswax, rubbed to a hard sheen by Nadine. On the table is an old brass schoolbell, used to summon the *patronne* from the kitchen. A green and white chintz sofa stands alongside a red leather wing chair, studded with brass nailheads, and the bombé cabinet has the dull sheen of silver leaf, personally applied by me. Currently, it's topped with a mixed bunch of lilies and marguerites, plonked hastily into a blue pottery jug by someone who obviously had little time to bother with fancy flower arrangements. A fake Louis-the-something love seat on spindly gilt legs is covered in traditional blue and yellow Provençal fabric found in the local market, and next to it a reed basket holds a pile of sweet apple logs.

Now, walk through the arch from the hall and you're in the salon, a big room fringed with those tall French windows leading onto the terrace and the gardens. This is the room with the oversized limestone fireplace that looks like one of my mismatched auction finds, but is in fact original to the house. This room is furnished with a pair of rather grand high-backed, tassled silk sofas, "rescued" from a decrepit château, as were the rugs, admittedly a bit threadbare and faded but still beautiful.

Beyond the salon is the small dining room, used only in bad weather, when the mistral blows the sand from the beach and the leaves from the trees, wrecking my jasmine and wrenching the vines from the arbor, and rattling everyone's nerves. It's kind of cozy in there, though, with the lamps lit and the wind howling, a bit like a storm at sea.

Anyhow, by the time you finally leave the terrace and the delights of a long, winey dinner, and climb the central staircase, you'll be almost asleep. You'll find six identically sized bedrooms, with an extra-large corner room anchoring each end of the hallway. Instead of numbers, I've named the rooms for famous French artistes and writers: there's Piaf and Colette, who, by the way, once owned a house in Saint-Tropez and sold her makeup line in a little store there. There's Proust, Dumas, Zola, and Mistral. I also named one for Brigitte Bardot, who famously lived just down the road from here. Plus Miss Nightingale's room is named for Marie-Antoinette, because I've always had a sneaking suspicion the woman had been misquoted and then blamed for all the French royal family's problems. Somewhat similar, Miss Nightingale had reminded me, to a recent princess's own problems.

Most of the rooms have balconies overlooking the leafy fig arbor and the terrace, with perfect views of the Mediterranean. If you want, you can lean from the windows and pick the ripe figs. When you bite into them, still hot from the sun, the sweet juices run down your chin.

In some rooms, the beds are all gilded ormolu and padded damask, which somehow turned out to look more country bordello than seaside villa, but which has a certain charm. Others are plain country iron, painted white and draped in gauze so that lying in bed with the soft slur of the sea in your ears, you could imagine you were in the tropics.

Everything else in the bedrooms is very simple. A table under the window; an amber-shaded lamp, a comfy chair, a soft rug for your feet. The soap in the small, Provençal-tiled bathrooms is made from local olive oil and is scented deliciously with verbena; the bed linens smell of being dried in the sun and the wind, and the bunches of flowers on the nightstands smell like wild strawberries.

Occasionally, a nightingale pays us a visit, or a blackbird, which in my view has the prettier song. I like to hope it sends those guests already drifting off to sleep closer into each other's arms, because there's surely nothing as romantic as a nightingale's song, heard while lying in your cool bed with the tall windows flung open to the sea breeze. "Hear that," I sometimes imagine a delighted lover whispering, holding the long, cool length of his woman against his warm tanned body, as they love each other.

I'm back on the terrace now, the focus and general meeting place of the Hotel Riviera. Worn terra-cotta pavers, verdigrised iron railings under a burden of blossoms, old-fashioned globe light, and, overhead, a thick canopy of fig leaves.

Enchanting is the word that comes to mind as I look down over the tangle of colorful plants spilling onto the sandy path below. At the end of this path, there's the clump of boulders and a flight of wooden steps leading down to the cove. Just above this is my own house, a miniature single-story version of the hotel, in the same faded-rose pink, with the same tall silvery shutters framing its windows, and a tiny porch tacked onto the front. The sea laps practically at my door and I sleep with my windows open to its soothing music.

I pick a sprig of jasmine and tuck it into my hair, as I take that sandy path, back to my little house, and Scramble, and my lonely dreams. Is there any wonder I love this place?

CHAPTER 13

THE NIGHT HAD TURNED SULTRY, THAT STICKY KIND OF heat that foretells a summer storm. I peeled off my clothes and headed into the shower. Five minutes later and many degrees cooler, I was in bed.

I lay there, eyes wide open, sheet thrown back, rigid as a soldier at attention, staring into the semidarkness at the vague shapes of the old blue-painted ceiling beams with the yellow spaces of plaster between them, Scramble rustled around on my pillow, clucking softly and occasionally touching my hair with her beak. I was glad of her company.

Sleep was impossible. I was too worried, too distracted, too *lonely.* I flung myself out of bed and sat by the open window, leaning on the wooden ledge. I felt the sun's warmth still locked there and rested my head on my arms, listening to the distant rumble of thunder and the soft background sigh of the sea, thinking how fortunate I was to live in such a beautiful place. I reminded myself that I had Patrick to thank for that.

I suppose I'm what you might call a nester, partly because as a child I never really had a home. Due to Dad's financial ups and downs, we were always on the move; one month I'd be a country cowgirl on a ranch, the next I was an urban schoolgirl striving to make instant best friends. We lived in so many different apartments I lost count. I yearned for a place to call my own.

My mother had simply picked up and left one day without taking six-year-old me with her. She'd dubbed my father, scathingly, Mr. Charm, and it was true, he was Mr. Charm, but oh, how I loved him. I'd hang on to his hand and on to his every word, gazing proudly up at my handsome daddy, who to his credit, and unlike my runaway mother, always showed up for PTA meetings, charming every mother there, beaming his "shy" smile while looking searchingly into their eyes. Looking for what? I wondered. It was a long time before I found out it was "would the answer be yes? Or no?"

After Mom left, somehow too, it was always me looking after Dad, instead of the other way around, making sure he got to appointments on time; that he'd booked the sitter; that there was milk for the breakfast cereal.

"You have to make a left turn here," I'd remind him from the backseat of the car, because even at age six I realized he had zero sense of direction. "I have to be at school by eight," I'd say, or "What shall we have for supper tonight, Daddy?" I knew if I didn't remind him he'd forget all about it and it would be take-out pizza one more time. Even a little kid can get awfully sick of pizza.

Anyhow, Mr. Charm or not, I adored him, and of course, he was the standard by which I measured every other man. I found out too late he wasn't the best yardstick to go by.

When I met Patrick I was at a vulnerable point in my life, but then somehow I always was. Vulnerable, that is. I'm sure a therapist would tell me it all stemmed from my childhood, it's simple common sense; though of course common sense has never stopped me from falling for the wrong man.

I was just emerging from a two-year odyssey with a movie actor (*odyssey* was the only way to describe that long, hard haul) when I'd arrived at this conclusion. The "actor" was a wanna-be actor when I met him, then he started to climb the ladder: a small part in a small film; then another, larger part; soon he was escorting young actresses to premieres and parties and showing up in *People* magazine and the tabloids. Even blinded by love, I guessed where it was heading—absolutely nowhere—and called an end to it.

With a pang of genuine grief, I decided there was no such thing as "true love." It was a myth invented for novels and movies, perpetrated by poets who wrote sonnets about it, and by writers of popular songs. *True love did not exist.* It was gone from my life forever. And then I met Patrick Laforêt and plunged in, Eyes Wide Open, Head Over Heels. All the clichés. All Over Again.

CHAPTER 14

IT WAS STARDUST ALL THE WAY, THAT FIRST YEAR WE WERE married, and Patrick made me feel like a bride every day of it.

I wish I could explain why a man falls *out* of love with a woman. With Patrick it was as quick as this. One day we were laughing and holding hands as we walked through the steep streets of Eze, a village perched on a mountainside above Cap-Ferrat, where we had gone for a precious day off from the demands of renovating our hotel. The next, he was heading off alone for Saint-Tropez with a casual "be back later, *chérie*."

For a year we had made love, morning, noon, and night, and as often as we could in-between times, when the workers weren't around and we could sneak some privacy in our still-unfinished cottage. And then suddenly we didn't make love so much anymore. It was as though Patrick had turned out the lights and left me in a puzzling twilight zone, not knowing why or what or how.

Of course, my first thought was there was another woman. After all, Patrick couldn't pass any woman without giving her the eye, and it would be a rare woman who could resist his looks and gentle charm.

Plus, let's not forget I was a simple, amber-haired, round-eyed chef from the suburbs when Patrick met me, and he was French, and handsome, and rich (at least I thought he was then), as well as a man of the world. I don't think a day went by that I didn't question why he'd picked me to marry.

It wasn't all bad. I mean, there were times when it would be perfect again, just for a day or so, and Patrick would be his old self, flirting and laughing and enjoying life and enjoying me. We would drive to a country auction, up in the hills of Provence to Orange, or even farther to Burgundy, where we once stayed the night in a grand converted château, living temporarily in the lap of luxury. It was so far removed from the daily chaos of our in-transition Hotel Riviera, it was like another world, and one where, to my surprise, I became another woman, throwing my cares and problems away and living just for the moment. We held hands, we kissed in shady bowers, and made love in a sumptuous feather bed.

I went to the local auctions and bid crazily on old stuff no one else seemed to want: the threadbare Oriental rugs, the out-of-fashion twenties marble-topped washstand; the crazy lampshades with the dangling bead fringes; and the gold lamé curtains from the thirties, swagged and tassled in purple, which to this day drape our—*my*—bed, looking like leftovers from a Fred and Ginger movie.

Sometimes, on those rare days we were together just before the opening of our hotel, we'd drive around and find an odd little sheep farm in the Sisteron hills where we'd spend the night tucked into a tiny room beneath the eaves, listening to the bleating of sheep outside our window and the splatter of rain on the tiled roof. Or we'd stop at a tiny *hostellerie,* just a couple of rooms over a little restaurant where we ate like kings and made love like bunny rabbits, as though this giddy world might never stop.

Did Patrick ever *really* love me, even then, when he was making love to me? It's a question destined to haunt me forever. I so want to believe he did, in his own way, which sadly in the end was not enough. And in the end my love was not enough either. I still care about where Patrick is, though, about what's happening to him, and who he's with. In my heart I believe he's with another woman, a younger, prettier, richer woman who can give him everything his material heart desires. Which, as I said before, doesn't make him a bad guy—just a bad husband.

So, there we are; I've bared my untidy heart to you—what's left of it anyway. For the past six months I've lived an independent life, running my little hotel, looking after my guests, cooking good food every night, and keeping myself busy so I don't have time to think about Patrick.

What I'm really dreading is the winter, when my guests have gone back to their own worlds and I'm here alone on my little peninsula, listening to the mistral blowing from the Siberian steppes, crashing through the Rhône valley, gathering speed until it finds my cottage, rattling the doors and windows, shrieking through the pines and toppling the heavy planters with a sound like cannon shots, making the silence inside even more lonely.

It will no longer be the season for cold rosé wine and instead I'll light the apple wood in the grate, praying that the wind won't blow the smoke back down the chimney. I'll brew up the chamomile tea that's supposed to soothe my shattered nerves and maybe I'll make some of those comforting toast soldiers and soft-boiled eggs that always remind me of my father and my childhood, because he would make them for me when I felt bad. Later, in bed, Scramble will snuggle into my neck, nibbling occasionally on my ear, and together we'll get through another long night.

Did I mention I wasn't looking forward to this? Did I mention how angry I am with Patrick? Did I mention I don't know what to do about his disappearance, where to look for him, or even who to ask to help? Well, here's the truth: the only good things to come out of this whole scenario are three facts. The first is that I still want to believe Patrick loved me, once upon a time. The second is I'm no longer in love with him. And the third is that I still have my true "true love": the Hotel Riviera.

CHAPTER 15

THE NOISE OF A CAR PULLING INTO THE GRAVEL PARKING lot broke the silence. Surprised, I glanced at my watch. Almost two A.M. All my guests, with the exception of the brutish Mr. Falcon, were home, and in any case Falcon drove the Harley. Car doors slammed, then I heard heavy footsteps crunching on the sandy path heading to my cottage.

A trickle of fear ran up my spine. It was the middle of the night, everyone was sleeping, I was alone. Even if I screamed no one would hear me, tucked away in my private little corner, shaded by thick hedges of oleander and honeysuckle.

I was suddenly so hot with fear, I could *hear* my heart thudding. I ran to the door, threw on the bolt, ran back, locked the windows, grabbed the phone . . . *I'd call the police. They'd be here in what? Five minutes? Ten? Fifteen? . . . Oh God, it would be too late.*

The bead curtain clanked as it was thrust aside, then someone knocked. I forced myself into absolute stillness, hoping whoever it was would think no one was here and just go away . . . after all, there was nothing worth stealing anyway . . . But did robbers knock?

"Madame Laforêt," a commanding French voice said. "Open up, please. It's the gendarmes."

The police. At two o'clock in the morning? I was already fumbling with the bolt and the lock. And then my heart stopped its thudding and sank like a stone. It must be about Patrick, I thought. They've found Patrick.

I got the door open and stood looking at the man facing me, big and bulky in a battered Panama hat and a crumpled white jacket. The top buttons of his shirt were open and a tuft of black chest hair stuck out above his loosely knotted yellow tie. He didn't look like a policeman and I edged quickly back behind the door. Then I noticed the pair of uniformed gendarmes behind him.

I clutched my hand to my sunken heart like a soap opera queen. "What is it, what's happened?"

The big man removed his battered Panama and held it to his chest. "Madame Laforêt," he said, "allow me to introduce myself. I am Detective Claude Mercier of the Marseilles police. These gentlemen are my colleagues from the local precinct. I need to talk to you."

The *Marseilles* police? It couldn't be *good* news. I held open the door and they strode past me. Their authoritative masculine presence seemed to suck all the air out of my small pretty room. I couldn't breathe . . . Anything could have happened, I told myself, sinking legless into the sofa. Anything . . . But these were the *good* guys, they were on *my* side . . . weren't they?

"Vous permettez, madame?" Detective Mercier pulled up a

chair. He sat facing me, leaning forward, elbows resting on his spread knees, twirling the brim of his Panama between his fingers. He stared into my face.

When I could stand his silence no longer, I blurted out, "For God's sake, why are you here at two in the morning? What's happened? Is it Patrick?"

The detective placed his hat carefully on his knees. He sighed as he sat back, hands clasped, fingers linked, thumbs twirling slowly.

"Madame Laforêt, your husband's car, the silver Porsche Carrara, has been found abandoned in a garage on the outskirts of Marseilles." He held up his hand. "And no, madame, your husband was not in the vehicle. Right now the Porsche is being gone over by forensics, with the proverbial fine-tooth comb, for any signs of . . ." His voice dropped a dramatic register. "Of violence."

That final softly spoken word echoed through my brain.

Detective Mercier was suddenly gentle. "Madame Laforêt, why don't you tell me everything you know about your husband's disappearance. It would be in your best interest. And of course, madame"—he leaned conspiratorially toward me, speaking so softly only I could hear him—"I will look after you *personally*. I'll see that you are well taken care of, that you are treated with respect." His eyes locked onto mine. "After all, a woman like you, *a lady* . . ."

So that's why the police were here at two in the morning. They thought I had killed my husband. Detective Mercier was being nice to me to get me to confess.

"I've already told the police everything I know," I said, suddenly cautious.

Mercier's dark brows folded into a straight line. "Are you telling me you know nothing? That your husband simply left one sunny morning and never came back?"

I nodded yes, and I felt the sweat slide icily between my shoulder blades. I said, "But now you've found his car, surely you'll be able to track him down? You and your colleagues in forensics . . . ?"

The detective stopped me with that upraised palm again. "Forensics deal in *death,* Madame Laforêt."

I gaped at him. "What do you mean? Where is my husband?"

Mercier lumbered to his feet. He walked to the door with the gendarmes following him. As he opened the door I heard the thunder, rumbling closer. He turned and looked back at me. "We were hoping you would be able to tell us that, Madame Laforêt," he said. "Since you were the last person to see him, and you are a suspect in his possible murder."

CHAPTER 16

Miss N

MOLLIE NIGHTINGALE COULDN'T SLEEP EITHER. IT WAS HER talk with Lola that was the culprit, she decided. Mentioning Tom had been a mistake. This always happened: it triggered off her subconscious, bringing him back again, larger than life—and twice as dead.

Tom was a man who'd lived dangerously and he'd died violently, as she had predicted he would.

"Rubbish," he'd said, dismissing her fears with a contemptuous curl of the lip as he stood in front of the mahogany cheval mirror that had been her father's, knotting his tie—always a striped silk rep, he must have had two dozen of them, all the same style but in different colors. It was Mollie's task each morning to select the "colors of the day," which pleased her, made her feel in some small way she was sharing part of his life. Silly, she knew, but that was the way it was between them.

Tom had lived his life as the hard-nosed detective at Scotland Yard with a reputation for pushing the envelope into dangerous territory. And she'd had her life as the refined schoolmistress, head of a select London day school for girls where calm and decorum were the watchword and the only crimes were sneaking a smoke in the bathroom or—the worst—cheating in a test.

Her and Tom's lives could not have been more different and, like creatures from alien planets, they met cautiously in the neutral territory of her tiny London flat, and also—when Tom the workaholic could no longer claim he had to work weekends and was actually forced into going—at her favorite place, the equally tiny cottage in the village of Blakelys.

Mostly, though, Miss Nightingale was at the cottage alone on weekends, soaking up the peace and quiet, and quite often, the drizzle as she gardened enthusiastically, spilling her spare love and emotions—those not reserved for Tom—into the heavy brown earth where she'd created a tangled beauty of a garden from the simplest of country flowers. She had sculpted daisies into topiaries; built great banks of delphiniums and hydrangeas; and scattered spring primroses under the lime trees, the true old-fashioned pale yellow primroses that came after the great clusters of daffodils, which, corny though Tom said it was, somehow always caused Mollie to quote Wordsworth:

"A host of golden daffodils," she'd say, admiring that springtime bonanza, while huddling from the cold wind under several layers of jumpers and cardigans. She thought Wordsworth had got it exactly right. Then, in summer, came her joy of joys, the roses, especially the climbing variety, the Gloire de Dijon with its huge cabbagy blooms in palest buff tinged with yellow and apricot and with a scent that knocked her socks off on a fine summer morning. And Golden Showers, which, true to its name, shimmered over the honey-stone cottage walls with golden abandon.

"A difficult plant," Tom had said about her Gloire de Dijon, "but like a beautiful woman, worth the extra attention." Which had left her wondering what on earth Tom knew about beautiful women who needed extra attention.

She'd taken a long look at her husband of five years (they had found each other later in life when she was in her fifties and he a couple of years younger), contemplating what it might be like to have been young and beautiful and courted by the handsome, dangerous Tom Knight. Her Knight in Shining Armor, she'd called him when he'd finally suggested, after drinks in a pub on the Kings Road—a place to which she was unaccustomed—that perhaps their lives should be joined.

Not exactly at the hip, of course, he'd added jokingly. After all, I've got my life and you've got yours. But it seems to me, Mollie, we get along very well. We've known each other a few years now, and you are exactly the kind of woman I need to add ballast to my life.

And she'd smiled and flushed a rosy pink that he said matched her dress, and two months later she found herself "plighting her troth" as she liked to call it, with this world-weary man with the eyes that said he'd seen it all and then some, and an expression in his taut, lean face that said, better not mess with me, fella, I'm smarter and tougher and harder than you are.

Blakelys Manor had been her girlhood home, but all Miss Nightingale had inherited, after the tax man had taken his share, was the gardener's old cottage, crammed now with treasures from the Blakely Nightingales' exotic past. She and

Tom had "honeymooned" in that old cottage, which was to become their "true home." Then finally, *her* home. Alone.

Sighing, Miss Nightingale sat up in the comfortable bed in the Marie-Antoinette room at the Hotel Riviera, bringing her thoughts deliberately back to her plans for the following day. And what exactly were her plans? she wondered as she pushed her plump feet into pink velvet slippers and shrugged a pink cotton robe over her Marks & Spencer lavender nightie. She smiled, remembering Tom saying how she looked like a summer garden in her favorite pastels, and how later she'd worried about whether that was a compliment or not.

He was difficult to read, Tom was, or at least in the beginning he was. Later, though, he'd opened up to her. He enjoyed her simplicity, he said, and her uncomplex, unworldly approach, and that's when he'd begun to share his "other life" as a detective with her. His *real* life, he called it. And of course Mollie's own life became more exciting as she began to live vicariously through him.

It was at the cottage over after-dinner brandies in front of the fire on a bitter cold winter's night, that she first coaxed the story of his latest case out of him.

It was a real toughie, he said worriedly, because it was a particularly gruesome murder and there was a dearth of clues. Plus it involved a child, something that incensed every cop who had to deal with such perversion.

It's the loss of innocence I keep thinking about, Tom said to her, brandy glass clasped between his big hands, staring into the flames leaping in the grate. I can't stop thinking about what the poor little thing must have gone through before the bastard finally killed her.

How do you know it was a man? she asked quietly. Tom

turned and looked at her, his eyes narrowed into slits. Bloody hell, Mollie, he said, you know what? You're a bloody genius. Excuse the bad language. Then he'd gotten up and made a phone call or two, slung on his anorak, said goodbye and see you when I see you, and hurried into the frosty night in the old green Land Rover, heading for the M4 and London.

It turned out the mother and her boyfriend were the killers after all, and after that, Tom would often talk to Mollie about the difficult cases. She learned a lot about violent crime: about the murders; the rapes; the gang assassinations; things she'd previously only read about in newspapers. And Tom found her lucid mind and simple reasoning a great help. For a while.

Sighing, Miss Nightingale pulled open the shutters leading to her tiny balcony and stepped out into the sultry night. Lightning flickered across the sky and the heavy scent of night-blooming jasmine filled the air. She couldn't grow jasmine in the Cotswolds, at least not in her little patch of garden; it just wouldn't "take," didn't like the chilly nights, she supposed, so it gave her special pleasure to smell it now and catch the gleam of its white petals in the darkness.

Her room was the smallest in the hotel, and because it was on the shady side and quite dark, Lola had sponge-painted it a yellow that was meant to be primrose but had turned out more egg yolk. There was a comfy double bed with an iron frame and gauzy curtains, a pair of mismatched nightstands painted Mediterranean blue and a bleached-pine farmhouse armoire found on one of Lola's country antiquing expeditions. On the small table by the window were a water carafe and a glass, a pile of books, and Miss N's knitting—currently a long stretch of stripes, a winter muffler that, in fact, she would give Lola as a parting gift.

A comfortable blue velvet chair was placed near the window and two pretty lamps with country-toile shades completed the décor. This room was the cheapest in the hotel because it was on the corner overlooking the parking lot. Not that Miss N found that a hardship, because the straw matting strung over the graveled space to keep the sun off the guests' cars was now covered with deep blue convolvulus and it made for a pretty sight. Plus, if she craned her neck a little as she did now, she could catch a glimpse of the sea, and the red and green riding lights of the small sloop still anchored there.

She was just thinking, how wonderful to be aboard that little sloop with the waves lapping outside your window and the sea rocking you soft as a baby in its cradle, so calm, so peaceful, so silent, when headlights beamed down the lane. A large black car gunned into the lot, then squealed to a stop, gravel crunching, right beneath her balcony.

Miss N shrank back; she didn't want to be spotted in her bathrobe and slippers with her hair in a net to preserve its careful waves. And besides, who could this be, arriving so late? The car had Marseilles license plates and it certainly did not belong to any of the guests.

The passenger door was flung open and a weighty man in a crumpled white jacket with a broad-brimmed Panama hat slammed over his eyes hauled himself out. He didn't bother to close the door; he left that to the two gendarmes who slid quickly out after him. He stood for a minute getting his bearings, then with a grunt and a wave of his arm for them to follow, he strode down the sandy path toward Lola's cottage.

Miss N drew in a shocked breath. The police! At this time of night they were definitely here on business. And that could only mean Patrick.

She sank into the white rattan balcony chair, staring after them, waiting, wondering. It seemed a long time before they came back, and when she heard their footsteps, she leaned over the balcony to get a better look. The big man lifted his head and looked right back at her.

Oh dear! Oh my! she said to herself, shrinking back against the wall, flushing with embarrassment. And then she thought about her Tom and how this pasty-faced, overweight, sweating detective in his white jacket and Panama hat couldn't hold a candle to him, and she pulled her dignity together and stepped silently back into her room, closing the shutters behind her.

She waited until the sound of the car disappeared into the distance. Lola's alone, she thought. Lord knows what they have just told her. It's about Patrick, though, I'm sure of that. Maybe they have found him . . . or found his body is more like it.

Wrapping her pink robe tightly around her, she opened the door and crept along the hallway. She padded down the stairs and out the front door, hurrying softly in her slippers, down the path to Lola's cottage.

Rounding the thick oleander hedge, Miss N stopped. No lights showed. No sound came from within. She hesitated, wondering. Should she knock and say, it's me, Lola, it's just Mollie Nightingale wondering if everything is all right?

Sighing again, she shook her head, then she turned and walked slowly back through the gardens. Something bad had happened, though, she felt it in her bones. And her old bones surely knew a thing or two about trouble.

She turned for one last look at the shuttered house by the sea. The only lights were the red and green ones on the small sloop anchored out in the bay.

CHAPTER 17

Lola

MY EYELIDS WERE ON SPRINGS. EVERY TIME I TRIED TO shut them they just snapped right back open. And there I was staring at the ceiling again, counting the cracks between the beams in the emerging dawn light. You'll know the questions I was asking myself over and over as the hours ticked past, slow as a night-bound snail. Those *where, why, who* questions. And especially the *why me? Why* did the police suspect me of being involved in my husband's disappearance?

All I knew was that Patrick would never have dumped his Porsche in some parking garage in Marseilles. That car was his image, his alter ego. In his silver Porsche, Patrick became the rich south of France playboy. It was not an image he would have forfeited lightly.

I was out of my hot rumpled sheets at five, pacing the terrace beneath my windows, arms folded, head bent, hardly noticing the lovely dawn transition from opal to pearl to aquamarine to sunlit gold. All I saw was the pale terra-cotta floor tiles and my long brown feet with the chipped red toenail polish. I told myself sternly I really must get a pedicure, then shook my head, astonished I could even be thinking of such trivia.

I scanned my little bay, loving its gilded early-morning stillness. The black sloop still rode at anchor, drifting gently on the breeze-rippled sea. I remembered the Naked Man and the hedonistic pleasure he took in the elements. I thought of his hard body as he stretched, his head tilted to the sun and the wind. And then I remembered his sleek blond girlfriend, young and gorgeous.

I sighed as I went back indoors, envying their carefree lives, while I had a hotel full of guests to look after and a restaurant to run; menus to be planned; marketing to be done; coffee to be fixed; croissants to be baked. I could not afford to indulge myself in my problems.

In the shower I let the cold water slide over my skin, shocking me awake. I dressed in a minute in pink linen shorts and a cool white camisole, shoved my in-need-of-a-pedicure feet into the beribboned wedgie Saint-Tropez espadrilles that laced around the ankles, wondering why I'd ever bought them. Like everything else in my wardrobe they were purchased on the run, either on my way to, or on my way back from, Saint-Tropez market, or else in the fall sales, which was the reason nothing in my closet went with anything else. I shook my orange hair to dry it a bit, remembered too late that I should have lathered on the UV lotion, did a hasty touch-up on the parts of me that showed, then grabbed my car keys.

Car! Hah, that was a laugh! It's only resemblance to Patrick's Porsche was that it was silver. It was also old and small. Tiny, in fact. An ancient Deux Chevaux, of the kind that used to be called a sardine can because it looks as though you could stick a key in and peel back the top. It wasn't even a real car, it was a flatbed and just right for my early-morning marketing activities, though not for much else. Still, it had seemed the perfect vehicle when Patrick and I were just starting out, the two of us getting into this "dream" hotel on the cheap.

Look how much money we'll save, I remember saying oh so naïvely, when I'd discovered the car parked on a cobbled street in Ramatuelle with an *À Vendre* sign stuck on its windshield. And if you disregarded the monthly bills from the mechanic I was almost right. What I hadn't factored into the keeping-the-costs-down equation was Patrick. Sure, I could have the sardine can if I wanted. Meanwhile, he'd bought himself the first of a series of supercars. I'm only now beginning to suspect how dumb I was. And still am. Probably.

Anyhow, the one place I'm not a dummy is in my kitchen. There, I know I'm in control. Marit, who was in before me, raised a floury hand in a greeting, told me that coffee was already brewed, and went back to arranging her croissant dough in neatly folded semicircles.

The smell of baking rolls and freshly ground coffee raised my spirits a notch and I sat at the long table under the windows with my notebook. With an effort, I shoved all the bad news about Patrick to the back of my mind, reserving him for quiet moments at the end of the day when I would be alone and free to pace the floors, free to agonize over his fate, free to be myself. Right now I had a business to run, guests to take care of. Today, they would be my salvation.

It was Saturday and market day in Saint-Tropez. There was sure to be good fish, fresh as it came. I'd also look for tiny golden beets and buy roulades of cheese made from the milk of Madame Auric's special herd of white goats, and which seemed to me to have a creamier flavor than any other. I'd slice the beets and the cheese and some sweet tomatoes, stack them in a line like a little train in a pool of creamy basil dressing on a bed of arugula with perhaps, if I were lucky, slices of bright orange persimmon, and if not then kumquats or golden plums.

I'd be sure to get crevettes too, the large ones called bouquet, and hopefully, I'd find Saint-Pierre, the delicate flat white fish that was heaven simply grilled or sautéed, served with a green sauce made from fresh herbs and lemon.

Anyhow, my specials were in my head if not yet in hand, plus whatever else I could find that was interesting. Not a difficult task in Saint-Tropez market on a September morning, I can assure you.

Glancing up I saw Jean-Paul's head float past the open window. His eyes were closed and he looked half-asleep. I heard the crash as his bike hit the rosemary hedge, sending a waft of Provence into the kitchen. With a muttered *"merde,"* he kicked the bike into place against the wall, then sauntered back past my window. The bead curtain rustled behind him and he stood, dusting himself off, looking sleepily at Marit and me. *"Bonjour, Madame Laforêt, bonjour, Marit."*

"Bonjour, Jean-Paul," we replied, eyeing each other and wondering where he'd been all night because he surely looked the worse for wear. I sighed; he was young and carefree and living in Saint-Tropez. I was grateful that at least he'd shown up.

I said, "Okay, Jean-Paul. First get into the shower, then some clean clothes, then set up the breakfast tables, there'll be guests wanting coffee before you know it." He stared blankly back at me. "Well, go *on,*" I said irritably in very bad French. "*Et dépêche-toi,* if you know what's good for you," I added.

Hands stuck in his pockets, Jean-Paul moved sleepily toward the bathroom behind the kitchen.

I slugged down the rest of my coffee, told Marit to see that our youth-of-all-work got his act—and the breakfast tables—together, grabbed my shopping list and headed for the car, making a small detour to the front desk to check on the day's arrivals and departures.

So far only the Oldroyds, the sweet Yorkshire honeymoon couple, were due to depart. I would make sure to see them before they left, give them a big hug and wish them well, and say, sincerely, that I hoped they would come back. And of course they would; guests always returned to the Hotel Riviera.

I was leaning on the pretty rosewood table gazing absently through the open front door when I saw Miss Nightingale in an apple-green jersey skirt that drooped a bit at the hem and a matching many-pocketed safari shirt. She stood, sandaled feet apart, head reverently down, hands behind her back, admiring Mr. Falcon's gleaming red and chrome Harley. She put a hand over her heart and heaved a big envious sigh. Her own little wasp-yellow rented Vespa looked almost comical parked next to it.

I waved to her and she walked back inside and gave me a long look. "No news from the husband yet, my dear?" she said.

I shook my head, glancing round to see if anyone had overheard, though it was certainly no secret that Patrick had left me. There could have been no more public local departure since Charles left Diana: the whole town knew, as well as all my guests.

"I saw the police last night," Miss N said. I threw her a surprised glance. "I didn't mean to pry, my dear," she added. "I just happened to be out on my balcony when they arrived." She hesitated, then said, "I trust it wasn't bad news, Lola."

"They found Patrick's Porsche in a parking garage in Marseilles."

"Marseilles? Now I wonder, why *there*?"

I shrugged. "They're checking it for forensic evidence."

Miss Nightingale's eyes narrowed but she made no comment and I couldn't bring myself to tell her that I was Detective Mercier's prime suspect.

"I'm just on my way to the market in Saint-Tropez," I said, gathering my wits. "Where are you heading?"

"I thought I might take it easy today," she said, as we walked outside together. "Perhaps I'll visit the market, pick up a gift for Mrs. Wormesly at the Blakelys Arms. She always looks after my Yorkie, Little Nell, when I'm away."

I asked if she'd like a lift, but she shook her head and said she'd just as well take the Vespa in case she felt like wandering farther afield.

I watched as she planted herself firmly in the saddle, adjusted her straw sunhat, hitched her handbag farther up her arm, then started up the motor and jolted up the driveway.

My own "silver chariot" awaited me. I should have been at the market half an hour ago. As I climbed into the car I remembered Detective Mercier telling me that forensics were going over Patrick's silver Porsche with a fine-tooth comb. With a foreboding shiver, I wondered what they had found.

CHAPTER 18

Jack

JACK FARRAR WAS STROLLING THROUGH THE SAINT-TROPEZ Saturday market in the Place des Lices, feeling at peace with the world. His black and white dog roved in small devoted circles around him, sniffing busily.

There was something about Jack's broad-shouldered rangy stride that was unmistakably American, and something about his craggy tanned face and the fine lines around his eyes that marked him as a man of experience. It was definitely a lived-in kind of face. His brown hair was short and spiky, his eyes were the color of the Mediterranean on a perfect day, and there were washboard abs under the old blue T-shirt that bore the logo "Rhode Island Regatta." As he walked women met his eyes, smiling interestedly at him. He gave them a somewhat lopsided smile back and kept on walking.

Both he and Bad Dog loved the hustle and bustle of the French markets: the dog for the good food smells and the tasty treats that might drop his way, and Jack for the miraculous way the markets sprang up out of nowhere in the early hours, filling the silent cobbled square with the harsh stutter of motors as the trucks arrived; then the rattle of iron struts on the cobblestones and the flapping of canvas as the stalls were assembled. Then came the fish trucks with their loads of shining silver, and the stallholders shouting greetings to each other as they artistically arranged their wares. He loved the way each scarlet berry seemed to bloom with velvety temptation and the way the graceful zucchini blossoms lay delicately in line, and how the small shiny potatoes were piled high, waiting to be picked over by the choosy French housewives.

He enjoyed the early heat of the sun on his bare arms, and the faintly bitter tang of that first steaming cup of coffee at the Café des Arts, where he liked to slather sweet butter of a kind only the French can make onto a still-hot baguette and munch it happily, watching the Saint-Tropez world go by. He liked looking at the hardworking locals, the suntanned tourists, the chic celebrities, and the snooty Parisians, plus there were more cute girls to the square mile here than anywhere else in the world.

Heading for that cup of coffee, he edged his way through the swarms of housewives clutching their *filets,* their net shopping bags. He was passing the cheese stall, sniffing the pungent odors appreciatively, when Lola Laforêt turned abruptly right into his path.

She took a quick step back, stuck out an arm to balance herself, and dropped her bags. Big Dog was quick; he'd wolfed down a perfect roulade of Madame Auric's goat cheese before she even had time to move.

"Oh, you bad dog!" she yelled, stamping her foot, making Jack laugh.

Her brown eyes blazed at him through a disorderly fringe of taffy hair.

"It's all *your* fault," she said accusingly.

"I agree. And I'm sorry." He bent to rescue whatever he could from the cobblestones. "You got Bad Dog's name right, though, but he considers anything on the floor fair game. Of course I'll replace the cheese," he added, glancing at the dog, still hopefully sniffing the cobblestones. "And Bad Dog will apologize. Come on, boy, say you're sorry."

The shaggy black mutt rolled his dark eyes at Jack in a give-me-a-break-why-don't-you look, then flopped reluctantly onto his belly. He rolled over, paws in the air, and gazed beseechingly at Lola.

"Fraud!" Lola snapped, unmoved by his charm.

"Hey, you can't say he didn't try."

"Yeah, *after* he ate the cheese."

Looking at her angry face, Jack thought she was definitely cute, if a little edgy. He held out his hand, giving her the smile that had wowed many women but had no effect on this one. "Anyhow, how are you this morning, Lola Laforêt?" He grinned as he said the name and she said defensively, "I used to be plain Lola March before I married the *Frenchman*."

"The Frenchman, huh." He eyed her thoughtfully. "Correct me if I'm wrong, but do I detect something ominous about that phrase?"

Lola clutched her string bags to her chest; she wasn't about to spill her problems and her life story to a stranger. "I don't know what you mean," she said defensively, but Jack Farrar was looking over her shoulder.

"Then maybe you also don't know why a guy who looks very much like a cop is following you?"

"*Bonjour,* Madame Laforêt." Detective Mercier tipped a careless hand to his hat, ignoring Jack. "I trust you have not yet heard from your husband?"

Lola bristled like an old hairbrush, every ginger hair seeming to stand angrily on end. "Would I be here, doing the marketing, if I had?"

"I must warn you to be careful, madame," the detective said. "Do not stray too far. We need to know exactly where you are at all times. Please remember that." And touching a finger to his hat brim again, he melted back into the crowd.

"Sounds like the French version of 'lady, you'd better not leave town' to me," Jack said, with a grin. "So, what have you been up to, Lola Laforêt?"

To his horror she looked ready to burst into tears. He glanced quickly around for help and saw Sugar making her way toward him.

Actually, you couldn't miss Sugar. She was in a skimpy red bandeau top and a white skirt that just about covered what was necessary. Plus she was in the company of a couple of bronzed young guys who might have stepped out of the male-model-of-the-year calendar. Jack guessed his time with Sugar might be up, and anyhow she certainly wasn't the right woman to comfort another woman.

He glanced uncomfortably at Lola, who looked very definitely upset.

"So, what's up, Lola?" he said, wishing he'd never met her.

She looked back at him, brown eyes wide and scared. "The police think I killed my husband," she said.

From out of the corner of his eye, Jack saw Sugar's pouty red mouth form a silent *wow*. He flung an arm around Lola

Laforêt's shoulders, grabbed her string bags, and called to Bad Dog.

"Tell you what," he said, "why don't I buy you a cup of coffee and a brandy, and then you can tell me all about it."

CHAPTER 19

He found a quiet table under the sycamores at the always bustling Café des Arts, then helped Lola into a chair facing away from the other customers. He summoned a waiter, ordered *deux fines* and *deux cafés*, then added a couple of croissants in the belief that if drink didn't make her feel better, then maybe food would.

"So, okay," Lola said, pulling herself together. "And thank you, Mr. Farrar."

Jack leaned back in his chair. He took a good long look at Lola Laforêt. "That's okay," he said. "And it's Jack."

"Jack." She managed a smile and he thanked God she wasn't going to cry.

Sensing his concern, she said, "You don't need to worry that I'm about to bawl my eyes out."

"So what's wrong with crying? It's the normal thing to do when you're upset."

"And how would you know?" she said.

He shrugged. "I've had my moments."

"Hah," she snorted. Jack grinned; she actually *snorted*. "I doubt that. And anyhow, I'm supposed to be the strong one."

"Sure," he said, though he wasn't sure about it at all.

"The strong woman, that's me," Lola added. "I'm the one who always looks after everybody."

Jack put the glass of brandy in front of her. She gazed doubtfully at it. "Aw, come on, Lola Laforêt," he said, exasperated. "I'm not trying to get you drunk. I'd just like to get you back to the point where when my dog eats your cheese you don't fall to pieces."

"It wasn't the *cheese*."

"So it was the detective. *And* the Frenchman. The husband you might—or might not—have killed. You'll notice I'm giving you the benefit of the doubt here."

"Thanks a lot." She threw him another glare, then took a sip. *"Jack,"* she added, giving his name a sarcastic emphasis.

Jack piled sugar into his espresso, then drank it down in one long sweet gulp. "So now we're friends, *Lola,* why don't you tell me the whole story."

"Why? So you can have a little spicy gossip to share with your girlfriend over dinner tonight? Well, let me tell you—*Jack*—I did *not* kill my husband. Patrick just disappeared . . . like smoke."

She picked up the croissant and took a bite. God, she was *famished*!

"Okay, so tell me what happened," Jack said.

She took another bite of the croissant as though wondering why she should be telling a stranger her story. Then she told him the whole truth and nothing but the truth. At least that's what she said.

"I went crazy trying to find Patrick," she finished. "I tried everything, I hounded the local police, I even hired a private investigator but all he did was spend *his* time and *my* money hanging out in bars in Marseilles."

She had already finished the first croissant and now she took a big bite out of the second; nothing like food in a crisis, he supposed.

"Of course, I questioned Patrick's friends," she went on, "*and* his girlfriends, *and* the local bartenders. Nothing. It seems when a person wants to disappear, he just can."

"Or else something happened to him."

"But what? And why? Patrick wasn't a bad *man*. He was just a bad *husband*. Of course, I knew about the other women," she said. "I confronted Patrick about his . . . philandering. He told me it wasn't his fault. He said they were just girls looking for a good time, they almost fell at his feet.

"Let me tell you something else, Jack Farrar," she said, looking him in the eye. "If I were going to kill Patrick, it would have been there and then. But I didn't. And before you ask, yes, I wanted to leave him, but I couldn't leave the hotel. It's my home, my own little oasis, a safe, beautiful place in this big, wide, difficult world."

"The police seem to think you might. What are you going to do about that?"

She heaved a sigh, dredged up all the way from her beribboned espadrilles. "It's simple, really," she said. "All I have to do is find Patrick, then they'll know I'm innocent." She thought for a minute then added, "There's another reason I need to find him, though. I want to ask him, face to face, what the hell he thought he was doing just going off like that, leaving me with all the worry, the problems, the suspicions."

"So if you find Patrick, do you want him back?"

She shook her head. "No. I don't. And you know why? First, he's too handsome; second, he's too sexy; and third, he's too French." She laughed. "Sounds like every girl's blueprint for the perfect man, right? Only trouble is, he shared those qualities around quite amiably with all and sundry. Hey"—she lifted a shoulder in a shrug—"let's face it, it *was* all displayed for him to choose from, right here on the beaches in the south of France. As tempting and available as ice cream on a hot summer day."

"And it probably meant as little to him."

"Well, isn't that the old alpha-male myth." She snorted *again*. "Tell that to today's woman-scorned, Mr. Farrar, and you'll find yourself in double-standard trouble."

"And what if you find him, only to bury him?" Jack Farrar said. She stared, horrified, at him, unable to answer. "I guess you must have really loved him," he added gently.

"Oh, I loved Patrick all right," she said. "In the beginning, I loved him. I believed everything about him, everything he told me. But you know what? Even now, six years later, I still don't know *who* Patrick really is. I guess I never *really knew* him."

CHAPTER 20

Lola

MOLLIE NIGHTINGALE HEADED PURPOSEFULLY TOWARD US, straw hat slammed over her eyes, handbag clutched close to her chest in case of muggers.

She checked my bewildered face and threw Jack a stern glare. "This young woman has enough troubles without you adding to them," she said.

"Ma'am, you've got it all wrong. I'm the rescuer."

"It was the police that upset me," I said quickly, letting him off the hook. "I was shopping, I dropped my stuff and Bad Dog ate my cheese, then Jack heard Detective Mercier say I'd better not leave town, so I told Jack the detective thinks I've killed Patrick, and he bought me coffee and brandy, and now I've eaten all the croissants and I've told him all about Patrick's disappearance or at least everything I know about it and . . . and well, now I don't know what to do. Except I have to find Patrick so they won't think I killed him." It all came out in one long breath.

Miss N turned to the waiter. "Three espressos and make

them strong," she ordered. Then she said to us, "Of course, had we been in England I would have ordered a nice pot of tea. There's nothing like it for helping solve a problem."

Jack looked bemused, but he offered her his hand. "My name is Jack Farrar," he said.

"And mine is Mollie Nightingale. Ex-headmistress of Queen Wilhelmina's, the best girls' school in London." She took a sip of her coffee and nudged me to do the same, glancing at Jack over the cup's rim. "And what do *you* do, Mr. Farrar?"

He grinned. "Isn't that considered bad form in England? Asking people what they do?"

"That may be, but you understand I need to know *who* and *what* you are."

Jack got to his feet. "Truth of the matter is, Miss Nightingale, I have no personal interest in Patrick or in his disappearance, except that my dog ate his wife's cheese. And since my role in this affair is now complete, I'm happy to be on my way."

"Not so fast." Miss Nightingale waved him imperiously back into his seat. Jack probably hadn't felt like this since he was ten years old and had been called before the principal for carving his initials in his desk.

Miss N pushed her glasses farther up her nose, the better to look him up and down. She liked what she saw and she nodded, then took another sip of coffee and said, "Lola is in serious trouble and she needs all the help she can get. Mr. Farrar, I may look like a simple old lady, but I want you to know that I was married to a Scotland Yard detective." She gave him a piercing glance over the rim of her coffee cup. "And that's no small change, as you Yanks would say. He was a powerful man, my Tom. A dangerous man too, because he had no thought for his own safety.

"Tom would often talk to me about the criminal mind and his theories on how it worked. He said it wasn't all that difficult. Criminal minds seem to think alike, and most of them are not all that clever, though there are a few exceptions, mostly in the corporate world. However, I helped Tom solve several of his cases, always behind the scene, of course, because no man wants to think his wife is cleverer than he is, do they?"

Her pale blue eyes behind those big glasses were so innocent that we both laughed.

"Anyhow," Miss N said, "I'm pledging Lola my help and the benefit of my criminal experience. No matter what has happened to Patrick, we shall find out. And if he's run off with another woman, my best advice to you, Lola, is get rid of him. And if it's . . . *the worst*"—she phrased it delicately—"then our job is to find out who did it."

It felt so *good* to have someone on my side, someone who believed in me, someone to help me. I leaned over and clasped Miss N's hand in mine. "Thank you. Again," I said, and Miss N smiled and patted my hand soothingly. "There, there, child," she said, as she must have a thousand or more times to distressed schoolgirls. "It'll be all right in the end, I promise you."

Jack Farrar was looking at us, obviously wondering how he'd gotten himself into this and no doubt looking for a way out.

I still don't know what made him say it, but say it he did.

"Okay, so we have to find Patrick," Jack Farrar said. "Count me in."

CHAPTER 21

JACK WALKED ME BACK TO MY CAR. I DIDN'T SAY MUCH EN route, I'd finally run out of steam. My rusty CV2 looked about to collapse under the strain of age and hard work. It hadn't been washed in weeks and was covered in a fine layer of dust. Bad Dog circled it then lifted a contemptuous leg on a rear tire.

I scowled, then turned to glare at Jack.

"Hmm." He looked at the car again.

"It works for me," I said, my stiff posture betraying my irritation.

"Looks as though that car's been working for you for a very long time." He gave the hood a little thump with his fist. "Damn good little workhorse, always was, or so I heard. Never owned one personally."

"You don't know what you're missing, but then people like you probably run around in silver BMW convertibles, or red Ferraris."

"Just goes to show how little you know about 'people like

me.' Besides, don't you know it's bad to make generalizations?"

He opened the car door; it groaned and when I switched on the engine it trembled like a tired old mare.

I wound the window down. "So what *do* you drive?"

"Certainly not a BMW, or a Ferrari."

"How about a red Corvette?"

He laughed. "Red's right. A Ford F350 quad-cab pickup. I'm a working man. Like you I need to haul stuff, only in my case it's boat stuff, not the marketing."

I shoved my hair back with an impatient hand and pushed my sunglasses on top of my head. I doubted Jack Farrar thought there was a beauty lurking under all that hair. I was a mess. He slammed the car door. The catch was loose and, like everything else, it rattled.

"Are you sure this thing is safe?"

"It's been safe for more than six years, no reason it shouldn't be now."

"Good feminine reasoning."

"Good masculine answer." My exasperated sigh made him laugh.

"You take dates out in that Ford pickup?" I asked.

"Depends. But my other car's a Porsche."

"Hah!" I gave a triumphant snort. "I knew it."

"An *old* Porsche, but it's built for speed and I guess I'm a speedster at heart."

I put on the sunglasses and leaned out the window, looking up at him. "I don't know why you're doing what you're doing, Jack Farrar," I said, suddenly humble, "but . . . thank you."

"Truth be told, I don't exactly know why either." He

grinned at me. “There’s just something about you, I guess.”

I backed the car out of the tight parking spot, made a quick U-turn and bounced off down the narrow street, and he lifted his arm in a goodbye wave.

CHAPTER 22

Jack

HEY, JACK," SUGAR SAID, "WHAT'RE YOU UP TO WITH THAT miserable-looking babe?"

"Saving her from a fate worse than anything you could imagine."

He linked his arm through Sugar's and they walked toward the Quai Jean-Jaurès followed by Bad Dog, still sniffing for fallen treasures among the market debris. Sugar's flesh was smooth and warm under his hand, cool and fresh as if she'd just emerged from the sea. Which he knew she had, not too long ago, because he'd swum with her off the boat early that morning.

"You jumping ship?" he asked, over an omelette fines herbes at Le Gorille. Helping women out of their troubles had whetted his appetite and he was suddenly starving, and besides, the damsel in distress had eaten all the croissants.

Sugar's blue eyes met his. She hitched up her red top and crossed her long brown legs. "Thinking of it," she said casually.

"No time like the present, Sugar," he said.

She flashed him a wide white smile. "Great," she said. "Just want you to know we'll always be friends."

He reached across the table for her hand. "Sure," he said, "and it was great while it lasted."

"Fun," Sugar agreed. "It was fun."

He finished his omelette and called the waiter for the bill. "Come on, I'll take you back to the boat. You'll get your stuff and I'll take you wherever you want to go."

Sugar's eyes lit up but she was looking beyond him at the two bronzed young gods heading her way. "Thanks," she said, "but no need. The guys will help me."

Jack got up and wrapped himself around her in a bear hug, which made Bad Dog prance on his hind legs and bark jealously. "Take care, Sugar," he said.

"See y'all around," she called as she headed into the arms of both bronze gods.

He watched them go, Sugar in the middle, their muscular young arms wrapped around her waist. Have a good time, Sugar, he thought, you're only young once.

And that brought him back to the problem of Lola Laforêt, the Bambi-eyed waif with a missing husband and a possible murder rap hanging over her ginger head. Just what had he gotten himself into? And what was he going to do about it?

He looked at Bad Dog sitting faithfully at his feet, awaiting the next event. No use asking him, Jack thought, patting the dog's scruffy head. He'd just have to find out for himself.

CHAPTER 23

Miss N

"Young man!"

Miss Nightingale bore down on Jack, straw hat slammed firmly over her eyes and tied under her chin with a scrap of green ribbon that did not match the green of her safari outfit. Nor did it match her sensible sandals, the sort middle-aged English ladies have always worn on holidays: flat and beige, strapped around the ankle and good for walking on seaside promenades, or in this case, for strolling cobbled marketplaces in the south of France and riding a small Vespa along sandy hill roads.

"Young man," she called again.

Jack pointed a finger to his chest. "Me?"

"Of course, *you*." She was a little out of breath from her dash.

He grinned. "It's been a while since anyone called me a young man."

Miss N pushed her glasses back up her aquiline nose. She

looked him up and down. "Young enough. Exactly how old are you anyway?"

"Miss Nightingale," Jack said with a sigh, "are you always this blunt?"

"Blunt?"

"I mean, do you always go around asking total strangers what they do for a living and where they're from and exactly how old they are? Next thing you'll want a copy of my bank statement."

"Your finances are the last thing on my mind. What's more important is the state of Lola's head."

"Who can blame her? It sounds like she might be arrested for the murder of her husband any minute."

"Let's not count our chickens before they're hatched, Mr. Farrar. There's still no body."

"There's no body *yet*."

They stood looking at the massive yachts gleaming with brass, and the beautiful bronze people glittering with gold and jewels and very little else.

Jack shoved his hands in the pockets of his ancient shorts. "Saint-Tropez in the summer," he said. "Good-looking women and men up to no good. Too much money and boats nobody loves. Most of 'em are rentals anyway. Nobody cares who built them, what they can do, only how big and expensive they are. There's not much 'love' out there in the marina."

Miss Nightingale shoved her hands in her pockets too. She thought he'd called it right. "Is that why you moored your sloop in the Hotel Rivera cove?"

"You mean, was it because I couldn't afford to join the world-class players here? Or did I just like it better there?"

"That's exactly what I meant. And I can see there's no use beating about the bush with you, Mr. Farrar. You're the kind that calls a spade a spade."

She met his eyes frankly, assessing him the way he was assessing her. "You have nice eyes," she said. "Blue like my Tom's, only his were more of a Nordic-blue. Kind of icy if I were truthful; to match his icy personality some said. He was never icy with me though, but then only I knew the *true* Tom. He was a shy man, you know, a loner, uncomfortable with his colleagues except when he was on the job. He was never one to prop up the bar with the boys after work, unless it was to talk about a case, of course. Though I don't get the feeling you're a shy man, Jack," she added. "Just a bit of New England reserve, I'd guess. Anyhow, I don't mind your sizing me up. It's always good to know who you're dealing with, especially in tricky situations."

"Who exactly *are* you, Miss Nightingale, behind that façade of the nice English lady?" Jack said with a smile, and Miss N thought that smile was the kind most women would find too seductive for their own good.

Jack asked Miss N if she'd fancy a little boat ride, then he apologized for calling her Miss N, and said he'd heard Lola call her that. "Somehow it fits," he added. "Kinda Agatha Christie, everybody gathered in the library to find out if the butler did it."

Miss N threw back her head, laughing delightedly. "That's just what my Tom said. A latter-day Miss Marples, he called me. The original one, in the books, he meant. Not that he was right, of course, it's just that I've always been nosy and that doesn't hurt when you're looking for criminals. It's amazing how people will talk: neighbors, friends, barmen."

"But not in Lola's case. Seems nobody round here wants to talk, and if they know anything they're certainly not saying. Anyhow, Miss N, what d'ya say about that sail around the harbor? It's a bit of a walk, my dinghy's moored all the way at the end. I wouldn't have liked to see her tucked in with all these big boys, not quite her style."

Miss N trusted her gut instinct with Jack Farrar: he was definitely better than he'd seemed at first sight. Of course, she'd had her doubts on the second sighting when she'd seen him hugging that sexy blonde so tightly she'd thought he might squeeze her right out of that tiny red top.

"Who's the blonde?" she asked, with her prim Queen smile. "Is she your girlfriend?"

Jack threw her a startled look, then he groaned. "The answer to that is Sugar is an *ex,* though I admit that's only of recent vintage."

"Like ten minutes ago in Le Gorille? I must say that that certainly didn't look like a kiss-off hug to me."

"And what exactly do you know about kiss-off hugs?"

He was getting exasperated, and Miss N let it go, even though it was important, because if Jack Farrar were going to get close to Lola, she needed to vet him first. There was no time for any more "mistakes" in Lola's life.

"You've got me there, young man," she said. "And it's true I don't know much about goodbye kisses, but that's because I never had one. Never had boyfriends, you see. Tom was my first and only."

Just speaking of Tom conjured the two of them sitting companionably in their pretty cottage garden as they often did after supper, watching the sunset. On evenings like these,

Tom would finally be at ease with himself. They would slip off their shoes and socks and wiggle their bare toes in the grass, which Tom said, quite romantically for him, somehow made him feel at one with the earth. Or at least their own small part of it. She laughed at his huge feet, size fifteen. "Proper policeman's feet," she teased, making him laugh too. He put on the woolly jumper she'd knitted, which he said was his favorite and that he wore to keep out that dratted north wind. "That wind will kill the tulips and one day it'll kill me," he said one extra-chilly spring evening.

"Don't say that, Tom," she cried, alarmed, unable to bear the thought of him dying even from so remote a possibility as the English spring wind. And he gave her a quick kiss on the cheek and said thanks for worrying about me, darling Mollie, but no cold wind's ever going to carry me off—not as long as I've got you to knit jumpers for me and keep me warm in bed. Then he gave her the eye and said how about it, girl, gesturing to the narrow wooden stairs leading to their bedroom, smiling at her.

She swore she'd turned beet-red because she was always rather shy about things "like that." Shy in a way that Jack Farrar and his gorgeous girlfriend would never have been, not in their entire lives.

But Tom had taught her a thing or two about sex as well as love. And knowing about sex, really understanding it as a primal urge, had helped in her detective "work" too; knowing how men felt about it and what they really thought about sex and women, and how often "love" was not even in the equation.

Sex was sex. Tom said it stood alone as the primary motivating force in murder. Nothing else touched it for a motive, not even money. And that's what she needed to talk to Jack about.

"How about it, Miss N," Jack said again, and she came back to the present, startled. "The boat ride around the bay?" he added.

"Oh. Oh, of course," she said, and she smiled, a very mischievous smile, because her head was still up in the past, in bed with Tom.

"I'm not made of Wedgwood china, you know," she said as Jack helped her too carefully into the dinghy. She hated to be thought "old" when, inside, she was still that spring chicken.

"Sorry," he said. Then, exasperated, "Between you and Lola I seem to have been saying 'I'm sorry' all morning."

Once they were out of the marina, Jack let out the throttle. Dangling a hand over the side, Miss N gazed into the clear turquoise water, enjoying the cool spray on her arm. In all her years of coming to the Côte d'Azur she had never once been *on* the water, only looked at it from the shore. Now she was enjoying herself.

Over the clatter of the little outboard, she shouted, "So how old are you anyway, Jack Farrar?"

"Bloody hell," he said, sounding almost as English as Tom. "You never give up, do you."

"My husband said that was one of my better characteristics." She thought Jack was a really handsome man, especially when he laughed.

They were alongside the sloop now and Jack shut off the outboard, letting the dinghy drift astern. He grabbed the line trailing in the water, tugged the dinghy alongside, and secured it with what Miss N sincerely hoped was a good strong nautical knot.

"I'm forty-two, Miss N," he said, climbing aboard the sloop. "Young enough."

"Young enough for what?" she asked, innocent as a cherub.

He really laughed then, throwing back his head delightedly, as he helped her aboard. "I'm beginning to think you're a very wicked lady. And the answer is young enough for sex, love, and rock 'n' roll—in that order."

"Well, of course I'd prefer to reverse the first two, but at least you included love." She sat on a pile of coiled rope, beige-sandaled feet tucked neatly under her. She pushed her glasses up her nose, pushed up her sleeves, straightened her sunhat, and accepted Jack's offer of a cold drink. "Lemonade is fine, thank you," she said.

"No lemonade. Coke, orange juice, Evian."

"Evian will do nicely."

She liked that he poured it into a glass for her and didn't just hand her a bottle as so many people did these days. Manners count, she'd always taught her Queen Wilhelmina's girls, and so does politeness; they smooth the rougher edges of our lives, keep us civilized.

"Now about Lola," she said. "Or to be more exact—about Patrick." She gave him a sharp look. "What d'you think's happened to him? Has he run off with another woman and left Lola in the lurch? Is it money trouble? Or is he dead?"

"There's only one answer to that," Jack said. "He's dead. I feel it in my bones."

"Hah! So do I. And my bones don't lie. And that, my dear Jack, leaves us with the dilemma of whether Patrick was murdered. And whether or not Lola did it."

Jack took a long slug of the icy Stella Artois. "Do *you* think she did it?"

"Of course not. This is an outside job, and to tell you the truth I haven't any idea where to start looking for Patrick, or his killer. But there has to be a *motive.* Whoever killed Patrick had something to gain. This is no spur-of-the-moment crime of passion, it's too clean, too neat, and the body has been cleanly disposed of. It took the police six months just to find the car, which leads me to believe it was dumped in that Marseilles garage recently. No silver Porsche is just going to sit in a public garage space unnoticed for six months, now is it?"

Jack nodded in agreement. "I knew Patrick, of course," she added. "I've been coming to the hotel ever since it opened. He was always in and out of the place. Handsome chap, a bit smooth, a lady-killer. And he loved that car almost as much as he loved himself. That Porsche gave him an image, a façade he presented to the world. That car *was* Patrick. Or at least he thought it was."

"So, the car disappears, Patrick disappears, the car reappears . . . what next?"

Miss N leveled a look at him from behind her Queen Elizabeth glasses. "What do you think?"

Jack looked across the stretch of shining blue water at the Hotel Riviera. So beautiful, so peaceful; a place where a man could unwind and leave his daily cares behind, nurtured by a taffy-haired woman called Lola.

"I think Lola might be in danger," he said quietly. "I feel that in my bones too."

Miss N nodded. "I'm afraid you're right," she said, but she was also thinking it would be jolly nice for Lola to have a man around the house. Especially one like Jack Farrar. "A girl couldn't ask for a better bodyguard," she said.

Jack's eyebrows rose. "Me?"

"Who else?" She smiled. "And thank you for offering," she added, leaving him totally bewildered, and somehow saddled with the responsibility for Lola Laforêt's safety.

CHAPTER 24

Lola

Miss N had made arrangements to meet Jack Farrar for drinks and a "conference" here at the hotel at six-thirty, but I was afraid to look at the clock, ticking away the minutes, because it meant soon I would have to face reality, and somehow I knew it would not be good.

I wandered forlornly into the kitchen. Nadine took one look at my worried frown and said in French, "Is this going to become a habit then, this moping? Because if so it's highly unbecoming."

"I have a headache," I said. So she wrung out a cloth in ice water, sat me into a chair, and held it over my eyes. It was so damn cold I yelled at her and heard her laugh.

"Get your nerves together, Lola," she said, "this is no time to fall to pieces. We have a dinner to produce. Besides," she added curtly, "Patrick's not worth the tears."

So I pulled myself together one more time and worked out my tensions preparing dinner.

I was in a frenzy of cooking, pounding my opinion of

Detective Mercier in the mortar and pestle along with the tapenade, that earthy blend of olives, anchovies, tuna, capers, and oil that I would later serve with drinks. After that I put a batch of Roma tomatoes, halved and topped with a touch of garlic and a hint of thyme, salt and pepper, into a slow oven to melt down to a sugary sweetness, to be served on slices of oven-crisped foccacia, with a sprig of rosemary.

Marit was painstakingly cleaning the Saint-Pierre which I would cook quickly in a little butter, and serve with a sauce flavored with wine and fresh herbs. And before you ask, yes, like most French chefs, I do use cream and butter. Anyone visiting the Hotel Riviera must put away their city fears for a while and just indulge; after all, it's not going to put pounds on you in just a couple of weeks. Besides, that's what a vacation is all about.

Jean-Paul, moving fast for once, was cleaning the fruits and vegetables brought to our door, as they were every morning, by a local *maraîcher,* a market gardener. There were tiny carrots with the little tufts of green left on top; white radishes that crunched when you bit them; creamy baby cauliflower; zucchini the size of my pinky; and tiny beans, crisp as twigs. A pile of salad greens awaited his attention, plus the ingredients for the vinaigrette: olive oil from Monsieur Alziari in Nice—in my opinion quite simply the best; champagne vinegar from Reims; mustard from Dijon; salt from the sea; and peppercorns from Morocco—how I love their aroma when they are crushed. Add a clove of our local purple garlic and a little fine sugar to taste. Whisk it until it emulsifies—and you've got yourself a great salad.

I had to keep moving, keep working; I couldn't allow myself to think about Patrick. I slid Barry White onto the

CD player and turned up the volume. Grabbing a knife I butchered the hell out of a leg of lamb, then I threw myself into preparations for dessert.

A clafoutis would be my special tonight, the easiest and tastiest of "puddings." A simple batter made from flour, eggs, sugar, cream, and cherries or other fruits layered in the bottom of a gratin dish, a lathering of kirsch, a good sprinkling of sugar, then the batter poured on top. More shavings of butter layered on that and another sprinkle of sugar, then bake the whole thing in a 400-degree oven for about twenty-five minutes. This is best served just warm when the batter is custardy and the cherries pop in your mouth like little taste bombs.

I went outside and picked figs from my own trees. They were ripe and sweet, and I'd serve them simply with a little raspberry sorbet and a splash of raspberry eau de vie.

I whirled around that kitchen, throwing brownies together, wiping off tiled surfaces, inspecting work in progress. Finally, I walked out onto the terrace for a breather.

I paced, arms folded tightly across my chest, head down, not even glancing at the view, at least not at first, then my eyes slid sideways. The sloop swung gently at anchor with no sign of life on board. I thought of the Naked Man, aka Jack Farrar, and his sculptured Blonde taking a siesta together and felt a surprising pang of something I suspected was jealousy. Then I told myself, of course I couldn't be *jealous,* I hardly knew the man, I just envied his carefree lifestyle is all.

There was a familiar squawk as Scramble lumbered around the corner. I caught her in my arms, kissing her silken feathers, and she crooned a soft little hen-tune in my ear. "I love you, you funny little creature," I said, smoothing her kissed feathers back into place. She gave me that sideways chicken look again and I asked myself one more time, was it really too much to believe that look meant "I love you too?"

Barry White's deep voice rumbled over the terrace. Was that man sexy or what? I wondered whether Jack Farrar could hear Barry singing about "lurve" and how he was "never gonna let you down, baby." Oh, for a man like Barry, I sighed, just as my sweet honeymoon couple, the golden-headed pair of lovebirds themselves, appeared on the terrace.

"Are you all right, Lola?" Mr. Honeymoon asked.

"Of course we know what's going on," Mrs. Honeymoon added sympathetically. "Everybody does. It's just we didn't like to mention it. But I can see you're upset. Has there been, I mean, you know . . . *bad news*?"

"Not that kind of bad news," I said. "Just general bad news."

Mr. Honeymoon's arm tightened around my shoulders. "Lola, my dad's a solicitor, an attorney you'd call him. He has associates in Paris and in Avignon. A lot of Brits have bought property in France and they're always in trouble, so he knows a lot about how things work here. If you need legal help, he's your man."

They were so sweet, so concerned, and so staunch in their support. I thanked them, thinking for the second time that day how lucky I was to find I had friends and that I was not alone. Then I remembered. "Weren't you supposed to be going home today?"

"Of course we were, but we're enjoying ourselves so much we decided to stay another week," Mr. Honeymoon said. "Nadine told us it was okay and that we could keep our room. I hope it's all right with you," he added anxiously.

"All right? Why, that's wonderful," I said. "This calls for more champagne. I'll send Jean-Paul out with it."

I hurried back to my kitchen. Everything was immaculate, everything in its place, everything gleaming, in complete contrast to my perennially cluttered little house where I headed next, with its bunches of mixed flowers jammed into pots, and the branches and leaves I picked up on my walks tossed onto the hearth. The aroma of spilled scent permeated my bedroom and yesterday's clothing lay where I'd stepped out of it. A pair of sandals were kicked under the bed, the gold lamé curtains drooped, and the gardenia candles were burned down into stubs. I sighed, regretfully. It was the perfect metaphor for my life: the hotel, my kitchen. Perfect. My cottage, and my private life. A mess.

I told myself sternly I must get myself together. I must get my hair cut, get that pedicure, buy some new clothes. But then I gave myself the same old excuse: I was too busy, there was just no *time*.

I stood under the shower, lifting my face to the cool water, rinsing away the fears. I thought this had been one of the strangest days of my life. But it was about to become even stranger.

CHAPTER 25

It was early afternoon and I was in my black leotard, attempting a few desultory exercises, trying vainly to get everything back into the place it used to be, including my mind. I swear I heard my spine creak. Probably from lack of use, I thought, disconsolately, since I was turning out to be spineless anyway. But then what I definitely *did* hear was someone walking down the path. Light footsteps. I wiped the sweat from my brow with a towel and went to greet whoever it was.

I had never set eyes on the woman standing on my front porch, but she knew who I was, all right.

"Lola," she said, smiling. "We meet at last."

"We do?" I said, astonished.

She was somewhere in her mid-forties, beautiful, petite, curved yet slender, with a long fling of dark hair and narrow turquoise eyes. I was just thinking they were so brilliant they had to be contacts, when she said, "I may call you Lola, may I not? After all, I feel as though I already know you."

"You do?" I said, astonished again.

"Because of Patrick," she said. "My old friend."

Trying to decide why the emphasis had been on *friend,* I invited her in. There seemed no option; she was obviously here to see me.

"Sorry about the mess," I said, quickly plumping up the cushions and waving her into the best chair.

"Thank you." Her accent was too charmingly French to stand; even just a *thank you* sounded soft, throaty, sexy. Oh Patrick, not another one, I thought with that familiar sinking of the heart. I asked, would she like iced tea, a diet Coke, water? It was so hot out this afternoon.

"Iced tea would be wonderful," she said, giving me a long assessing glance from beneath her lashes. "But first, I must introduce myself. I am Giselle Castille, an old friend of Patrick's. He was best man at my wedding, though of course I'm a widow now. Patrick and I have known each other since we were children." Her turquoise eyes nailed me. "But surely Patrick mentioned me? Ours has been such a *long* friendship."

Suddenly aware that I was hot and sweaty and half-naked, I tugged the leotard out of my butt and quickly wrapped the towel around my waist, wishing this glamorous woman out of my life and wishing that if Patrick's females were going to come and call, at least I could have warning and be looking my best. Madame Giselle Castille was tough competition; sexy, worldly, charming.

"Patrick didn't mention you," I replied, "but then he knew so many people." I didn't say he knew "so many women" but Giselle smiled. She knew what I meant.

"Ah," she said, "but you see, that's the way men like Patrick are, *ma chère.* Freedom is their raison d'être, they are like migrating birds, flitting from country to country following the weather, and the beautiful women. But I'm sure I don't need to tell you that."

I took a deep breath, excused myself, and went to get the iced tea. My hands were shaking as I took the glass pitcher from the refrigerator and put it on a tray. I sliced a lemon, managing to cut my finger, added a bowl of sugar, tall glasses, and long silver spoons, then carried the tray into my tiny sitting room.

Giselle Castille was examining the photos arranged on the console table behind the sofa: family photos of myself when young; with my father; with our dogs; and with my horse when Dad had a ranch for a while, in one of his many financial ups—as opposed to his financial downs, when we moved back to a condo in the suburbs of L.A.

Giselle was holding a picture of Patrick, a close-up shot I'd taken on a misty day in the gardens of the grand château in Burgundy where we had spent the night. His eyes are narrowed in a smile and his hair is ruffled by the wind, and he looks so handsome you could just die.

"Tell me, Madame Castille," I said, setting down the tray and pouring iced tea. "Why should I know about you? And why you are here?"

"You must call me Giselle." She put back Patrick's photograph and settled into the chair again. I offered lemon, which she accepted, and sugar which she did not. "I finally came to see you because I've heard rumors that the police suspect you of being involved in Patrick's disappearance. I know how upset you must be and, as Patrick's friend, I am here to offer my help. If there's anything I can do for you, anything at all, Lola, I want you to let me know. A friend is always a friend, you see, and for me that extends to Patrick's wife."

I wasn't sure I believed this, but why else would she be here? "Thank you for the kind thought," I said, "but there's not much anyone can do. I don't know where Patrick is, and neither do the police."

"They found the car, though," she said, catching me by surprise. I didn't know how police business had become public, but apparently my life was now the subject of local gossip and speculation.

Giselle stirred her tea slowly. Her long delicate hands were the color of fresh cream, the short nails painted dark red. In Pucci-patterned Capris, jeweled thong sandals, and a tight turquoise top that matched her eyes, she was a man's woman if ever there was one, with her languorous glances and the subdued sexiness French women seem to acquire without any effort at all.

"I've known Patrick since we were children," she said. "We grew up together, you might say."

I looked interested. I had never met anyone who knew Patrick when he was a child.

"We lived in Marseilles," Giselle said. "Both our families were in the fishing business. Patrick's caught the fish; mine bought it to sell on to restaurants, or to process it, to freeze it and ship it throughout France and most of Europe. My family was rich. Patrick's was not exactly poor, but not in the same league."

The long silver spoon clinked against the ice in the glass, as she stirred her tea again, a delicate summer sound, the kind you might associate with two women sharing secrets about their lovers on a hot, lazy afternoon.

"Patrick and I went to the same schools, then on to university at Grenoble, though he didn't stay the course. I went to live in Paris, and Patrick lived anywhere in the world where the living was easy and the women beautiful and the gambling available. From time to time, we would see each other, usually in Paris, and in the summer here at my villa in the hills above Cannes. Patrick would come to stay and we'd 'hang out together,' as you would put it." She eyed me from under her lashes again, the turquoise of her eyes shocking me with their cold gleam. "We were always . . . *good friends* . . . ," she said in a voice like a purr. "*Always*. And now, *ma chère* Lola, I am here as *your* friend."

"You are?" I said.

She gave me that hard glance again. "Patrick talked to me about his problems, you know. And you too can speak freely to me. I'll do my best to advise you."

"Well, thank you," I said, because she was my guest and Patrick's "good friend" and I couldn't exactly tell her to get lost and get out of my life before she even got into it.

"Of course, I lent Patrick money," Giselle added suddenly. "A lot of money. I don't know whether you know this, but Patrick was in bad financial trouble. Gambling debts. There were . . ." She hesitated. "There were 'threats . . .' "

"Threats? What kind of threats?" I said, shocked. "Maybe you should tell the police this."

She shrugged. "The police are already aware of Patrick's problems. But don't worry, Lola," she purred again, "I'm not going after *you* for the money." She gave me a long look. "Though legally, of course, I could." She glanced around. "And I suppose this little parcel of land with the so-called hotel is worth quite a bit."

Was there a hidden threat behind those words? I wondered as Giselle got to her feet, the iced tea undrunk.

"Were there signed notes for these loans?" I asked, worried now about the security of my beloved hotel.

"There was no need for notes and signatures, between Patrick and me," she said, smiling a feline little smile, "but trust me, I have other 'evidence.' "

She took a card from her designer handbag and handed it to me. "Here's my number," she said, "call me anytime. Call me if you hear from Patrick."

I walked with her to the door. She held out her hand and I shook it. It was as cool as if the day were a winter one.

"And of course," Giselle said, "we still don't know where Patrick is. Or even *if* he is," she added, sending a chill through my heart.

I watched her walk back down the path, stepping light as a panther, her long dark hair swaying in rhythm with her hips. You bastard, Patrick, I thought. Wherever I go in the world, there'll be women like this, "old friends," coming to warn me off you—dead or alive.

CHAPTER 26

I PUT GISELLE CASTILLE OUT OF MY MIND, AND MADE AN EF-fort with my appearance that evening, though it wasn't be-cause of Jack Farrar's blue eyes. Or if it was then I wasn't admitting to it. Anyhow, my freshly washed hair had dried shiny in the sun and I'd put on my best lacy underwear, purely for self-esteem purposes, and nothing at all to do with the Naked Man. I wore an apricot dress that fluttered, charmingly I hoped, around my knees, though looking in the mirror I suspected knees were not my best feature. But then whose knees are? You have to have confidence in these matters, I told myself, gazing upward and sweeping mascara over my lashes. I took another doubtful look. Maybe I should have used black instead of brown.

I turned away, exasperated. *This* was who I was and it would have to do. I sprayed my neck with Dior's Tendre Poison, bought because I loved the green glass bottle but now I also loved its light feathery scent. I touched up my chipped nail polish, promising myself a pedicure tomorrow, and slid my too-long feet into the strappy bronze sandals I'd bought in the end-of-season sales which, by the way, are always terrific in Saint-Tropez, after the tourists have departed and the hotels are beginning to close. I tested the three-inch heels cautiously, wondering whether they'd been a mistake, but they were so pretty and reduced to almost a gift that I hadn't been able to resist.

I didn't remember dressing up as being such hard work, but maybe that was because I hadn't done it in such a long time. I took a final look and decided I'd do. Besides, I should have been in the kitchen fifteen minutes ago, or else serving drinks and telling my guests about tonight's menu, and asking about their day. I headed for the door, thinking how surprised they'd be when they saw me; all they usually got was me in chef's white's or, at most, a T-shirt and Capris.

I stopped, my hand on the doorknob, thinking about it. Maybe I'd overdone it. Jack Farrar was coming to talk about Patrick, he wasn't coming to see *me*.

I ran back to the bedroom, flung off the dress and the heels, tugged on my usual Hotel Riviera tee and Capris, shoved my feet into comfortable thong sandals, and shook my hair out of its unaccustomed neatness. Without a further look in the mirror, I marched firmly back to my rightful place in the world. *My kitchen.*

Out on the terrace, Jean-Paul was setting out bowls of olives and crudités and Miss Nightingale was already at her table, sipping pastis. I admired her blue and white dress and said I thought she looked like a piece of Wedgwood china, and she laughed and gave me a conspiratorial wink as I hurried by. I sneaked a quick glance across the bay at *Bad Dog.*

Nothing doing there. But it was still only six-fifteen. Too early for the Naked Man.

I checked Nadine and Marit in the kitchen, then piled tomato bruschetta onto platters and garnished them with sprigs of rosemary cut from the bush outside the kitchen window. I mounded tapenade into small bowls and piled straw baskets with different breads. I checked my figs; checked the fish; checked the lamb and the salad and the clafoutis; then went back outside to check on my guests.

To my surprise Mr. Falcon was in conversation with Miss Nightingale. She must have waylaid him on his way to his table.

"That's a wonderful machine you have out there, Mr. Falcon," I heard her say.

"Er, thank you, ma'am. I kinda like it myself," he replied.

"My husband had a Harley. Turquoise it was. An odd color for a Scotland Yard detective, don't you think?"

Falcon shifted his expensively loafered feet, obviously uncomfortable. "Er, yes, ma'am. I guess so."

"Still, a powerful machine suits a powerful man, I always say." Miss N cocked her head to one side, smiling at him, but he was already edging away.

"Yeah. Well, I'm sure you're right, ma'am."

"It's Miss Nightingale, Mr. Falcon," she called after him. "And it's very nice to meet you too."

But he was already hurrying to a table at the end of the terrace, as far away from her as he could get.

"Why Miss N, I do believe you scared Mr. Falcon away," I said, depositing tapenade and bruschetta on her table.

"Just thought I'd break the ice," she said serenely. "See

what he's really like under that tough-guy façade."

"And did you?"

"Just as I thought, he's dangerous." She nibbled on an olive. "The question is, what exactly is he doing here? The Hotel Riviera is clearly not where he wants to be. Logically, my dear Lola, it must have something to do with Patrick."

Suddenly legless, I dropped into the chair next to her. "But what?" I said, just as Jack Farrar turned the corner onto the terrace.

CHAPTER 27

I TOOK IN THE FADED OLD JEANS ON THE LEAN HARD BODY, the crumpled white shirt rolled at the sleeves. Obviously they were not into ironing on the sloop though they *were* squeaky-clean. I also noticed the healthy sheen of his tanned skin, or maybe it was just weather-beaten to that warm gold. His face was long, his jaw square, and his blue eyes matched his jeans and had the same sort of crinkles as his shirt. His brown hair was cropped short and looked as though he might have cut it himself. His nose was what you might call positive, a bit bumpy, a little crooked, and he had a smiley mouth with the best teeth I've ever seen. He looked too good to be true.

I was glad I'd changed out of the dress; it would definitely have looked as though I were trying too hard. And I had been. And I shouldn't have.

"Miss Nightingale, Lola." Jack Farrar gave us a funny polite little bow. He gave me a long glance. "You're looking better."

"Almost human, you mean," I said, defensive about the

mascara and the lipstick and that he might think I'd fancied myself up specially for him.

He grinned. "Almost."

"Wine?" I asked.

"Wine is perfect, thanks."

This time I served a bottle from our own vineyard, around the corner and up the hill. Not up to Cuvée Paul Signac's standard, perhaps, but very soft and drinkable. Jack nodded his approval, which pleased me more than I thought it should.

"You look smart tonight, Mr. Farrar," Miss N said, and I caught the underlying note of approval in her voice that meant that she thought Jack was okay.

"Miss N has one of my guests under suspicion," I said. "The man sitting at the far end of the terrace."

Jack twisted his neck and took a peek. "I noticed him last night," he said. "I think I know him from somewhere, but I can't place him. Looks as though he wishes he were anywhere but here," he added.

"That's his Harley out front," Miss N told him in a conspiratorial whisper. She leaned closer. "I told Lola the first time I saw Mr. Falcon, he's a dangerous man."

We all stared at Falcon sitting with his back to the view, drinking whiskey and chomping down the sweet tomato bruschetta as though it were airline peanuts. His hands were large and pale with matted dark hairs along the fingers. Like some kind of creepy-crawly, I thought with a shudder. Plus he was built like a bull: the wide neck, the powerful shoulders, the long arms.

"Brutal," I found myself whispering too, though he was too far away to hear. "That's exactly how he looks. Like a brute."

"He's obviously shadowing you," Miss Nightingale said.

"Why else would he be here at the Hotel Riviera? And as I said, I'm willing to bet it's something to do with Patrick."

"And I'm willing to bet on your instincts, Miss N," Jack agreed. "I can't think of any other reason a man like that would be here." He looked at me. "Has he said anything to you?"

"Only to demand a room—our *best* room—and to order his food. Other than that he's pretty much ignored me. In fact he's ignored all of us, though he does take frequent walks around the property. Admiring the garden, I suppose."

"That man's no gardener," Miss N said.

I was watching the movement of Jack's tanned throat as he swallowed the cool pink wine. I told myself nervously I'd better get out of this sensual mode; just because I hadn't been with a man in a couple of years, not even been *near* one if truth be told, didn't mean I had to fall all to pieces when the first attractive stranger took my fancy. Besides, there was always the question of Patrick.

"I checked with an old friend in Marseilles," Jack said. I raised my eyebrows, surprised he knew anyone there. "You meet a lot of people in the sailing fraternity," he added. "A friend in every port, y'know how it goes. Anyhow, this guy is an ex-cop who does a little fine-tuned private investigating on the side. He's agreed to use his contacts, find out what he can about the Porsche—where the garage is, what state the car was in—and exactly what the police think happened to Patrick."

He gave me that long calculating look again, then blunt and to the point, said, "You know this might mean that Patrick is dead."

I stared down at my hands. I didn't know if I could handle that. I could not bear to know that beautiful disloyal Patrick was dead.

"Closure," Miss N said firmly. "That's what Americans call it."

I refilled the wine glasses with a shaky hand and asked Jean-Paul to bring another bottle, then I told them about my afternoon visitor, Patrick's old friend Giselle Castille.

"Patrick's longtime lover," Jack said, catching on immediately.

"And no doubt she's jealous," Miss N added.

"Did you know anything about gambling debts?" Jack asked.

"Only that we never seemed to have money, but you know this is just a small hotel, there's not a lot of profit to be made."

"It's Lola's 'labor of love,' " Miss N explained.

"And obviously gambling was Patrick's. Bad enough for 'the boys' to be after him, if Madame Castille is to be believed."

"I believe her," I said, suddenly sure. "I met Patrick in Las Vegas. He was always there. Sure, he was a gambler."

"And a loser," Jack added quietly.

Just then Red Shoup emerged onto the terrace. As always she looked pulled together in a way I never could hope to emulate, in a coral silk dress with an agate-green pashmina thrown around her shoulders to protect her from the breeze that had a new autumnal edge to it.

"Bonsoir, mes amis," she said. "And how are you tonight, Lola?"

I said that I was good and she turned her smile on Jack. I made the introductions, then Jerry Shoup arrived and they stayed to drink wine with us, telling us about their day.

I left them to it and went to check the kitchen again, greeting Budgie Lampson and the boys en route. I realized with a pang that the season was rapidly drawing to a close and soon all my guests would be gone. I wondered what I would do when they had left and I was here alone with my problems and the police on my tail, and gambling debts and the mysterious Mr. Falcon lurking in the background. I shuddered just thinking about it.

"Ghost walking over your grave," Budgie said cheerfully, then clapped a dismayed hand across her mouth. "Oh, dammit, I said the wrong thing *again.*"

I had to laugh because, with her frizzy mop of blond hair and baby-blue eyes, she looked the exact picture of a naughty little girl. "That's okay. And anyhow, it wasn't really a ghost, it was just a cool wind blowing up. Makes me think that autumn's coming too soon."

"Not soon enough," she said feelingly. "Then these little buggers will go back to school and I'll be reprieved. It'll be back to London for me, and back to the cold and the snow, I suppose. Oh boy, am I going to miss this place. And you too, of course, Lola." She patted my arm encouragingly just as Jean-Paul arrived with Oranginas for the boys, who were already halfway through a platter of bruschetta.

Then my adorable golden Honeymooners arrived, she simply glowing, and he sturdy and pink-cheeked and yellow-haired, with kind gray eyes behind his rimless glasses. I was so glad they had stayed on, even though they'd told us it would destroy their budget for the entire year, but they thought it was worth it. I got them settled, sent Jean-Paul around with the menus, then went back to Miss N and Jack, and the Shoups. They were all talking about the mysterious Mr. Falcon, and I supposed, about me and Patrick.

I stood there for a moment, thinking that anyone looking at

us would not see the sinister undercurrents. All they would see was a happy group of people on a flowery terrace overlooking the blue Mediterranean on a gorgeous September evening. And that's who we were, I thought, suddenly feeling better. I'd hit bottom last night with Detective Mercier and I'd gone under again this morning in the market. But now I felt a sudden lightening of my heart. I was on the way up again.

"Madame Laforêt?" I hadn't heard the man coming and neither had the others. A little man, squat and soft-footed, plump and pale; no Saint-Tropez tourist tan here. He peered at me from behind his gold glasses like a sharp-eyed little bird.

Everyone turned to look. Even Mr. Falcon stopped chomping bruschetta and looked interested.

"I am Madame Laforêt," I said.

"And I am Maître Dumas. I'm a Paris attorney representing my client, Monsieur Laurent Solis."

The silence on the terrace was palpable. Like Onassis and Safra, Solis was a name to be reckoned with. I stared at Maître Dumas, astonished.

"I have to inform you, Madame Laforêt," he said solemnly, "that Monsieur Solis is taking legal action against you in the matter ownership of the Hotel Riviera."

He held out a document tied in legal-pink ribbon and stamped with a lot of official-looking red seals. Stunned, I reached out and took it from him.

"Here is my card, madame," he said. "If you wish to contact me, as I am sure you will, you can reach me at the Hotel Martinez." He stared at me for a long moment through his tiny glasses. "*Eh bien,* I will say good evening, Madame Laforêt," he said with a little bow. "And may I wish you all *bon appétit.*" And he hurried away as silently as he had come.

CHAPTER 28

SUDDENLY, DINNER BECAME A COMMUNAL AFFAIR. TABLES were pushed together and my guests, with the exception of Mr. Falcon who had roared off on his Harley, huddled around, pouring wine and offering theories on Maître Dumas's statement, examining the legal documents, speculating on Laurent Solis's wealth and reputation, and exactly why he'd want to take my home from me.

"It's not only your home, it's your *living,*" Jerry Shoup reminded me sternly. Then Miss Nightingale said, "Patrick's at the bottom of this, I'm sure of it." Not knowing Patrick, Jack Farrar stayed on the sidelines, but he did say, "This is more complicated than I thought," which Red Shoup said was the understatement of the year.

By now I was in a state of shock and had no head for cooking, so Marit coped with dinner and Jean-Paul served, and for once everybody ate the same thing. I apologized, of course, but nobody minded; in fact, the table became almost partylike as more wine was poured and everyone tucked in to stuffed artichokes, seafood risotto and salad, then the clafoutis and tiny thin-crusted apple tarts, little wheels of brown-sugary sweetness that Marit had thrown together. More wine was poured, and the discussion shifted to what to do next.

"Maître Dumas was right," Jack said, "the only way to find out what's really going on is for you to meet with Solis."

It was said that he had made his first fortune selling arms to any country's enemies, including his own. Now, though, he was "a citizen of the world," directing his global business operations from his luxury yacht, and those businesses included hotels, property, and oil. Solis was said to have the largest fleet of tankers in the world.

Noticing my terrified expression, the whole table offered to come with me, but in the end it was decided only Jack and Miss Nightingale would accompany me. Jack went off to make the call to Maître Dumas, but he wasn't there, so we poured more wine and waited for him to return the call.

It was almost midnight when the phone rang. The Honeymooners were looking sleepy, Budgie had put the boys to bed, and the Shoups were playing cribbage. We looked silently at each other as Jack went to answer it. When he came back I asked, breathlessly, "So . . . ?"

"That was Maître Dumas. We have an appointment with Solis at eleven A.M. on the *Agamemnon* in Monte Carlo. Dumas said we can't miss it, it's the biggest yacht there."

"The *Agamemnon*," Miss Nightingale said thoughtfully. "Now that's an interesting choice, a Greek naming his yacht after a man at the root of classical Greek tragedy. Agamemnon, as you may know, was the king of Mycenae and commander of the Greek army in the Trojan War. He captured Cassandra, the daughter of the enemy king and she became his lover. Agamemnon brought her back to Troy, where he was murdered by his wife, Clytemnestra, and her lover."

I hadn't known Agamemnon's story and I found myself wondering why Solis had chosen such a name. I knew I was not going to enjoy meeting a man who could link himself so closely with such a story.

JACK WALKED ME BACK TO THE COTTAGE. "YOU SURE YOU'LL be all right?" he asked, standing, hands in his jeans pockets, on my little front porch.

"No," I said, because I could already feel my guts shriveling at the thought of losing my little hotel.

"I'm not surprised, I'd probably feel the same if somebody just told me they were about to take away my home."

"Where is your home exactly?"

"Newport, Rhode Island." He looked at me and grinned. "You wouldn't like it, it's too cold."

"Then why d'you stay there?"

"My family's always lived there. It's where I build my boats."

I leaned on the rail separating the porch from the path. There was no moon and the sea looked black, with just the sloop's riding lights gleaming green and red.

"Newport," I said. "Old family money, I suppose."

"I make my own living, doing what I like to do."

"Me too."

He came to stand next to me, his back to the sea, arms folded. I could feel him looking at me. He said, "Did you always like to cook?"

"Right from when I was a kid. Actually, my dad taught me." I laughed at his surprise. "Girls don't usually learn cooking from their fathers, and if you'd known him, you would have thought it even weirder. He was such a man-about-town, so handsome, dark hair, blue eyes, six two, and charming. All my girlfriend's mothers fell for him. And so did my girlfriends, when they were old enough." I stared into the darkness, seeing my father's handsome face, smiling at me.

"So you were a daddy's girl," Jack said, bringing me back to the present.

"Oh, I was *such* a daddy's girl. When I wasn't feeling well he'd fix soft-boiled eggs and toast soldiers for me. He'd bring them to me in bed and dip the toast into the egg yolk, feeding me like a little bird. I always felt better right away. Somehow it all seems so simple when you're a kid," I added. "You just love one other and enjoy life. When Dad died, I thought I'd die too."

We stared at each other in the dim glow of light coming from the house, then to my surprise Jack put his hands on my shoulders. He held me at arm's length, smiling at me. "I'm sorry, I've got no toast soldiers to make you feel better tonight," he said. "See you tomorrow. Nine."

"It's a date."

He gave my shoulders a little squeeze then strode off down the path to the beach.

I waited on the porch until I saw the sloop's lights go on before heading for my lonely bed.

CHAPTER 29

THE NEXT MORNING AT NINE A SAILOR IN WHITE SHORTS and a white T-shirt with "Agamemnon" printed in deep blue, was waiting for us in Saint-Tropez, in a thirty-seven-foot Sea Ray that would have been anyone else's idea of luxury. Until they saw the *Agamemnon,* moored in deep water off Monte Carlo, that is.

Picture any luxury yacht, then double it in size. The *Agamemnon* was 240 feet. Add a helicopter and a seaplane on top, a small fleet of powerboats tucked inside, and fifty or so crew, including, so the sailor told me, round-the-clock chefs, and you had your own private love boat.

I was glad I'd made an attempt to look dignified and adult, in a white cotton skirt, a yellow shirt, and my espadrilles. I'd clamped back my hair with a tortoise comb, and was wearing lipstick and dark glasses—in case I got emotional. Miss Nightingale was in her Wedgwood-blue and Jack wore his usual shorts, sneakers, and a crumpled linen shirt, untucked. We looked like a bunch of tourists taking in the big time.

"The Ritz Carlton afloat," Jack said, as the dazzling white cliff of the *Agamemnon* loomed over us. Another white-uniformed sailor helped us up the steps into what looked like heaven, but might turn out to be hell. I had a bad feeling in my stomach about which it would be.

A steward ushered us along a corridor carpeted in *Agamemnon* dark blue dotted with silver stars, then up a sweeping mahogany staircase to the grand saloon. He offered us refreshments which, though we were dying of thirst, we refused on the basis of not being seduced by the enemy. We were told that Monsieur Solis would be arriving soon and left to cool our heels in the enormous art-filled room.

I took in the view of Monte Carlo from the huge picture windows. I'd never seen it from this angle before, with the Corniche roads snaking above and below, and was surprised of how green and lush it looked.

I stared around at the tables inlaid with precious woods, at the creamy leather club chairs and sofas deep enough to get lost in. I took in the Léger, the two Picassos, the Matissse, the Brancusi sculpture, and the huge, colorful, rotund sculpture of a dancer by Niki de Saint Phalle. I noticed the antique Venetian mirrors and all the priceless bibelots and trinkets scattered around, and fear crept up my spine. There was no way I could fight this kind of wealth. For some reason, Solis wanted my little hotel and now I had no doubt he could get it. In fact, he could get anything he wanted. The puzzle was, *why* did he want it?

Jack pointed to the Niki de Saint Phalle dancer. "Remember, it's not over till the fat lady sings," he said, making me laugh, just as Laurent Solis walked into the salon.

A flicker of surprise crossed his face at our laughter,

quickly replaced by a smile as he walked toward us, both hands held out in greeting. He was older than I'd expected from his photographs; a big bear of a man, silver haired and perfectly attired in a white linen suit and dark glasses, which he did not remove.

"Welcome, welcome to the *Agamemnon*," he said.

A couple of strides behind him came a gorgeous blonde, young enough to be his granddaughter, over six feet tall in a pair of killer yellow mules, a tiny yellow bikini, a lime-green sarong, and a blinding amount of carats in diamonds—in her ears, around her neck, on her wrist, and on three of her fingers. I glanced at Miss Nightingale to see what she thought of this vision, but her face showed no reaction. Solidly queen-like in her Wedgwood-blue and pearls, she inclined her head regally as first Solis introduced himself, then said, "And this is my wife, Evgenia."

Evgenia did not bother even to nod. She took a seat in one of the club chairs immediately behind her husband, crossed her legs, lit a Gitane, and eyed us impatiently.

Laurent Solis picked me out immediately as the victim. He smiled as he took my hand in both of his. "Madame Laforêt, I'm charmed to make your acquaintance," he said, and to my surprise, I could have sworn he meant it. "It's just a pity the circumstances are so . . . unfortunate. Yes, *most* unfortunate."

I found my voice and introduced Miss Nightingale. Solis bent his head reverentially over her hand, as though she were truly a queen. "And this is Mr. Farrar," I said, touching Jack's arm for comfort more than anything. "He's a friend," I added, quickly defining the relationship, just in case Solis was wondering.

Solis shook Jack's hand, then indicated where we should

sit, lining us up on a sofa like ducks in a row at the fair, with the light from the picture window dazzling our eyes. He took a seat immediately opposite. He now had the advantage of being able to see our faces—and our reactions—perfectly, while we remained dazzled and, so to speak, in the dark about his.

"First," he said, "are you sure I can't offer you some refreshment? It's so hot today. Evgenia," he said over his shoulder, "call Manolo, tell him to bring cold drinks for my guests, and some of that baklava." He turned to us. "Unless you would prefer something else? Wine? Champagne? Bourbon?"

Behind him, Evgenia lifted a phone and relayed his order. Then she took another drag on her Gitane and crossed her legs the other way.

Solis looked at me, still behind his dark glasses. "I'm about to tell you my life story, Madame Laforêt," he said, ignoring the others, "so you will understand why I am what I am. A businessman. If it were otherwise, I would not be here today. And neither, madame, would you."

He smoothed back his thick silver hair, indicating to Manolo, who'd appeared so promptly I suspected he'd been waiting outside the door, to put the silver tray of drinks on the table next to him. Manolo did so, then stood with his white-gloved hands behind his back, awaiting further orders.

"Miss Nightingale?" Solis asked. She primly said, no, thank you. "Then perhaps a little of the baklava?" He looked greedily at the plate. "It's my favorite, in fact you might say it's my downfall."

Manolo took the silver tongs, placed a square of sugary baklava on a starry blue fragile china plate and set it on a small table, alongside Miss Nightingale. He repeated the performance for myself, then Jack. He stepped back, hands folded behind his back again. I noticed he did not serve any to his master, and we did not touch ours.

"Ice water for everyone," Solis told Manolo, looking as delighted as if he'd just given us the keys to the kingdom, or at least to his ship. "Let me tell you," he said, "baklava was not the kind of delicacy I ate in my youth. Oh no. It was years before I could afford to put anything in my mouth other than the most basic of foods. Bread, couscous, rice." He twinkled at us from behind the dark glasses. "I was, you might say, a third-world orphan before anyone had coined the phrase 'third world.' And I was alone in that world of poverty and no education."

He took a sip of his iced water. "Not a good position to be in, you might say. And I would agree, it was not."

Behind him, Evgenia closed her eyes, as if feeling her husband's pain.

"Poverty is the same in any city in the world," Solis went on. "Athens, Rio, Caracas . . . you sleep on the street, you eat whatever you can steal, you live by your wits—and if you have no 'wits,' then you die on the street. Life can be short and death sometimes merciful, for the poor."

He paused for another long swallow of ice water. "But of course," he said, and that smile appeared again, "my story, as you can see, has a happy ending. Though not without its travails. I'll begin, as all stories should, at the beginning."

CHAPTER 30

I WAS JUST SIX YEARS OLD WHEN MY MOTHER WAS RUN DOWN by a truck in the road and killed," Solis said. "It was then I learned my first lesson of real poverty. *Life is cheap.* My mother counted for nothing. I don't even know where she is buried, just somewhere by the side of that forgotten road."

My face must have registered shock because he leaned forward, elbows on his knees, hands clasped loosely, looking into my eyes.

"We were living in Morocco," he said, "but my father was Greek. He took me back to Athens to live. We were poor, as you know." He paused, looking at us. "In fact you *don't* know," he added, "because only a person who has been as poor as I was, can *know* what true poverty is like."

He opened his arms wide, embracing the sumptuous salon, the treasures it contained, his glossy young wife, the whole incredible ship that was his to command. "All you see is this," he said, "and sadly for me, that's all anyone sees of Laurent

Solis. All anyone knows about, or cares about, is that I am rich."

"And are you going to give us any other reason we should care, Monsieur Solis?" Miss Nightingale said sharply, obviously resistant to his charm.

He eyed her for a moment from behind the dark glasses, then gave a deep sigh that I thought came from the heart. I felt myself melting with sympathy. "I doubt that's possible, in the short time I shall spend in your company, Miss Nightingale," he said. "But I shall try my best."

I glanced at Jack out of the corner of my eye. His arms were folded across his chest, his face impassive. Only I seemed affected by Solis's personal charm, and his sad story.

But I was wrong, there was one other. Evgenia unraveled her long legs and came to stand behind her husband. She draped her arms around his neck. "Poor darling," she said, in a heavy Russian accent. She dropped a kiss on his silver hair and Solis took her hand and pressed it tenderly to his cheek.

"Evgenia has heard this before," he said.

"But it never fails to hurt me," she murmured, retreating to her chair again.

"Soon after we arrived in Athens, my father abandoned me," he said. "Or perhaps he just died. I never knew for I never saw him again. I was living on the streets of Piraeus, the port city southwest of Athens, finding whatever odd jobs I could, running errands, fetching, carrying. I was a little workhorse, but I was also a fast learner, and I knew there was something better than this in my destiny. And that destiny was in my own two work-scarred young hands."

He extended those hands as if for us to see—smooth, well-manicured, the hands of a rich man, if not a gentleman.

"I had no family, nothing to keep me in Greece, so I lied about my age and signed on as a cabin boy—a kind of slave you might call it—on a tanker. They were much smaller in those days." He paused for a moment, as though remembering, then, "Bound for Marseilles," he added.

"Marseilles?" I heard myself echo his words and he took off his dark glasses and for the first time I looked into his eyes. Dark eyes, gentle eyes. The windows to his soul. I felt myself sinking into them.

"I can see you are ahead of me, Madame Laforêt," he said. "And yes, Marseilles is the connection. I was a boy with nothing in the world and in Marseilles a woman I had robbed because I had no other option helped me. Her name was Nilda Laforêt and I have never forgotten her act of kindness. She refused to hand me over to the gendarmes. She gave me food, talked to me the way no one had ever talked to me in my short life. She treated me like a human being and I never forgot her.

"Many years later, I was able to repay that kindness—ah, it was more than mere kindness or even charity, it was an act of pure love on Nilda Laforêt's part.

"I revered this woman," he said, still holding my eyes with his. "Though I had no contact with her after that initial year when she helped me. But when I heard she had died, I commissioned marble angels for her grave." He paused, then added, "And of course Patrick Laforêt was her grandson."

Evgenia slithered to her feet. She stood looking down at me. She was beautiful, a natural beauty, from the blond hair to the pert breasts and the flawless golden skin. Solis glanced at her over his shoulder and again she wrapped her arms around him.

"You are such a good man, my darling," she whispered, loud enough for us to hear, then she walked to the window and turned her back, staring out at the dazzling Côte d'Azur.

"Patrick Laforêt was a notorious gambler," Solis went on. "When you met him in Las Vegas he was already drastically in debt. The casinos had allowed him a big line of credit and for a while everything was good. But gambling is like love, you win some, you lose some. Patrick had nothing left by the time he came to me, begging for a loan to stall those creditors."

Solis took time out to smile at me. "But creditors are cold-hearted people and business is business. Patrick was in an all-or-nothing situation. And all he had left to pledge against this loan was the Hotel Riviera. So I gave Patrick his money, I assumed he paid off his creditors, then he defaulted on my loan.

"And so you see, Madame Laforêt, I am now the sole and legitimate owner of the Hotel Riviera."

"But that can't be," Jack said. "As Patrick's wife, Madame Laforêt is co-owner of the hotel."

Solis shook his head slowly; his smile had suddenly lost its charm. "Patrick signed the loan document before the marriage."

Shocked, I snapped out from under his spell. Solis had spun me the story of his rise above poverty, about what a compassionate man he was, only to thrust the knife in at the end.

"Monsieur Solis, tell me exactly why you *want* the Hotel Riviera?" Miss Nightingale said.

"There's an obvious answer, Miss Nightingale, and it's the only reason Patrick was able to borrow against the property. It's rare to find undeveloped land directly on the sea, here on the Côte d'Azur. I am certain that Madame Laforêt is unaware that the land on either side of the hotel's peninsula is included in the property. Patrick was sitting on quite a little nest egg. Pity he gambled it away, but then"—Solis spread his hands again, giving us that smile—"a gambler never learns. And what's more, a gambler never cares. You see, *gambling* is all that matters."

Like magic, Maître Dumas had appeared at Solis's side. I had no idea he was even in the room. Evgenia was still looking out the window, still smoking, nervously tapping ash into a crystal ashtray clutched in her other hand.

"Evgenia, must you smoke in here?" Solis said coldly. 'It's not good for the art."

Evgenia stubbed out the cigarette. Maître Dumas stood by Solis's chair, awaiting instructions.

"Sir?" he said.

"Show these people the documents, Dumas."

"Yes, sir." Dumas stepped toward me and handed me a copy of the contract pledging the property and land known as the Hotel Riviera to the Consortium Solis. It was dated six months before my marriage and signed clearly by Patrick.

I handed it to Jack. "I presume it's Patrick's signature?" Jack said. I nodded.

I was glad I hadn't taken so much as a sip of Solis's damned ice water.

"And so now you hate me, Madame Laforêt," Solis said, "for a business transaction that turned out in my favor. Let me remind you all, it could have gone the other way. Patrick gambled, he could have won money, paid back the loan, and all would have been forgiven. Surely, it's *Patrick* you should be blaming, Madame Laforêt, not me? And the only reason I lent Patrick the money and saved his skin was because of his grandmother. The woman who helped a young boy on the streets, so many years ago."

I struggled out of the depths of the sofa and smoothed down my now-wrinkled white cotton skirt. Jack and Miss N stood by me as I said, "I will have my attorneys look at this document, Monsieur Solis."

"I can assure you they will find it in order."

Miss Nightingale clutched her handbag firmly and pushed her glasses farther up on her nose. She looked, I thought, solid as a rock, a bastion of decency. She cast a glance at the sulky beauty. "And Madame Solis, what does she think of all this?" she said.

Evgenia jerked her eyes from the view of Monte Carlo and fixed them soulfully on Miss N.

"It's very simple," Solis said. "I'm giving Evgenia the Hotel Riviera as a little present. She can do whatever she wishes with it."

Evgenia flashed him a heartbreaker of a smile, then leaned her back against the window and folded her arms, gazing silently up at the ceiling.

Again, Manolo appeared from nowhere, as everybody seemed to on this ship. Our audience with Laurent Solis was obviously over. He did not get up, nor did he bid us goodbye.

I turned for one last look at him. He was still sitting where we had left him, but he was looking at Evgenia. I couldn't see his face, but I saw the look on hers. I thought it could be described as happiness.

CHAPTER 31

WE WERE SITTING ON THE SIDEWALK TERRACE OF A LITTLE café in Antibes, contemplating ice-cold drinks that seemed unable to slake our thirst, and mulling over the conversation on the *Agamemnon* with Laurent Solis.

"My dear, you know what's at the heart of all this, don't you?" Miss N said.

I looked up at her. "What?"

"Why, sex, of course. *Cherchez la femme,* they always say, and in this case I believe we have found her."

"Evgenia," Jack said. His brow cleared as something dawned on him. "My God, now I remember where I saw Falcon. It was in the Caves du Roy. He was Evgenia Solis's bodyguard. He kept everybody at arm's length, even the waiters had a tough time getting through."

"You noticed her then," I said.

"Of course I noticed her. She's unmissable just walking down the street, let alone in a nightclub when she's dancing on the table and flaunting it."

"In front of her husband," Miss N said thoughtfully. "How interesting."

"She must be mad," I added.

"No, not mad," Miss N said, "she just has her husband exactly where she wants him and she's a woman who knows how to play the game. Beauty is her asset—money his."

"She wants my home," I said bitterly. "And what's more, she's got it. She's probably going to pull it down and build herself a splendid forty-room villa with a helicopter pad and twenty servants and throw wild parties where she'll dance on the table so her hangers-on can admire her style."

"Spoken like a true woman," Jack said.

"It's the truth, I'm sure of it."

"I'm sure of it too," Miss N said thoughtfully. "But there's more to this than meets the eye, I'm sure of that also."

"What *I'm* sure of is that Lola is in trouble," Jack said.

I stared at my iced drink, knowing I had lost my little hotel, my true "home," and all because of Patrick and his gambling.

"We must contact young Oldroyd's lawyer father in Avignon," Miss N said, sounding very efficient and in charge. "We'll get legal advice on this."

Jack reached over and took my hand. It was wet from clutching my icy glass of *citron pressé,* but he didn't seem to notice. "One thing I do know," he said, "is that legal matters take a long time to unfold here in France, especially property matters. The old Napoleonic code takes care of that. There'll be years of bureaucratic haggling, everything has to go through the proper channels, and even with big money, those channels can be hard to cross. In fact, sometimes it can stall things even longer. So we'll have time to sort things out."

I noticed his use of the word *we,* and instinctively I squeezed his hand. He wanted to make me feel better but I wasn't sure I was buying his explanation.

Jack paid the *addition* and we drove silently back to the hotel. All was quiet, there was no one around, not even Nadine in the kitchen. Miss N said she thought she would go to her room for a rest and to think things over, Jack was going back to his boat, and I was going to my cottage to try to brood over what I could do to save my home.

"Thanks anyway," I said to Jack as we walked down the path together. He glanced at me, his eyes narrowed.

"For what? So far, I haven't helped one bit."

"You tried. That's what counts."

He turned me to face him. I could feel the heat of his hands through my shirt. "Look, I really wanted to help you. A man shouldn't leave his wife in this situation, it's not right."

"Nothing was right between me and Patrick for a long time." I shrugged. "That's just the way it was."

We stood there, his hands on my shoulders, looking at each other.

He said, "It's true what I told you, bureaucracy will hold this up forever. You're not going to be kicked out tomorrow or anything like that."

I nodded, still holding his eyes with mine. "Yes," I said. And then he bent his head and kissed me.

His lips were warm, firm, his breath sweet. It was not a passionate kiss, it was just a kiss between two people who suddenly might care for each other. A preliminary, you might say, in the game of romance. Why I cared for him, or he for me, I didn't bother to analyze. It was just there, that spark between us.

"Get some rest," he said. "I'll see you later, on the terrace for dinner."

I nodded, watching him walk over the rocks to the jetty and his dinghy. He didn't look back as he sped across the calm turquoise cove.

WE TOLD MY GUESTS THE BAD NEWS, OVER DRINKS ON THE terrace later, and also that Falcon was Evgenia's bodyguard and obviously working for Solis.

"So why is he staying here?" Red asked.

"Checking on me, I suppose," I said gloomily. "Or more likely checking on Evgenia's property. You saw him walking around, making notes."

"Mr. Falcon left this afternoon," Miss N said. "I was on my balcony and saw him go. He had his bag and he just roared off on the bike. I assume he paid his bill?"

I gaped at her. I hadn't known anything about Falcon leaving. "Nadine must have taken care of it," I said.

"Did it occur to you that Falcon might have been checking on Patrick?" Jack said, and I turned and gaped at him, as did everyone else. "He might have thought you knew where Patrick was," Jack added. "I found out today it's very difficult to complete a real estate transaction in France without the presence of all the parties concerned. Also, here in France, a man cannot be presumed dead until ten years have elapsed since the time he went missing. That might just throw a bit of a wrench in Solis's works."

"Ten years," I said, thinking of Patrick, dead. It didn't seem possible.

"Ten years in which you're better off without him," Red said firmly, making me laugh. Dammit, I knew it was true.

I poured more wine, my own rosé from that vineyard up on the hill where the moon-dusted grapes hung ripe and heavy in the crisp autumn mornings, and which tasted like the essence of summer. My eye caught Jack's as I filled his glass; there was a hint of a smile in his.

"I'll call my father right now." Mr. Honeymoon removed his arm from Mrs. Honeymoon's golden shoulders. She smoothed back her short blond hair, gazing lovingly up at him, and my heart melted, as it always did when I saw them together. Oh, to be young as they were, and so in love, to be newly married with all of life in front of you, without any of the mistakes I seemed to have made.

"So," I said briskly, taking out my order pad, "I can recommend the fried zucchini flowers stuffed with tiny shrimp in a basil sauce, the *soupe au pistou,* or there's the vegetable terrine with a spinach cream sauce. Then there's the homemade pasta with a fricassée of pintade, guinea fowl; or there's simple grilled lamb with rosemary and garlic served with a crisp gratin of wafer-thin potatoes. The fish today is rouget, the small ones, grilled with fresh herbs. Oh, and there's mussels, moules marinière. And for dessert, as well as the usual sorbets, we have a nougat glacé au coulis de framboises, a frozen fruit-and-nut-filled creamy nougat with raspberry sauce. Plus a chocolate cake I made this afternoon."

Cheers greeted this recital, just as Mr. Honeymoon came back with the news that his father would help and wanted to know all the details. Mr. Honeymoon said he'd already told him "all the details," but anyhow his dad would call me tomorrow.

I thanked him again, took the orders, and disappeared into my kitchen. Scramble was already in her hibiscus pot, head tucked under her wing, oblivious to the fact that she might soon be homeless.

And speaking of homes, all my guests were due to leave this weekend. In just a few more days, I would be alone here in my personal little paradise that was mine no longer.

CHAPTER 32

IT WAS MIDNIGHT WHEN, LIKE CINDERELLA LEAVING THE ball, I finally left the terrace and walked home. I'd said good night to my guests about an hour ago, but then I'd lingered, cleaning up the kitchen with Jean-Paul and going over food plans for the next day with Marit. The truth was, though, I didn't want to be alone.

I looked across the dark water at the lights of *Bad Dog,* wondering about Jack Farrar, then I noticed that his dinghy was still moored at the jetty.

He was waiting for me at the cottage, sitting on the rattan porch sofa, one leg hitched comfortably over the other.

"I knew you'd have to come home sometime," he said.

I caught the gleam of his smile in the midnight-blue darkness and felt my heart do that little flip that always means trouble. Stop it, I told myself sternly, this man means nothing to you, you mean nothing to him. He's just a friend, a new friend, who's trying to help you out, that's all.

"Well, I'm here," I said, plumping down next to him.

"Yeah."

I could feel him looking at me.

"You okay?" he asked.

"I think so. Thank you for asking, though."

"That's okay."

We listened to the soft slurp of the Mediterranean washing the shore.

"I spoke to my detective friend in Marseilles," he said. "Forensics found nothing in the Porsche. Just fingerprints. They were all Patrick's."

I nodded. "Thanks." I was just glad it wasn't blood.

"You're a terrific cook, y'know that?" Jack changed the subject.

"That's my job."

"Yeah, but some cooks hate what they do. You cook with love."

"Gotta spread that love around somewhere," I said flippantly, but he didn't laugh. "So, if you think I'm such a good cook—and by the way the word is *chef*—why not come to dinner tomorrow night?" I said out of the blue. "It's my night off, we could dine here." I didn't add *alone,* a word which was cropping up in my vocabulary a lot tonight, but he knew what I meant.

"Thank you, I'd like that." He got to his feet and stood, looking down at me. "You sure you'll be okay tonight?"

I nodded. "I'm sure."

"So what time?"

"How about nine?" I said. We dine late here in the south of France and nine was early enough so as not to look as though I were asking him to spend the night.

"I'll be here."

We stood, looking at each other.

"Lovely night," he said, scanning the stars.

"Do they look the same from your boat?" I asked and he smiled.

"Better."

"Everything's better on a boat, I suppose."

"Not everything," he said, reaching out for my hand.

Those little electric tingles filtered from our clasped fingers as we stood, looking up at the stars. I felt him turn slightly, sensed he was looking at me. I met his eyes.

"Lola?" he said, and then he bent his head and kissed my hand.

It was the sweetest gesture, so gentlemanly, but in a way, sooo sexy, I turned to liquid gold. He ran his hands up my bare arms, lifted my heavy hair from my nape, grasped my head, pulled it toward his. Then we were kissing.

They say the eyes are the windows to the soul, but lips are the first wonderful link in the game of love, that first gentle kiss, hesitant, seeking each other, searching for that moment when, eyes wide open, you link body with soul.

My first kiss from Jack Farrar was like nothing I'd experienced before. I wanted to melt into his body, to become part of him. All my ladylike pretensions were swept away in one tiny moment, and I was no longer Patrick's abandoned wife. I was a woman again and, even though it was for this night only, Jack Farrar was my man.

After a long while he lifted his mouth from mine and we stood wrapped in each other's arms, weak-kneed with longing.

"More," I said, running my tongue across his lips and he laughed and said he was just about to say that himself. Then, to my astonishment, he picked me up and carried me through my own front door, straight to the bedroom.

"No messing about with you," I said, smiling back at him, because this was a truly happy occasion. In fact, it was one of the happiest moments of my entire life.

"Come here," I said, flinging off my shirt and reclining on the bed like a true Jezebel. And he laughed, flinging off his own shirt, and then his pants, his underwear. I couldn't take my eyes off him. Up close and getting closer my Naked Man was even more perfect than through the binoculars.

"Nothing you haven't seen before," he said, laughing, "but all *your* secrets are intact."

"I want to share them with you," I whispered, licking his ear, shivering with delight at the touch of his hands.

"Beautiful," he murmured, "so beautiful, Lola, here, let me touch you, let me find you . . ."

His lips searched my body, sending ripples of pleaure through me, and I smiled. "Delicious," I said, tasting him, "you are the most delicious man . . ."

And my old four-poster rocked to our rhythm as we made love through the night.

"Never," I said to him softly, "it was never like this before . . ." And he sealed my mouth with kisses and entered me again, and again, until I was one delicious dish of pleasure myself. And nothing else mattered.

We woke to the dawn and the sound of Big Dog whining and snuffling along the crack under the bedroom door. We lay on our backs, his arm under my shoulders. I turned and smiled at him. *"Bonjour,"* I said softly.

"How're y'doing?" he replied with a grin.

And then we were laughing and kissing, and I had to dash

into the shower and get ready for my day and he had to rescue Bad Dog from near-abandonment, and get out before any early guests wandered down the path to the beach.

He caught my chin and planted a kiss firmly on my bruised mouth. And then he was gone.

And I had a big smile on my face.

CHAPTER 33

WITH THE DREAM OF LAST NIGHT'S LOVEMAKING IN MY head, I was excited as a girl at her first prom. Tonight, everything must be perfect, including myself.

I rechecked the table I'd checked at least ten times before, I smoothed the linen cloth and refolded the napkins, feeling them between thumb and finger to make sure they were crisp. I adjusted the position of the plates, fussed over the silverware, and gave an extra polish to the bubbled green glass goblets. I fiddled with the bunch of white daisies, then, dissatisfied, hurried back to the kitchen and changed the crystal vase for a squat yellow jug. My fingers itched to light the candles but it was too early, and instead I rushed around redistributing lily-scented candles on the stone fireplace and floating votives in bowls of water on the coffee table.

It was all as ready as it could be, I decided, as I ran back up the path to the kitchen.

The restaurant was closed and the staff had the night off. The kitchen was all mine and I twirled, surveying "my home."

It was *still* my home, and I wasn't going to think about all the worries and problems. Tonight was "tonight" and my love, Jack Farrar, was coming to dinner.

I piled everything for our *dîner-à-deux* into containers, took them back to the cottage, and set the food out on the counter ready to serve.

Then I ran a bath, flinging in perfumed oils with abandon, lying there with the water up to my neck, thinking lascivious thoughts about my Naked Man that I told myself if I were a "lady" I should certainly not be thinking. So I pulled out the plug, turned the shower onto cold, and stood under it as long as I could bear.

Now I was freezing, I even had goose pimples. I toweled my hair, shook it free to dry; then lotion, powder, and the Tendre Poison scent.

I hurried into the bedroom to dress, and caught sight of myself in the mirror. I stopped and took a long, severe look. Tan lines and goose bumps notwithstanding, I thought there was a kind of glow about me tonight. I lingered over my reflected image, running my hands over my breasts, still high and firm; then over my belly—a little too curved and a touch Rubenesque, but hey, I'm a chef; then along the length of my thighs—firm and muscular because I'm on my feet all day. Somehow my fingers managed to tangle in the bush between my legs—it's redder than the hair on my head and almost qualifies me as a true redhead. I stared at myself in the mirror, pink-cheeked, red-haired, and glowing like the votives I had so carefully arranged, and felt last night's thrill all over again.

I took a deep breath and turned guiltily away, tugging on my underwear—lace of course, but a bikini not a thong, which I've never been able to get accustomed to. And cream, not black, because I think black seems to say, hey, here I am, ready and waiting and all yours. Even though I was, I didn't want to advertise it. The matching bra felt like a whisper against my skin, and I heaved a deep sigh of pure pleasure. Was that just great sex? Or was I falling for him? Who knew? Right now, all I knew was it was the best thing to happen in a long, long time.

I wore the gauzy apricot dress I'd almost worn the time Jack had come to the Hotel Riviera, then taken off at the last minute in favor of Capris and a tee. I still thought it swirled rather charmingly around my knees, especially when I had on the beribboned espadrilles, though I doubted they were meant to go with the dress. Big gold hoops in my ears—the thin kind; a jangly bead bracelet bought in Saint-Tropez market; a run of the hands through the hair so it ended up in its usual disarray. And there I was. Ready.

I headed outside, waiting until I saw the dinghy heading for my cove. Then I went back inside and lit the candles.

CHAPTER 34

Jack

JACK STRODE UP THE PATH TO LOLA'S HOUSE ON THE DOT OF nine, bearing flowers. The door stood open, the bead curtain was swinging in the breeze, and he almost expected Scramble to poke her head out and give him the once-over. Instead Bad Dog galloped up from the beach with what could only be described as a big silly grin on his face.

"Better behave yourself," Jack warned, pushing aside the curtain. And she was looking at him, looking at her in her slinky little peachy dress, with those silly espadrilles strapped around her skinny ankles in cute little bows.

"Sorry, guess I should have dressed." He glanced down at his crumpled cotton pants, the old loafers, and the ancient denim shirt he would never part with unless his very life depended on it.

"You look . . . *scrumptious,*" Lola said.

"Do you relate everything to food?"

"In your case, yes. You're edible," she said, moving into his arms.

"And you." He gave her the same up-and-down look she'd given him. As he kissed her, he thought she looked so girly and vulnerable, it almost brought a lump to his throat.

She pulled away from him. "For a minute there, I thought you hated the dress."

"I *love* the dress." He was still standing on her doorstep, still clutching the bunch of flowers. Suddenly Bad Dog dashed past, almost knocking them off their feet.

He aimed a mock-kick at Bad Dog's butt. "Sorry, he's a street dog, never could teach him manners."

"Hey, boy, sweet dog," Lola said, and the dog came running.

Jack watched as she put her arms around him, murmuring, "Sweet baby dog," and darned if the mutt didn't give her his soulful "good dog" face and also a good lick that took off a swathe of makeup, but Lola just laughed.

Then Bad Dog spotted Scramble perched on top of the armoire, her eyes fixed unblinkingly on him. After a minute Bad Dog gave a plaintive little whine and slunk off, ears and tail down, a bewildered look on his face.

"Meanwhile . . . ," Jack said, handing Lola the flowers.

"Meanwhile . . ."

She was looking at him from under those long Bambi lashes, clutching the flowers to her breast. Then the flowers fell forgotten to the floor, and he was kissing her and she was kissing him, and they were telling each other how long they had been wanting to do this . . .

"What about dinner?" Lola asked when they finally came up for air.

"What about it?" He claimed her mouth again, felt her

body sink into his. He was trembling as he whispered, "Lola, are you sure you're ready for this?"

Her voice was soft, breathy, in his ear. "Yes, I'm ready," she said.

CHAPTER 35

Lola

HAVE YOU EVER FELT YOUR BODY MELT INTO A MAN'S SO that you're not even sure you exist anymore, except as a part of him? That's how it felt, making love the second time with Jack Farrar.

Under his exploring hands I was suddenly delicate as spun silk and slippery as fresh cream; I was Cinderella turning into a princess, I was a starburst in the sky, and I was a long way, baby, from that ingenue chef in Encino, California. I was a woman again. And I loved it.

"I knew you'd look like this," I said to him, stretching my body the length of his, stroking his golden flanks, licking his cheek, his neck, anything I could get my tongue around. I loved the texture of his skin, the crisp hair on his chest, bleached gold by the sun, his hard sailor's hands.

"That's because you already saw." He was biting my lips now, shutting me up so he could kiss me properly.

I giggled because it was true. "I would have known anyway."

"Can't say the same," he said, exploring my mouth with his tongue until I had to turn away to catch my breath. "You're a complete surprise."

I pushed up on my elbow. "A *nice* surprise?"

"The best."

Then he pulled me back under him, slid his mouth the length of my body, sank his face into me, breathing me in, gentling me with his fingers and then his tongue. I arched into him, I was a starburst again, the planets had never looked so lovely and real life was forgotten as he entered me, lifting me onto him with a gentle expertise.

"Sweet, sweet, sweet," he murmured in my ear as he made love to me. "Sweeter than honey, my lovely Lola," he groaned later as we trembled together, and then that delicious fall over the edge into that starry starry night.

After a while, he edged his body off mine and I lay there, clutching his hand, hardly knowing where I was, who I was, only that I was in France, making love on a summer night with the breeze from the sea blowing through the open window and my man's happy sighs in my ears.

"Lost in France in Love." The memory of an old song flitted through my head and I hummed a few bars, happier than a kid with an ice cream—and smiling like the cat who'd got the cream. Or more likely like Bad Dog, who'd probably gotten our dinner by now!

I jolted upright. I'd left all the food on the kitchen counter. I scrambled out of bed and ran for the kitchen.

I surveyed the damage. Licking his lips, Bad Dog gazed at me without the remotest sign of guilt. I stamped my foot. "Bad dog!" I yelled.

Jack came in. He looked at the scattered remains of the

hors d'oeuvres; at the mangled bones of the lamb chops; at the greasy blob amid the chestnut leaves that was all that remained of the Banon cheese; and at the cracker crumbs.

"Jesus," he said. Then he threw Bad Dog outside and slammed the door. We could hear him snuffling along the gap at the bottom. He gave a disconsolate whine, then slumped with a thud onto the step.

"Serves him right," I said, still angry, but Jack was laughing. I glared at him, but he was naked and gorgeous and he was eyeing me in a way I liked to be eyed, and I began to laugh too.

"I already had dessert anyhow," he said, pulling me into his arms and kissing me again.

We stayed in that position for quite a while, then, ever the hostess, I said, "I have Parmesan cheese and a good bread . . ."

Jack groaned, still holding me. "Lola," he said, "do you ever stop thinking about food?"

"Not when I have a hungry customer on my hands," I said, leading him by the hand back to the bedroom, though not for the reason he thought.

I handed him a white cotton robe, the kind we supply all our guests with, slipped one on myself and went back to the kitchen. I took a bottle of my favorite champagne, Taittinger La Française, from the fridge, filled the ice bucket, went back into the living room and handed the bottle to Jack to open. I returned to the kitchen, put a slab of Parmesan on a plate and a crusty round loaf on a wooden board, along with knives, butter, and plates.

I plonked them on the coffee table and stood, hands on my hips. I thought how domestic we looked. In fact, I almost told Jack how "at home" he looked here in my cottage in his bathrobe, opening champagne, but I thought better of it. We said *santé,* clinking glasses, washing the taste of sex down in good champagne without ever taking our eyes off each other. Drinking each other in, I thought with a pleasant little shiver.

I said, "Surely you're hungry?" He nodded, still without taking his eyes off me.

We didn't bother to eat at the table I'd fussed over for so long, we just sat on the rug and ate off the coffee table. I hacked a couple of hunks off the loaf and some slivers off the cheese.

"There's nothing better than champagne after making love," Jack said, holding my hand, "unless it's a hunk of bread and cheese."

"Just think yourself lucky Bad Dog didn't get around to the bread," I said, with a full mouth. As usual I was starving but it was tricky eating with one hand. "And there's better yet to come. I kept the lobster salad in the fridge so you won't go hungry after all."

"What about dessert?"

"Depends."

"On what?"

"Whether you like lavender crème brûlée."

He stared at me. "You're joking."

I giggled and almost choked on the bread. He was definitely not a crème brûlée man, let alone *lavender* crème brûlée. "Didn't think you'd care for that somehow, so I made a chocolate cake instead."

He leaned over to kiss me. "Sounds good to me."

"Of course, it has pralines and cream and a few extra decorative and gastronomic touches," I added, "though I could be persuaded to serve it plain with ice cream."

"I'm your all-American boy. Just bring on the ice cream."

First, though, we had more champagne, then I brought out the lobster salad which, though I say it myself, was the perfect after-love food. Or before love, come to think of it, though now I *was* thinking about it, love had not been mentioned between us.

I was still thinking about that as I speared a particularly good morsel of lobster and fed it to Jack. He returned the compliment, kissing me as I chewed.

"Did I ever tell you I love redheads?" he asked, pushing my slippery bangs out of my eyes, running his hand slowly over my hair, and sending new shivers down my spine.

Then we forgot about dessert and made love some more, on the rug under the beady-eyed gaze of Scramble, still on top of the armoire.

CHAPTER 36

WE WERE IN BED WHEN I AWOKE TO THE SOUND OF RAIN against the windows. I turned my head to look at Jack. He was awake too, looking at me.

"Rain," he said lazily. "Who would have thought it, here in the south of France."

"Better let the dog in," I said, realizing too late how like a wife I'd sounded. "I mean, I wouldn't want him to get wet," I added hastily.

Jack had propped himself on one elbow and was looking at me. I didn't want him to think I was interested in a long-term relationship; he was a man who enjoyed his freedom, I'd just take what I could get now. Besides, I was never going to fall in love again. Remember?

"I don't believe in love at first sight," I said, nervously making my point. "You know, eyes meeting across the room, sparks flying . . ."

"It was across the water," he said.

I frowned, puzzled.

"Eyes across the water, remember, the telescope . . ."

"And the binoculars . . ."

Jack nodded. "Anyhow, you weren't looking so great, the first time I saw you."

"Yeah, well, probably not. But I just want you to know I don't believe in all that love-at-first-sight stuff."

"Me either." He lay back against the pillows, his face an unreadable blank.

"So. No falling in love, then." I sounded very firm, like a woman who knew what she was doing. Miss N would have been proud of me.

"You got it," he said.

"Right."

"So," he said. "Now we know where we stand."

"We certainly do. Anyway, what about the dog?"

Jack unraveled himself from the sheets, and sauntered to the door, naked as the first day I'd seen him and looking just as good as he had when I'd watched him climb from the sea, at one with his world. It was a world I knew nothing about, and one where I obviously did not belong. So I was right not to fall in love. Right?

I already felt my resolve crumbling. Oh God, you're such a dummy, I told myself. It's déjà vu all over again and you're falling once more, hook, line, and sinker—was that a suitable nautical term?—for the wrong man.

Jack had let the dog in. I dried him off with my best bath towel, while Jack took a shower (I gave him a clean towel, in case you're wondering). Then I sat on the edge of the bed with Bad Dog snuggled up to me, watching Jack put on his clothes. He slid his feet into the tired pair of loafers, then came and stood next to me.

"The food was great," he said, looking serious.

I nodded.

"So was the champagne."

"It's my favorite."

He pushed my hair out of my eyes. "You're beautiful, Lola."

I wanted to say, no, I'm not except when I'm in your arms. "You too," I mumbled instead, wondering whether that was the right thing to say to a man anyway.

"Tell me something," he said, "did you think of Patrick at all tonight?"

I gasped, shocked. Did he think I had no principles? That I would think of another man when I was in his arms? I shook my head.

"Thank God for that," he said, and I wondered if he viewed our lovemaking as some sort of therapy, a modern-day version of marriage counseling.

"I'd like to invite you onto my boat," he said. "I can't promise you a gourmet dinner, but a sunset cruise around the bay is pretty nice, and I'll supply the champagne this time."

"I hate boats," I said truthfully.

He groaned. "Learn to love 'em, baby," was what he said, then he lifted my hands to his lips, kissed them, called for his dog, and was gone.

I fell back onto the sheets, staring at the beamed ceiling, asking myself why I was such an idiot. Lack of practice, I suppose. Then I was asleep in minutes with Scramble on my pillow and the memory of Jack's body on mine, and the sound of the rain on the windowpanes.

CHAPTER 37

THE NEXT MORNING, LITTLE WHITE-SAILED BOATS SKIMMED past my cove, but where the sloop had been was just an empty shimmering expanse of turquoise water. Bad Dog and Jack Farrar were gone.

I turned away, unbelieving. I was a woman with a stone in her heart. I reminded myself fiercely that I had been wounded before. I could get over this. But somehow I showered, got dressed, got myself together. For the first time I didn't even notice how charming my kitchen was, didn't even think how I loved it. This kitchen was no longer mine, and Jack Farrar was not mine.

I muttered a *bonjour* to Nadine, who gave me a long searching look back, then poured me some coffee. I thought about what I had said to Jack about not falling in love. I didn't even remember exactly what I'd said, only that it was stupid, just because Patrick had hurt me.

Miss N had told me not to lock love and romance out of

my life because of Patrick? Well, I had gone and done just exactly that.

"Drink the coffee," Nadine said, in French, standing over me. "Then tell me what's the matter this time."

"Men," I said, staring gloomily into my coffee mug.

"A *man,* more like it," she said, hands on her hips, her brow furrowed. "I just hope it's not Patrick again; I've had about enough of him. He's at the heart of all your problems."

I agreed. "But now I've gone and done it again," I said. "I've gotten involved. I spent last night with a man, and this morning he's gone. He's disappeared." I stared at Nadine. "What is it about me, Nadine? What am I doing wrong?"

"Caring too much," Nadine said. "You should think more about yourself instead of others. You're a people-pleaser, Lola, and everybody loves you for it, but it's time you put more thought into your life, your own *affaires de coeur.* Forget Patrick and get your own life straightened out."

She stalked to the sink and began rattling dishes around. "And forget Jack Farrar too," she added. "He's like the other one, he'll live his own life and it won't include you."

This bit of advice, though well meant, did not make me feel any better. The hot coffee tasted like the bitter pill of truth. "You're probably right," I said. "And anyway, our main problem is you and I are soon going to be out of a job. What'll we do next?"

Nadine's dark eyes gleamed with sympathy. "I'm not saying it's going to happen," she said, "but if the time comes when you no longer own the Hotel Riviera, then maybe you and I should start up a little *bistro* in Antibes. A little storefront place. You'll cook, and I'll serve, and my sister will greet the customers, when she's not at home taking care of her babies, that is. In which case, you and I will do it between us. We'll make a go of it, you'll see."

She was so good, so stoutly supportive, wanting it all to come true for me, that I got up and gave her a hug. "Thank you, my friend," I said. "Let's hope it won't come to that."

Marit walked in. "Madame Laforêt," she said.

Instead of her usual working outfit of shorts and T-shirt, she was wearing a pretty summer dress and she was holding a suitcase. "My *maman* needs me at home, madame," she said.

"Oh dear," I said, "is everybody okay at home? Your mother?"

"Maman is fine, but I have to leave you right away. My boyfriend is picking me up at the end of the lane in five minutes." She glanced at her watch. "I'm sorry to leave so abruptly, madame, but as I said, *maman* needs me in Lyons."

I nodded. I understood, Marit was moving on. She'd probably gotten a good job in Lyons, a city of fine food and good restaurants. It would be a step up in her career, and I didn't begrudge it for an instant, though I would have liked more notice. Still, the guests would soon be gone; I'd manage.

"I hope everything goes well for you, Marit," I said, writing out a check for her wages. "You have true talent as a chef and I'll give you an excellent reference." I smiled up at her. "Let me know how you're doing. And thank you for working so hard, I appreciate it."

She seemed flustered by my calmness and good wishes; obviously she'd expected rancor, anger even. "You are *très amiable,* Madame Laforêt," she said, then she gave me three quick kisses instead of the usual two, a true sign of affection. *"Bonne chance, madame,"* she said, picking up the check and her suitcase.

"And to you, Marit," I said. Then she kissed Nadine and was gone.

Two gone, eight to go, I thought, just as Jean-Paul cycled past the window. As usual, he flung his bike into the rosemary bush, then sauntered into the kitchen, hands in his pockets, a dreamy look on his face.

"What happened?" Nadine demanded, hands on her ample hips again.

Jean-Paul stopped to look at her. *"L'amour,"* he said succinctly, then he added, "*Bonjour, Madame Laforêt*. I will attend to the tables right away."

He drifted into his room in back of the kitchen and we heard the shower go on. "Love," I said to Nadine, "has a lot to answer for."

The shrill ring of the phone blended with the sound of Nadine shunting plates around. I answered it. It was Freddy Oldroyd, Mr. Honeymoon's lawyer father. I went over the situation in detail, promised to FedEx him copies of the documents today. He told me not to worry, he would sort it out. He'd get back to me as soon as he'd read the legal documents. I thanked him, but I didn't believe him. In my heart I knew there was no way I was going to be able to keep my little *auberge*.

It was not a great beginning to the week.

CHAPTER 38

THE DAYS SLID PAST IN THE USUAL BLUR OF MARKETING, preparing, cooking, looking after my guests. Jean-Paul left early too. He'd found himself a winter job in Cannes.

"I'll be back next summer, Madame Laforêt," he promised. I advised him instead to go back to school, or apprentice himself to a good kitchen where he could learn, and progress up the ladder. But ambition was not in his makeup. Oddly, I missed him.

Before I knew it, my guests were leaving. They gathered in the front hall, suitcases piled around them, settling their bills with Nadine at the old rosewood table, exchanging addresses and promising to keep in touch. I helped them pile luggage into their cars, then stood back. The moment I had dreaded was here.

"Keep your chin up," Budgie Lampson said, and the two boys gave me bear hugs and said they would miss me and miss my brownies. I laughed and gave them a goody bag filled with those brownies. They climbed gleefully into the car, already devouring them. "Hey, those were meant for the plane," Budgie protested, but it was too late, and she drove away, laughing.

"We'll keep tabs on what's happening via my dad," Mr. Honeymoon said, giving me a kiss, and Mrs. Honeymoon hugged me tight and said, "We're on your side, remember, and of course we'll be back next year."

I waved them goodbye, then turned to Red Shoup who was standing quietly, looking at me.

"So, now what?" she said, brushing back her red curls and looking me in the eye. She was a straight shooter; I could expect no false sympathy or promises it would be all right from her.

I shrugged. "I'll just have to see how the cards play out," I said, unthinkingly using a gambling metaphor.

"That's the way it is, little honey," she said. "But let me give you some advice. Take time out, put yourself first for a while, stop looking after people. Especially men." She gave me a shrewd glance. "So what happened to Jack Farrar?"

"He left."

She nodded. "Not for good, though, I can promise you that." She kissed me on both cheeks, hugged me tight, said, "*Bonne chance,* little honey," then climbed into the car.

Handsome, kind Jerry Shoup, who'd been piling in the luggage and grumbling about the quantity of stuff his wife had managed to acquire in a month, came over and took me in his arms.

"We all love you, Lola," he said. "You're the best, remember that." He climbed in the car and started it up.

"See you next year," Red called, waving out the window.

I hope so, I thought. Oh, I hope so.

And then they were gone.

Only Miss Nightingale was staying on for another week. Meanwhile, she had gone off on a little trip up the coast by herself.

"You need space, my dear," she had said. She knew what was going on between me and Jack. "It'll all work out in the end," she promised, driving off in the little Fiat she'd rented.

Oh, but will it? I thought, standing in the empty lane, looking at my suddenly empty inn, and feeling completely alone.

CHAPTER 39

I WASN'T ALONE FOR LONG. A SILVER-BLUE JAGUAR CONVERTible came barreling down the lane with Giselle Castille at the wheel. The top was down and she was wearing a chiffon scarf over her hair and huge, very dark sunglasses, à la Grace Kelly in *To Catch a Thief*.

I stood on the front steps, watching as she climbed gracefully out of the convertible, swinging her long elegant legs out first, adjusting her short skirt, then sliding out without showing anything she shouldn't, as professional as a star exiting a limo at a Hollywood premiere.

A man was in the passenger seat; young, dark glasses, baseball cap. He looked at me, but didn't get out.

"Lola," Giselle said, walking toward me, cool and elegant in simple white linen.

"Giselle," I said. We stood awkwardly on the step, looking at each other.

"We need to talk," she said.

I nodded. "Please come in."

Inside, she stared around the comfortable hall, taking it in. She walked through the arch into the salon, then I heard her heels clattering on the tiles as she went out onto the terrace.

I looked around seeing what she saw and suddenly my charming little hotel looked not chic enough, not glossy enough, a little worn at the edges. Yet what it lacked in luxury, I had always thought it made up for in charm.

Giselle obviously didn't see "charm." She saw the rather battered antiques, the gaily patterned inexpensive Provençal fabrics, the chips on the rosewood table, and the flowers drooping in the battered silver urns.

"So, this is the Hotel Riviera," she said.

"This is it," I agreed.

"Patrick's only asset," she added, settling onto the fake Louis-the-something gilt sofa, covered by me in yellow and blue stripes and a lot of upholstery tacks.

"It was," I agreed with her again.

"I heard a rumor that Solis bought the property from you, for his wife?"

It was a question, not a statement. I put her straight. "Patrick owed Solis money. He pledged the property, then reneged on the debt. Solis is claiming the hotel. He plans on giving it to his wife."

"Ah, Evgenia." She gave me a knowing look from those turquoise eyes. "It's always *cherchez la femme* with Patrick."

That was exactly what Miss Nightingale had said. I wondered if it were true, about Patrick and Evgenia? And if so, how did Giselle know?

She said, "However, Madame Solis will have to fight *me* for the property. I have here a list of the monies Patrick owes me. I always gave him checks. I have a note of their numbers and the amounts, and all the checks were made out to him, in his name. I believe my claim will predate Monsieur Solis's. I have been lending Patrick money for many years."

"Is that what you came to tell me?" My chin was up in the air where Budgie Lampson had told me to keep it. I was haughty, cold, and angry with this rich maneuvering bitch, who wasn't satisfied just to have had my husband, now she wanted my home too.

"That is all, my dear Lola. Except, maybe, just one other thing."

"Okay," I said, a little wearily, because at this point Patrick's life was just too complicated even to fathom. "What is it?"

"Tell me where Patrick is," she said, surprising me. "Just tell me where he is, and I will drop my claim. I promise."

I stared stonily at her. "I have no idea where Patrick is."

"Oh, yes, you do." She was on her feet, heading for the door, immaculate in her white linen with the white chiffon scarf over her long dark hair, looking like a suntanned Madonna without the innocence. "I warn you," she said, "it's in your best interests to tell me where Patrick is."

I followed her to the door. "*Why* is it in my best interests?" I demanded, really angry now.

"Because, my dear Lola, Patrick belongs to me. He always has."

She left me standing on my doorstep, a stunned look on my face. Of course, I'd known the minute I met her, she had been Patrick's lover, but he *belonged* to her? The woman was crazy.

As if to prove my point, Scramble appeared from around the corner. She stopped to survey the scene, then with an almighty squawk, she ran at Giselle, wings flapping in a hen-jet takeoff. Giselle screamed, arms flailing, as she tried to beat her off, but Scramble pecked her arms, her legs, anywhere she could reach.

"Get it off me, get it off me!" Giselle yelled, along with a string of unladylike epithets. I just stood there, arms folded, thinking, Go to it, Scramble. I would have scratched Giselle's eyes out myself if good manners hadn't stopped me.

The young guy jumped out of the car. He grabbed Giselle and aimed a kick at Scramble. I grabbed her, clutching her under my arm.

"Get out," I said firmly. "You are not wanted here."

Giselle was still yelling as they drove off, but I didn't care. Still, I'd had the uneasy feeling I hadn't seen the last of her. She would be back and looking for revenge.

I STALKED BACK INTO THE HOTEL. IT WAS SUDDENLY QUIET, unnervingly quiet.

Clutching Scramble, still squawking, I walked back down the path to my cottage. As I rounded the oleander hedge I saw it.

The sloop was moored in my little cove, just like the first time.

CHAPTER 40

I STOOD LOOKING AT IT, MY HEART POUNDING, MY MOUTH dry with anger. Scramble fluttered from my arms, heading back to the terrace and her hibiscus pot.

So he was back, was he. It had been almost a week. Where had he been? Why had he left without saying anything? And especially why had he left without saying anything *right after we had made love all night*? Maybe I hadn't behaved in a very ladylike manner, but I was no one-night stand. If he thought he was just going to sail right back into my life as though nothing had happened, then he was wrong. I'd had it with men. *All* men. And that included Jack Farrar.

I flung myself onto the porch sofa. Head thrown back against the cushions, eyes closed. I willed myself not to care. Life had dealt me one more blow and, coming on top of all the others, I just couldn't take it.

A while later, I heard Jack's footsteps on the path. I didn't open my eyes; I didn't even move. But the sound of his voice sent a shiver down my spine.

"Lola? Lola, are you all right?"

I could feel him, standing next to me, hear him breathing. I imagined his frown as he stared at me.

"Go away," I said, finally.

"But I just got here."

"Hah." I snorted.

"Hey, what's up, honey?" he said.

I opened my eyes to narrow slits. He'd never called me honey before. He looked about the same: way too attractive.

He said, "I just got back from the States."

"Hah. A likely story." I'd bet he'd been hanging out with his cronies in the ports along the coast.

He lifted my feet off the sofa, sat down next to me, and rearranged my legs across his knees.

"There was an accident in Newport," he said. "Carlos was out with the rest of the crew on the big sloop, the one we planned to sail to South Africa. For some unknown reason the rudder came loose, in fact it parted company with the boat, leaving a gigantic hole. They tried the pumps but the hole was too big, the water was coming in too fast. The boat sank in fifty feet of water. I had to get back. I took the first flight out from Nice to Paris, and then on to Boston."

"Was he all right, Carlos? And the rest of the crew?" We had eye contact now, though still cautious on my part.

"They'd Maydayed, the rescue boats had them out of the water almost before they had time to get wet."

"That's all right then."

"Yeah, that's the good news. I had to get back quick to organize divers to check the damage, get the cranes to pull her up. It wasn't a small job. And my beautiful boat is a wreck."

I heard the sadness in his voice and I said, "I'm sorry."

He caught my chin in his hard warm hand. "Lola, I'm sorry you're angry and hurt. I tried to call you but you weren't there. I left a message with Jean-Paul, I told him there was an emergency and I'd be back in a week."

I gave a wry smile. My ex-youth-of-all-work had run true to form. "It's in one ear, out the other with Jean-Paul," I said.

"Apparently. But you were not in my life one day, and out of it the next," Jack said. "I promise that wasn't the way it was. You were on my mind all the way across the Atlantic on that flight from Paris. And back again."

"I was?" I could feel myself softening. "*Melting*" was actually a better word. His face hovered over mine, then his lips closed in the gentlest of kisses, like the first kiss ever, tender as butterfly wings.

"You were, and you are," he murmured. He was stroking my legs, propped across his knees, not sexy, just gentle, nice. "What can I do to make you forgive me?" he said.

I swung my legs down and sat up quickly. "I know what you can do," I said, with a desperate sparkle in my eye. "Everybody's left, even Miss Nightingale is away on a trip. I need to get away from here. Why don't you take this chef out to lunch?"

"You got it." Jack grinned at me in that way that could melt a woman in Antarctica. I was picking up the pieces again, and not looking to the future the way I knew I should have been. But somehow, right now, I didn't care.

CHAPTER 41

WE DROVE INTO SAINT-TROPEZ—THAT IS, JACK DROVE MY car, complaining about the gearshift all the way. First we went to Le Bar Stube, a sailors' hangout in a little hotel on the Quai Suffren. It's on the second floor and crammed with locals and clubby leather armchairs and dozens of model sailboats.

"Home away from home for you," I said, settling at a table out on the balcony overlooking the yachts lined up in the marina.

"Not as snazzy as your terrace."

"Thank you for the compliment," I said. "But I'm beginning to have doubts about its snazziness." He gave me a quizzical look so I told him of Giselle Castille's second visit, and how her cutting glance had made me look at my little hotel with new eyes.

"I never thought about it before," I said. "I just put the hotel together as though it were my own home. There was so little money and most of that went on structural repairs. I wanted to put in a pool down by the cove, the kind that looks as though it's spilling over the edge into infinity. It was going to be a deep marine-blue." I shrugged. "But there was no money left over for that. And now, of course, I know why."

"Patrick," he said. "Any news on that front?"

I shrugged again. "None." I looked at him across the table as the waiter poured flutes of champagne. "I missed you," I said honestly, even though it was probably not the right thing to say to a man who a short while ago you thought had left you in the lurch after your one and only night of passion.

"I missed you too." He gripped my hand tightly, sending rivers of delight through me. When he finally let go, he lifted his glass in salute. "To you, Lola March," he said, " 'a woman with a big heart.' "

"That heart is beating at twice the speed of sound," I said. "It must be the champagne."

"I hope not," he said, and we smiled, delighted with each other.

I told him more about Giselle's visit and that Scramble had attacked her, and that I was worried she'd be back, and he said obviously Scramble knew the woman was up to no good, and he might have done it himself had he been there.

Hand in hand, we ambled back to the car, on to Tahiti Beach and Millesim, a zen-peaceful beach club, wonderfully free of Saint-Tropez glitz, especially now, at the tail end of the season. Soon all the beach clubs would close, as would most of the hotels and restaurants. Soon, the mistral would be blowing and the Alpes-Maritimes would be capped with snow, and the sky would be misty-gray, or that hard winter blue. Soon, Jack would have the *In a Minute* back in the water, then he'd be on his way to South Africa with his friend Carlos. Soon, I would be alone again. And too soon, I might no longer have my home.

But life was to be lived now, for the day, for this very moment, so I ordered Charentais melon with Parma ham, and Jack had the moules marinière.

The place was almost empty, just another couple sipping rosé wine and watching people strolling along the beach. A sweet-faced little white dog came by to say hello, balancing on his hind legs, waving his front paws in a dance for food. So of course I fed him all my Parma ham while I ate the melon, and when there was no more he left me for another. He also left me with a row of flea bites up my left leg—a fine way to say thank you, I said, laughing.

I sat back, savoring the moment. There was the sound of the sea, the beautiful blue and green view of the peninsula where my hotel was tucked away, the warmth of filtered sunlight under the canvas awning, an old Aznavour record playing softly in the background. This moment was pure happiness, I decided.

Then I devoured an entire bowl of wild strawberries while Jack told me stories about Cabo San Lucas in Mexico, about how different it was from our south of France sophistication.

"It's just a funky little town with some high-decibel discos, a few strip joints, some good hotels, some cheap," he said. "There's a couple of places I like to eat, the Mocambo for the best deep-fried whole red snapper you'll ever eat, and a salsa hot enough to toast your innards. The best bar is known as the Office, out on Medrano Beach: feet in the sand, margaritas the size of beach balls, good food, fishermen getting drunk after a long day on the Sea of Cortez, good-looking women eyeing the fishermen . . . kinda like that."

"I'll have to go there someday."

"Don't expect too much, it's just a little Mexican seaside town, the *real* Mexico. Except now they're building grand hotels and big money is coming in." He sighed regretfully. "It's a pity that places you discover and really like never stay the same."

"Yes, it's a pity," I agreed, enjoying just looking at him.

Our eyes met; the message between us was clear. Jack took my arm as we walked out and back to the car. It was later than I'd thought, we'd been gone for hours, but it didn't matter, there were no guests. I was not den mother today. My time was my own.

CHAPTER 42

WE DROVE SLOWLY BACK ALONG THE BEACH ROAD, jammed so tight into my little car, I could feel the warmth from his body. I had a sudden longing to run my fingers over the hair on his arms, blond from the sun. A kind of breathless silence hung between us, that flickering tension that is the lead-in to love.

We turned down the shady lane leading to the hotel. Jack parked under the tumble of blue morning glory, and I thought that this would be the first time we would really be alone together, here. The place was completely ours. We could dine alone on my terrace watching the little jeweled lizards and the blue of the sky melt into the blue of the Mediterranean. We could hold hands and breathe the sweet fresh air, flavored with jasmine, and sip rosé wine. If we wished, we could cavort naked in the midnight sea. Tonight, the world was ours.

I unfurled my legs, hauling myself out of the car, remembering how gracefully Giselle had done it, but then she was in a Jag and I was in the Deux Chevaux. Anyhow, she hadn't had Jack Farrar sitting beside her with sex on his mind, just the way it was on mine.

We strolled toward the terrace, then Jack said he'd left the dog alone on the boat and he'd better go get him. He smiled at me, holding my shoulders the way he did before, tilting my chin until I was looking into his eyes. "And then, we'll take it from there," he murmured, brushing my lips with his.

I watched him stride down the path to the wooden jetty, turning at the oleander hedge to gave me a wave. I slipped off my sandals, enjoying the heat of the terra-cotta tiles on my bare feet. I was still smiling as I walked along the terrace toward the kitchen, where somehow I always ended up, guests or no guests, staff or no staff. The glass beads on the door curtain tinkled musically in a sudden gust of wind. Autumn was definitely on its way.

I felt something wet and sticky under my toes and looked down. I knelt and touched it. Blood! I stared around, not knowing where it could be coming from. And then I saw Scramble lying next to the hibiscus pot.

Her throat had been cut. I knelt over her, trying to push the edges of the wound together, but it was too late.

Tears rolled down my face. Scramble was my little love, my odd little pet, the tiny yellow chicken peering fearlessly at me from the palm of my hand. I stroked her feathers, crying softly.

CHAPTER 43

Jack

WHISTLING CHEERFULLY, JACK TIED THE DINGHY UP AT the jetty and strode back up the path. Bad Dog cavorted beside him, prancing on his hind legs like a circus dog, making Jack laugh.

"Better behave yourself tonight, old buddy," he said, giving him a friendly whack. "No wrecking dinner this time. Or anything else," he added, remembering the way Lola had looked as she got out of the car, the fall of taffy-colored hair, the way she swept the bangs impatiently out of her eyes; her bare brown knees and the sweet curve of her mouth as she turned her head and smiled at him. A secret little smile that held a promise.

He'd missed Lola more than he'd thought possible on the week's trip back to the States. His head had been full of worries about his sunken boat, but on that long transatlantic flight, lying back in his seat, eyes closed, she had crept into his mind. He remembered the way she looked and the texture of her soft skin under his hands. He remembered the way her brown eyes had rounded with shock when Solis told her he was giving the hotel to Evgenia, and her pride as she had gotten to her feet and told him her lawyers would see about that.

Lola March Laforêt was holding her own in the face of adversity and he admired that. He admired that she worked hard, keeping her little hotel together; and that she imbued it with charm and with love, and the way she gave herself to her guests in so many different ways.

Of course, he should have stayed in Newport and taken care of business. He had an expensive wreck on his hands and he shouldn't be in the south of France helping Lola Laforêt get her life back together. He had his own life to worry about. But business had taken a back seat this time. He'd left the rescued boat and the problems in Carlos's hands, promising himself he'd stay just a few days, a week max, just to make sure Lola was all right. Then he'd be back, getting the *In a Minute* back into shape for the South African trip.

He rounded the pink oleander at the corner of Lola's house, heading for the terrace, then turned to look back. The dark sky had blended into the sea; there was no horizon, just a limitless blue, the wind in the trees, and Bad Dog snuffling through the bushes. Endless peace.

He was smiling as he headed up the steps to the terrace; he was alone with Lola, and his boatyard and the urgent repairs were the last thing on his mind.

"Lola," he called, striding along the terrace, still smiling. "Lola, don't tell me you're in the kitchen again?"

Then he saw her kneeling next to Scramble, her hands

covering her face. "Jesus," he whispered. And knew Giselle had returned for her revenge.

He knelt, touched Lola's shoulder, felt her tremble.

He turned her to him, pulled her hands from her eyes, held them tight. "It was Giselle," she said. "I know it. She hated me because of Patrick, and she hated being made to look like a fool."

Jack helped her into the salon. He laid her on the high-backed damask-covered sofa. He arranged cushions under her head, brought her tissues and ice water and a cloth from the kitchen.

"Blow your nose," he said, dipping the cloth in the ice water, wiping Scramble's blood off her.

She lifted her head and stared at him. Her long Bambi lashes had stuck together in starry points, the way a crying child's did. She looked so *vulnerable.*

"I have to bury her," Lola said. "I want to put her by the oleander and plumbago next to my house."

"We'll do that," Jack said.

Jack cleaned Scramble and wrapped her in Lola's old blue cashmere sweater, then he cleaned up the terrace and threw the bloody cloth in the trash can. He found a spade and dug a hole where Lola showed him, while she sat on the rattan sofa, holding Scramble, wrapped in the sweater.

"That's about it, I think," he said finally. It should be deep enough.

Lola knelt by the miniature grave. She lowered Scramble into it. "Goodbye, little friend," she whispered. Then she got up and walked away.

Jack finished filling in the grave. He uprooted some of the

blue flowering plumbago and planted it on top.

Lola was sitting bolt upright on the sofa, staring into space.

He crouched in front of her and took her hands in his, gazing anxiously at her. "Come on, Lola, honey," he said gently. "You're coming home with me."

CHAPTER 44

THEY WERE SITTING TOGETHER ON THE DECK, THE DOG stretched out beside them, snoring gently. The inky sky was bright with stars and a half-moon that looked as though someone had pinned it up there. The sea rippled silkily, rocking the small boat, and a soft wind rattled in the halyards.

"Have you ever slept on the deck of a boat?" Jack asked.

She turned to look at him. He was lying on his back, his hands under his head, gazing at the stars. "No."

"It's the best. It's just you and the sky and the breeze. When the sun comes up it touches your eyelids, warm as a kiss."

She rolled over onto her stomach, chin propped in her hand, looking down at him. "It really does that?"

"Yup."

She rolled back again. "I want the sun to kiss my eyelids," she sighed. "I want to feel that kiss."

"And so you shall, Cinderella," he said, and went off to fetch blankets and pillows. He arranged the pillows under her head, and put the blanket over her, then knelt beside her.

"It was Giselle," she said. "I'm certain of it. She was jealous of me because of Patrick."

"More likely she got her friend to do it," Jack said.

"Don't go away." She clutched his hand.

"I'm staying right here."

"Good," she whispered, closing her eyes.

When he was sure she was sleeping, Jack walked to the bow. He stared out over the dark sea, worrying about what might happen next.

After a while, he poured himself a brandy, then went back and sat beside Lola. He thought, with that little stab of tenderness again, she looked the way she must have as a child.

He lay down beside her, liking the feel of the breeze on his skin and the familiar slap of the sea on the sloop's hull. He thought of Sugar and all the girls before her, and of how he'd enjoyed their company aboard the *Bad Dog*. But he had never felt like this before.

He was awake before the sun kissed Lola's eyelids. He sat up and looked at her in the soft gray light. She was still sleeping. He got up quietly, went down the steps to the cabin, took a quick shower, and put on the coffee. She was just stirring when he came back. The sun was peeking over the horizon and her eyes were still closed, but she was smiling. "I felt it," she said. "I felt the sun kiss me."

"How was it?"

"Good. It made me feel . . . good."

"Now you know why I like being on a boat."

She sat up and ran her hands through her tousled hair. "Don't look at me, I'm a mess," she said, knowing it was true.

"I'm not looking," he said. "I'm just the room-service guy."

Lola looked at the tray he was carrying. A pot of coffee, two mismatched mugs, two boiled eggs propped up in shot glasses, a paper plate with toast, cut into "soldiers" and oozing butter. She looked back up at Jack.

"It'll make you feel better," Jack said.

She nodded, smiling. "It will," she said. "I promise."

CHAPTER 45

Miss N

MISS NIGHTINGALE RATHER ENJOYED THE TINY FIAT SHE'D rented for her trip up the coast. It reminded her of her own Mini Cooper, though her little car was a daring red, not the everlasting silver like this one. She hadn't hesitated about the color when she'd bought her car a year ago, though she'd imagined Tom saying, now why do you want to get red, you'll catch the eye of every cop from Blakelys to London, and with your speeding, Mollie, you'll have more tickets than a theater kiosk. But of course Tom had not been there to caution her, and anyhow she rarely went to London anymore. When she did she took the train from Oxford to Paddington. It was so much easier than trying to park in the city these days.

So, red it was, a nice flashy scarlet that everybody in the village recognized. They waved to her, smiling the way they used to when she roared past on the back of Tom's turquoise Harley, probably showing more leg than was proper for her age, though her face was hidden by the safety helmet that always gave her claustrophobia. She hadn't been able to bear to get rid of the Harley; she polished its chrome every week until it looked as though it belonged on the showroom floor and not in her own little stone garage that had once been a gardener's shed.

She was thinking of Lola though, not Tom, as she drove along the autoroute toward Cap-Ferrat, where she planned to take another look at the old Leonie Bahri villa, abandoned and almost lost under an invasion of clambering vines. There was a "Private, Keep Out" notice tacked to the big iron gates but Miss N ignored it in the belief that no one could accuse a woman of her years of planning on stealing anything, other than a cutting or two from some of the plants that still flourished in the chaotic gardens. She made no attempt to get inside the villa; that would have been wrong. And since the windows were dirty and obscured by vines she couldn't even see in.

Leonie's villa intrigued her almost as much as did the disappearance of Patrick Laforêt, though of course, without the ominous present-day consequences of what might have happened to Lola's husband. Leonie Bahri was part of the past, but her story had been written up in the local newspapers and preserved in their morgue for any researcher to read. There were even pictures, soft focus and too old and blurry to make out very clearly, other than that Leonie was a tall woman with a torrent of blond hair rippling to her waist, like the women in Dante Gabriel Rossetti's paintings. Some pictures showed her dressed in what must have been the latest Paris fashions, hatted and gloved but still somehow looking like the "wild child" of her reputation.

Leonie's villa had once been La Vieille Auberge, white,

foursquare and green-shuttered, set amid a riotous garden on a rocky olive-studded slope leading to the sea. Now it was abandoned, pillars crumbling, roof tiles missing and no doubt letting in the winter rains.

Still, there was something magical about this place, Miss Nightingale thought, as she wandered the half-hidden paths through the once spectacular terraced gardens. It was a place of peace and silence, its secrets hidden forever.

She knew that Leonie had planted these gardens herself. She had also transformed the old place into a charming hotel just the way Lola had; and Leonie had been abandoned by her lover, the way Lola had. Were there more similarities between the two women? Miss Nightingale wished she knew more about Leonie's story than just the ones in the local papers, that said Leonie had been a star of the musical stage, a woman with a reputation, a woman with a powerful lover; a woman who had loved too often and too unwisely.

No matter, she put all thoughts of Leonie out of her head, swept the clutter of dried leaves from an old stone bench, and took a seat in the shade of an old flowering jacaranda tree. The only sounds were of birds and the faint thud of the sea against the rocky shore. She closed her eyes, at peace with the world.

When Miss Nightingale awoke the sky had changed from early morning gold to the hard bright blue of a hot afternoon. Refreshed, she got to her feet, not without a creak or two of the knees. Goodness, she thought, it must be lunchtime and you know how the French are. If you're not there by ten minutes to two they'll refuse to serve you. Going off to have their own lunch, she supposed. Still, perhaps she'd be a little more adventurous today, press on over the border into Italy.

It wasn't a long drive and nobody ever refused a woman a meal in Italy, regardless of the time.

As she turned to leave, she caught sight of a small marble slab beneath the jacaranda tree. Getting onto her creaky knees, she dusted it off with her linen handkerchief and put on her glasses.

A little cat was carved into the marble. Small and slender with pointed ears and a triangular face, it lay, half-curled on its back, paws akimbo, head coquettishly to one side. It was so charming it made her smile. She leaned closer to read the inscription. "Bébé," it said. "Always in my heart."

Bébé must have been Leonie's cat, and in truth the animal had a look of the woman in the photos: the pointed face, the grace, the pose of the eternal coquette. So, Leonie had buried her "baby," for that was the cat's name, under this very tree where they'd probably sat together, just the way she had today, looking out to sea and dreaming away the afternoon.

Miss Nightingale gave the little stone cat a goodbye pat, then wandered back through the garden to the quiet road. She closed the rusting iron gates carefully behind her, not wanting others to discover her private place, then she got back into the car and returned to the autoroute, heading east.

"Italy," she said to herself, smiling, "what an adventure."

CHAPTER 46

THE LITTLE FIAT CHUGGED UP THE STEEP CURVES OF THE SEA road, skimming round hairpin bends with views that, if you lost concentration for a split second, were literally to die for. Miss Nightingale had no such qualms, she could have driven roads like this all day, and possibly all night, without flinching at the sight of the sheer drop on her right and the huge trucks roaring past on her left. The drive was longer than she had thought, though, and she pressed her foot to the metal, urging the small car on.

When she finally crossed the border at Ventimiglia she realized it was too late to go any farther. Heading for the seafront, she slid the Fiat into a too small parking space, congratulating herself on her excellent driving. She found a small clean-looking café and ordered lasagna and a glass of lemonade.

Nothing like ice-cold lemonade on a hot afternoon, she thought, glancing around at her neighbors. No tourists here, just local workingmen hunched over a game of chess and a couple of grandmotherly types, like herself, she supposed, except they had the luxury of taking care of their grandchildren for the afternoon. Ah well, she'd had "her girls" at Queen Wilhelmina's for all those years and their memories took the place of grandchildren in her life.

She toyed with the lasagna. It was the first time she'd eaten a bad meal in Italy, though she'd stayed at *pensiones* and *albergos* throughout that land for many years. Even the lemonade was bad, sharp and acidic and not cold enough. Her little adventure had turned out to be not such an adventure after all, and now she had to face the long drive back. Sighing, she paid her bill, leaving an adequate tip even though they didn't deserve it. She decided to stretch her legs before driving on.

The new Ducati 748S parked near the café caught her eye immediately. She thought how Tom would have loved it. Slim, sleek, powerful, the epitome of motorcycle design. "Ducatis cost a small fortune," he'd told her, "sort of the Ferrari of the biker set."

Miss Nightingale walked in little circles, admiring the gray Ducati with bright red wheels from every angle. She wondered whom it belonged to. Then, smiling to herself, she walked on. A brisk ten-minute stroll and she would be on her way.

Tying the ribbons of her straw hat firmly under her chin, she stared around the square looking for something to admire: a statue, a store, an old carved doorway, but there was nothing and she wandered back to the parking area.

The owner of the Ducati straddled the bike. Miss Nightingale paused to look. Actually, her feet just stopped moving. She was frozen to the spot.

The Ducati owner put on his helmet. He looked right and

left, checked behind. For a brief second he glanced Miss Nightingale's way, then he roared down the street and was gone.

Miss Nightingale's nostrils narrowed like a hound sniffing the scent. She took off her glasses and polished them. She put them back on her nose and stared down the cobbled street as though expecting him to return. She took a little leather notebook from her handbag and wrote down the motorcycle's number. She had learned a thing or two from her Tom, after all.

And the man on the expensive Ducati was Patrick Laforêt or she'd eat her straw hat.

CHAPTER 47

Patrick

SOMETHING PATRICK LAFORÊT LOVED ALMOST AS MUCH AS HE loved women was speed. Especially on a machine like the one between his knees right now, with the exhaust pipes under the seat roaring like a jet at takeoff.

The Ducati 748S was a beauty, sleek as a stealth fighter-jet with its matte-gray paint job and red magnesium wheels. There was nothing to beat it, except maybe his Porsche. He regretted losing that Porsche but Evgenia had said it had to go. It was too easy to trace to him. She was right, of course. Evgenia was always right. She seemed to know about these things, the way other women know how to look after a baby.

He revved the engine as he drove onto the autoroute, streaking past the competition, leaving them in his dust like the ordinary people they were. Ordinary meaning poor. Patrick knew what it felt like to be poor and it was not a good feeling. Being broke did not make him happy; he was a man who enjoyed the finer things in life and the respect that money brings. He'd struggled with that problem for a long time, sometimes up and sometimes down, but now the future was all set to be up.

He patted the envelope tucked into the inner pocket of his denim jacket, feeling its edges hard against his chest. Evgenia had done it again; their nest egg was growing, but not fast enough for her. She was as ambitious as he was and twice as ruthless. For instance, he could never have come up with the plan she had devised, never in a million years. Maybe you had to be Russian, or a woman, or both, to come up with a scheme like that. Or maybe you just had to be beautiful enough to get away with it.

It was her beauty that had taken his eye, of course, the first time he'd seen her, lunching at Club 55. Le Cinquantacinque was the glitterati's favorite afternoon beach rendezvous. Everyone who was anyone and who was in Saint-Tropez or on their yacht came to the Cinquantacinque's terrace for lunch. There were flowers on the tables and champagne in silver coolers, and the best bodies clad in the best designer bikinis and shirts and sandals you'd see anywhere in the world.

It was a year ago. Patrick was sitting at a table under the white canvas awning, alone for once, since the guy who was supposed to meet him, and whom he was about to ask for a serious loan, had not shown up. Probably gotten wind of what was to come, he thought, gloomily sipping a beer.

Now he was stuck with having to pay for his own lunch, and though they knew him well here, they were not happy to have him taking up an important table that could be turned over more profitably. He understood. The season was short, everyone had to make their money while they could.

He finished his beer and was contemplating moving on,

lunchless, when he spotted the windblown blonde standing at the front of the motor launch cutting through the water, heading for the club. The boat was a Riva, slim as a cigarette, enameled a bright yellow that matched the blonde's bikini. She was as tall as any Las Vegas showgirl. And diamond studded. And knockout gorgeous.

"Rich girl" was written all over her but that was just an extra added attraction. She stalked past his table, following the maître d'." Like a hound rising to the scent, Patrick's sexual antennae reached out to her. She stopped dead and looked into his eyes.

"Is this seat taken?" she asked, with her hand on the back of the chair.

He shook his head. "I'm alone."

"I'm Evgenia," she said, in a voice like slow-poured cream, as electricity flickered between them. "And who are you?"

They didn't bother with lunch after all. They slipped out of the beach club and into his Porsche and to a little pied-à-terre he kept in the hills above town for just such moments as this. Electricity played no part in their "lovemaking." An earthier word would have been more suitable for their mating, for their hungry cries and her passionate screams. Patrick had never had a woman like her; Evgenia had never had a man like him. And she wanted to keep him. Forever.

They had been lovers for three months when the plan evolved in the aftermath of their love-play. They were lying on the crumpled sheets, she smoking her everlasting Gitanes filters, he stretched out, arms behind his head, still wet with sweat and sex.

"It's very simple," she said in that throaty whisper with an accent that sometimes sounded almost comic in its Russianness, as though she were playing the beautiful spy in a Hollywood spoof. And then she explained how simple it was. Patrick would get his land back and his hotel. She knew this was important to him because he'd told her so, endlessly. She could manipulate Solis; he would do anything at this point, he was so besotted with her. But not for much longer, not when he found out, as he would soon, that she had been selling jewels and cars and furs and stashing the money. "I'll just have to get rid of Solis," she said.

Patrick laughed, not taking her seriously. She'd thought it all out, though. She and Solis would go for a late-evening cruise along the coast, as they often did. The *Agamemnon* crew always went to their own quarters early. Solis liked to be left alone with her on deck. She would choose a moonless night, perhaps lure him to the rail—to look at the dolphins, she'd say. She'd make sure he drank a lot, add a little extra something to his drink . . . he was an old man, and even though he was big, she was stronger, and besides she'd catch him off guard. Just one big push and it would be over. And she would be free. It would be easy.

"And then," she said, crouching over Patrick and staring into his eyes, "you will get rid of your wife."

Shocked out of this dream of lust and money, Patrick paced the floor, naked and angry, demanding to know what kind of creature she was, how could she even think of such a thing. He would divorce Lola, never *kill* her.

But Evgenia had learned long ago always to watch her back. "Look at it from my point of view, darling Patrick," she coaxed. "If I run off with you, I'll get nothing. And trust me, darling, I'm not a woman who can be poor. I have to kill Solis."

He groaned and she pushed him away. "Don't pretend, we're alike, you and I, Patrick," she said. "Think about this. I leave Solis, I have no money. You divorce Lola, it'll take years in the courts and she'll take you to the cleaners. We would be *poor,* Patrick. And how long do you suppose our 'love' would last then? A year, six months, a week?"

He buried his face in the pillow and she knelt to whisper in his ear.

"It's time to get real, sweetheart. If I kill Solis, you'll be the only one who knows about it. Someday, who knows, maybe you'll get jealous. We'll have a fight and you'll tell the police what I did. You'll accuse me of murder. Hah! I'm not stupid enough to allow that, my darling Patrick. Oh no, it's tit for tat. I kill, you kill. I can never tell on you, you can never tell on me. And *we* get all the money."

She lay next to him, stroking his back, dropping soft wet kisses on the muscles of his shoulders. "Right, Patrick?"

"I can't do it."

She flung herself from the bed and began throwing on her clothes. "If you think I'm going to waste my life being a married man's mistress, Patrick, then you are mistaken."

She paused at the door, looked back at him, eyes burning. "You'll never see me again."

Patrick thought fleetingly of Lola. "I'll think about it," he agreed, stalling for time. He couldn't bear to lose Evgenia. She had him under her spell, the way certain women have with men from the beginning of time. He belonged to her.

CHAPTER 48

THE POWERFUL DUCATI ATE UP THE MILES, THREADING EASily through the traffic out of Menton. Patrick crossed the border into Italy at Ventimiglia, where he stopped to get a quick sugar-laced espresso at a small bar, before pushing on. He soon arrived at the small seaside town of San Remo, where there was a rather grand hotel, the Hotel Rossi.

He swerved into the circular driveway in a throttled roar, parked the bike in the prime spot reserved for him in front, next to his new metallic-blue Mercedes, cut off the engine, swung his leg over, and stretched his limbs.

"Signor March, welcome back." The doorman touched his cap, smiling.

"Grazie, Nico," Patrick said, tipping him a couple of euros, despite the fact that all he had done was open the big glass door for him.

Everyone here knew him as Signor March. His driver's license, his identification, all his papers now stated that he was Cosmo March, a French national, from Paris. His hair was closely cropped, almost shaved, and it was remarkable how just that had changed his whole appearance. Not that it mattered; nobody here in Italy gave a damn that he was someone other than Cosmo March. Which, by the way, was the name of Lola's father. Well, almost. Her father's name had been Michael Cosmo March, but Patrick had dispensed with the Michael when he'd taken on his identity.

To the people of this small resort town, he was just another rich guy, whiling away his time at a seaside hotel, though the puzzle was why he wasn't at some even grander hotel, in one of the more fashionable spots, like Portofino, or Santa Margarita di Ligure.

These were actually places Patrick would have preferred, but in San Remo he was half an hour from Monaco and the Solis yacht. And therefore close to Evgenia, who managed to slip away on the pretext of shopping to meet him in the small villa he'd rented in Menton. He never went there unless he was meeting Evgenia. He preferred the slightly more urban delights of the San Remo hotel and cafés and even the beach club where he met pretty girls. Nobody had written fidelity into the contract he'd made with Evgenia, though she probably would have killed him had she known. Still, a leopard can't change his spots and Patrick wasn't about to try.

And then, of course, there was the casino, second only to the one in Monte Carlo, and where he had become a well-known high-stakes player. Once a gambler always a gambler.

The Hotel Rossi was built in the grand style of the early 1900s when *luxe* was the word. The entrance hall, with its massive columns, soared to a great height, and there was a domed ceiling painted with clouds and cherubs and the rays of an everlasting sun. The marble floors rang under the clatter of high heels and the high chatter of children's voices as they hurried out with their parents for the evening *passeggiatina,* the stroll around the café-lined promenade that everyone participated in. They greeted those they knew with warm embraces and slaps on the shoulder, and eyed those they didn't know inquisitively, assessing their clothing and jewels and hairdos, because in Italy a *bella figura,* the way a woman was turned out, was essential to her standing.

In the hotel, gilded consoles topped with tall bouquets and enormous mirrors lined the hall. Stiff sofas and chairs in gold silk were scattered around, though no one was ever seen sitting on them. It was very different from the Hotel Riviera.

Patrick went directly to the bar overlooking the leafy courtyard at the back of the hotel. The white-jacketed barman greeted him by name and, without asking, brought him his usual Campari and soda.

"You have good day, Signor March?" he asked, and Patrick smiled and admitted that yes, he'd had a pretty good day, *grazie.* They discussed the weather, the latest soccer results, and the talent contest that was to take place that night at the beach club. Then Patrick took the elevator up to his suite on the top floor, not the grandest suite in the hotel but suitable for a rich man alone, like himself.

He took the packet from his jacket and inspected the seal. It had been sent FedEx to the Banque du Soleil in Menton, to Monsieur C. March, and the seal was intact. He put the envelope down on the Biedermeier desk, then walked into the bathroom, shedding his clothes. He stood under the cool shower for ten minutes, washing away the grime of the day and the exhaustion and anxiety that always accompanied his expeditions into France, when he wondered whether he would be recognized, what he would say if he were. And also how he would explain the contents of the packet.

Cool again, he put on the hotel robe, a waffle-weave fine cotton, white piped in navy with the hotel's monogram on the breast pocket. He took a bottle of Pellegrino from the well-stocked minibar, flung himself into the chair, and took a long drink of the water.

He turned the packet over in his fingers. Finally, he ripped it open and looked at the contents. A bundle of dollars, fifties, hundreds, folded inside a Post-it with the written notation "$110,000." Plus a pair of earrings, large tear-shaped pearls swinging on the end of diamond drops. The earrings were wrapped in a scrap of chiffon the color of the setting sun. He held it up, laughing. Evgenia had sent her underpants, the thong she'd been wearing yesterday when she had FedExed the package to him. He held it to his face, breathing in the scent of her.

He walked to the window and stood looking down at the busy street and the rows of striped cabanas dotting the long stretch of beach opposite. It was late and they were empty, the beach boys were cleaning up, shaking out the cushions, arranging the chairs back in straight lines, emptying ashtrays, raking the sand. At the edge of the water, a small girl played at chasing the sea, running forward when the wave receded, shrieking with delight when it chased her back again. Her blond hair shone in the sunlight and her happy cries delighted him. He wondered what a child of his and Evgenia's would look like. Maybe a blond miniature of Evgenia, sweet though like this one, innocent . . .

Patrick closed his eyes and took a deep breath. His days of innocence were almost over.

He paced the room. Back and forth, back and forth. He couldn't go on like this much longer. The good life in a small seaside town, even in a luxury hotel, was not his idea of a good time. He needed his freedom. He needed to be "alive" again.

He contemplated the pile of dollars on the desk. Then he went into the bedroom, got dressed, brushed his hair, dabbed a hint of cologne over his unshaven stubble.

He picked up the money, sorted it into denominations, the fifties and the hundreds, and put it in his inside jacket pocket. Life was to be lived. He headed for the San Remo casino.

CHAPTER 49

Lola

I NEVER WANTED TO LEAVE THIS BOAT, I WANTED TO BE rocked by the gentle sea forever. I wanted to shut out reality and curl up in Jack Farrar's arms and not even think about the future. But two days had passed, my time was running out.

I looked at Jack, sleeping beside me in the bed built into the bow of the sloop. Outside the twin portholes, the sea lapped, tranquil as only the Mediterranean can be on a perfect night. All the portholes and doors were open and a breeze blew through the cabin, stirring Jack's hair. I touched it; it was crisp and springy, full of life under my fingers. That's just the way Jack was. Full of life. And now he'd brought his personal energy force into my own life. A few wonderful nights of passion was all it was going to be, then he would be on his way again. He was a true sailor, happiest when he was at sea with only his dog for company.

What went through his thoughts out there alone? I wondered. Did he think about the girls he knew? Would he think about me? Would I soon become a distant figure, a mere ghost from his past? I sighed. Jack Farrar's future was set in stone, and my own future was dissolving before my eyes.

I wondered, briefly, where I could get the money to start up a restaurant. I'd just about scraped through financially this summer. What little "profit" there was would have to get me through the off season, though if I had to leave the hotel and find somewhere else to live, I didn't know how I would manage. I simply didn't have the funds.

Jack turned over, and I spooned into him, wrapped my arms around him. He was my knight in shining armor. He'd come to rescue the damsel in distress and he'd done everything he could. Jack Farrar had come to help me, not fall in love with me, and that's just the way it was.

I pressed my body against his, breathing in the soft male scent of his skin, remembering our lovemaking these past few days. He was a tender man under that tough mariner exterior, a man sensitive enough to bring me soft-boiled eggs and toast soldiers to make me feel better, a man gentle enough to bury Scramble and plant a flower on her grave. A man who'd taken me into his sea world for a few days and looked after me as though he really loved me. And perhaps he did, I thought as I drifted off to sleep, though I guessed only for the moment, because I knew that was the way Jack was.

When I awoke, the sun was up and Jack was gone. Bad Dog was at the foot of the bed, tongue lolling, staring wonderingly at me. I patted the bed and he jumped up and nuzzled my face.

"You're a good boy, you know that," I said, running my fingers through his wiry fur, smiling because there was something about the mutt's eager expression that made you smile.

Jack stood at the foot of the steps, barefoot and half-naked, looking at me. "How do you feel this morning, Lola March?" he said, coming toward me and planting a kiss on my mouth. His skin was damp from his swim and he smelled briny and fresh and of all things simple and good.

I flung back the sheet and wriggled to the foot of the bed. "I'm going swimming," I said, "catch me if you can." I dashed through the small cabin up the few steps onto the deck. I posed there, naked, arms above my head, just the way Jack had the first time I had seen him, then I dived. The cool clear water closed over me, shocking my sleepy body awake, sending tingles of pleasure through every nerve ending.

I opened my eyes and peered into a crystalline world. Tiny fish darted all around me, scared no doubt by my large presence. I stayed under until I could breathe no longer, then I shot to the surface like a cork from a champagne bottle, laughing and yelling. Next minute, Jack had jumped in, followed by Bad Dog, and we all dog-paddled around, chasing each other and laughing. Oh, it was so *good* to feel so happy, so carefree, so alive. I never wanted this moment to end.

But, as no doubt Miss N would have said, all good things must end, which I certainly hoped was not true, but in this case I knew it was. Back on the sloop, I showered the salt water from my body, pulled on my shorts and one of Jack's T-shirts—I hadn't brought any clothes with me in our spur-of-the-moment getaway. I ran a comb through my long wet hair, pushed the bangs out of my eyes, and scooped it all back in a ponytail. Then I joined Jack on deck.

"We're out of coffee and food," he said. "How about breakfast in Saint-Tropez?"

"Sounds good to me," I agreed, and we climbed into the

little dinghy. The dog jumped in after us, and we chugged across the sea toward the town. I looked back at the Hotel Riviera, alone and neglected, on its beautiful promontory. I vowed I would fight for it to the end.

CHAPTER 50

Evgenia

EVGENIA SOLIS STRODE PAST HER HUSBAND WITHOUT SO much as a glance his way. She leaned on the deck rail, watching a small boat carving a foamy wake through the calm blue Mediterranean. She heard Solis behind her but she did not turn to greet him. She didn't even want to look at him, though he owned her as surely as any other man owned a priceless piece of art. Evgenia was a rich man's wife, but that did not mean she was a rich woman.

She had been born Evgenia Muldova, in poverty in Russia, one of seven children, all girls. Her parents worked in a local factory and all nine of them lived in two rooms, considered lavish accommodation by local standards. But not by Evgenia, the youngest and the beauty. No one understood exactly what gene pool Evgenia had evolved from, since her siblings were short, brown-haired, and sallow-skinned like their parents. And all six of them followed their parents into the factory.

Evgenia took a long look at their lives: at their home and at the factory. The horror of it made her blond hair stand on end. She was destined for better things. At fifteen, she left—without a word. She never saw her family again. Lying about her age, she worked the clubs in Saint Petersburg, as a dancer/hostess, whatever euphemism you care to use.

Meeting men was easy; but meeting men who were willing to help her was not. Still, she was making money and they indulged her passion for clothes and the occasional bauble; nothing of any great value, but because she was young and had never had a gift in her life, they pleased her.

She'd finally been brought to Europe by a man who "handled" women like her, and it was there that she met Laurent Solis.

It was in Saint-Tropez at Les Caves du Roy nightclub at the Hotel Byblos. As always it was packed, jammed too tight even to dance. Impatient with the crowd, Evgenia clambered over the silver-haired man sitting alone on a banquette, then up onto his table, where she proceeded to dance.

She was aware of herself, of the impact she was making, and that all eyes were on her. Especially the man whose table she had chosen for her dance floor. Arms waving over her head, her silvery dress catching the light, tossing her long blond hair, totally abandoned to the music, she was also aware of the man. She took in the immaculate white linen shirt, the dark glasses, the pricey magnum of Cristal, unpoured. She noted his expensive watch and the fact that he was at the best table in a club where money and celebrity were the main virtues, followed only by looks and style. He was older, but he looked important, and rich.

She stopped dancing and stood, hands on her hips, swaying slightly to the music, looking down at him.

Laurent Solis looked up at her, a blond goddess on the

pinnacle of his table; he took in the length of her slender legs and the sheen of youth and sweat on her skin. And he wanted her. He took her back to his yacht, he showed her he was a powerful, rich man, that the world was his. And Evgenia, shrewd little peasant girl that she was, refused to sleep with one of the richest men in the world, even though he promised her a fur coat and a diamond necklace and just about any other darn thing she wanted. Evgenia wanted marriage, and she got it.

What she wasn't clever enough to get, though, being unsophisticated in the ways of the real world of the very rich, was a prenuptial agreement. And so now here she was, just a "rich man's wife."

It was better than being poor, certainly. She had unlimited credit at every store in Monaco and Cannes, in Paris and London and New York. She could buy as many designer clothes as she wished. She was a regular customer at top jewelers, though Solis had to approve purchases above a certain price. But he was shrewd, too, and knew that to keep her he had to allow her a bit of freedom. He bought her a Ferrari, but not a Gulfstream jet; a sable coat, but not her own house.

In any woman's terms, Evgenia would seem to have it made, but her mind worked on a more basic level. How to take Laurent Solis for as much money as possible, because who knew when he might trade her in for the latest Riviera beauty. After all, he was a serial bridegroom: Evgenia was his fifth wife. Her time was limited, she had better make it fast.

Ever the peasant, she began in a small way with the clothes, buying at the shows in Paris and Milan, then selling them on immediately, usually at half the price, which, the way she spent, amounted to a tidy sum. She bought a couple of expensive cars, then pouted sweetly to Solis that she didn't like them after all. Since she had taken care to buy them in her own name, she was able to sell them on and bank the change. Then she hit the jewelry, big time, only she didn't tell Solis she was buying and selling, and of course she still had the important pieces to flaunt whenever he wanted to see her dressed up, and plenty of diamonds to give her enough glitz to satisfy her and to fool him. Anyhow, for her, jewelry was as good as money in the bank.

But Solis was nobody's fool and he was dangerous. Evgenia knew she had to be careful. There had to be an end to all this; she couldn't just go on stealing the "petty cash." She had a couple of million stashed by now but she needed more. She needed big money. She needed to be rid of Solis. She was seriously thinking about pushing him off the yacht some dark night, remembering the way the newspaper mogul Robert Maxwell had been found floating in the sea, somewhere around here, wasn't it? But before she could do that, she would have to make sure she had the lion's share of the Solis estate.

And that's when Evgenia met Patrick Laforêt and decided he was her destiny. But now Evgenia had a plan. She knew it wasn't just Lola that was keeping him from doing what she wanted. It was that awful little Hotel Riviera. It had been Patrick's father's place, and his grandfather's before that, and he loved it. Sentimentality did not exist in Evgenia's vocabulary. With the hotel gone, the land would be free of "family memories." It would be free of Lola because she would be out of a job. It would be easy to make Lola disappear, just like the hotel. In fact, maybe she could arrange for both to happen at the same time. All she would have to do was strike the first blow. Falcon would take care of the rest.

Still ignoring her husband, Evgenia walked along the deck and up the flight of steps to the swimming pool, casting off her sarong on the way.

Following her, Solis picked it up, watching her long muscular legs as she strode up the stairs, the smooth upward tilt of her rump in the thong, the delicate curve of her breasts as she took off her bikini top. He held the sarong to his nose, breathing in the scent of her.

Evgenia could feel his eyes on her, like a vulture, devouring her flesh. She posed for a moment, giving him his money's worth. Then she dived cleanly into the smooth sparkly waters of the marble pool.

CHAPTER 51

Miss N

Miss Nightingale had failed; she had not got the number of the Ducati, only that it was an Italian plate. There hadn't been time and her eyes were not as good as they used to be. Bothered by what she thought of as her "dereliction of duty," she drove back to Saint-Tropez and onto the Ramatuelle road.

She heaved a small sigh of relief as she turned into the lane leading to the Hotel Riviera; she felt as though she were coming home. She parked under the blue morning glory, next to Lola's old CV2, noting that all the other cars were gone. She'd said her goodbyes to her fellow guests before she left on her little trip with a promise to visit Red and Jerry Shoup at their home in the Dordogne, and to keep in touch with Mr. and Mrs. Honeymoon, the sweethearts of the Riviera. Despite all the problems, it had been a good summer; her fellow guests were delightful, the view sublime, and Lola as kind and caring as always.

The only fly in the ointment of peace and perfection had

been Evgenia and Laurent Solis, and of course the mysterious Patrick. Only he wasn't so mysterious any more. Patrick Laforêt was alive and well and riding a very expensive motorcycle. She couldn't wait to tell Lola and Jack.

The front doors were open, as they always were, and Miss Nightingale pulled off her sunhat and stepped into the cool, silent hall. The hotel was closed for a week, for "renovation," Lola had said, though all it needed was a thorough end-of-season clean and a touch of paint here and there.

"Yoohoo," she called. "Yoohoo, Lola, I'm back."

There was only silence. There was a metallic tang in the air, and puzzled, Miss Nightingale walked out onto the terrace. "Yoohoo," she called again. Nothing. Lola was probably in her own house, taking a well-earned nap. She debated for a minute whether or not to wake her, then decided that her news was important enough.

As she rounded the oleander hedge, she noticed the freshly turned over patch of earth beneath Lola's bedroom window with a sprig of plumbago on it, wilting from lack of water. Odd, she thought, why would Lola take the time to plant something, then fail to water it?

"Lola?" She rapped on the French windows but got no reply. But Lola must be in because her car was here. The door was unlocked and she went in, but the little house was empty.

Tired, she plumped onto the porch sofa. She'd have to wait for Lola to get back, though she was bursting with her news.

After a while she got up again. No use wasting time, she would bathe and change, then wait out on the terrace. Lola had to come home sometime soon.

She was walking back up the path when she smelled that odd smell again. She paused, sniffing the air. And then she saw the plume of black smoke curling above the kitchen roof, drifting across the high blue sky.

"My God, oh my God. Fire!" she screamed. But there was no one to hear her.

Her legs were shaking as she ran onto the terrace to the kitchen, saw flames shooting out the door and out of the windows, which exploded suddenly in shards of glass.

She ran back along the terrace to the front hall, no fire here yet. She grabbed the phone, dialed the emergency number. *"Fire,"* she said, controlling her panic until she had got the message through. "*Fire at the Hotel Riviera,* off the Ramatuelle road. The kitchen is on fire . . ."

CHAPTER 52

Lola

WE WERE IN THE DINGHY, BACK FROM BREAKFAST, WHEN I heard the blare of the fire trucks, never a good sound in the south of France. Fires have scorched thousands of acres here, destroying part of the coastal beauty for decades to come. Trucks seemed to be coming from every direction, and I put a hand over my eyes, scanning the coast. I saw the black smoke curling into the air, spilling over the little coastal towns, borne by the brisk wind,

"Looks like a big one," Jack said.

I frowned, suddenly anxious.

Then we saw it, the smoke swirling up from the hotel, and orange flames licking from the kitchen windows.

"It's home," I yelled.

"It's the Hotel Riviera," he added, but Jack was already heading for the jetty.

I was out of the dinghy before he had time to tie the line. Ashes were in my hair, stinging my eyes, as I ran toward the terrace. A burly fireman waved me angrily back. "Get out of here."

I shouted at him, panicked. "You've got to save it, please, oh please . . ."

The *pompier*'s face was blackened with soot and smoke. "*Chère madame,* we will do our best. Right now it's dangerous, the trees could ignite any minute. You must get back."

Miss Nightingale ran toward me from the direction of the parking lot. Her eyes were red and she was coughing. "I found the fire, I called the fire brigade," she said. "I've searched everywhere for Scramble, but I'm afraid I couldn't find her."

My body sagged, first Scramble, now this. I put my arms around Miss N. "Thank you, my friend," I said, "but it was already too late for Scramble."

The chief was yelling at us to get out, we were causing a hazard.

I couldn't even look back. I took Miss N's arm and hurried down the path to the sea.

We went back to the sloop and sat on deck, watching the Hotel Riviera burn. Two small planes were dropping gallons of water, red with flame retardant, onto the roof and the surrounding trees. A single small ember blown by the wind was all it would take for the fire to sweep through those trees and along the coast, jump the road, and head up into the hills.

We sipped Evian water, pressing the icy bottles against our hot faces, not saying much. A couple of hours later, it was all over. The *pompiers* were sifting through the debris, wiping off their blackened faces, packing up their hoses, taking long draughts of water, talking among themselves.

We got back in the dinghy and went to take a look. My

beautiful kitchen was gutted. Choked, I shook each fireman's hand and thanked them for preventing a disaster. I would never forget them.

The chief took me to one side and told me there was evidence of arson. Fuel had been scattered around in the kitchen and ignited. He asked if I knew anyone who might have done such a thing.

I stared at him, speechless. Oh yes, I thought it could have been Giselle Castille. It could have been Evgenia Solis, or Jeb Falcon, or anyone else who had blighted my life for the past few months.

"I'm sorry, madame," the chief said finally, "but this is now a matter for the police."

CHAPTER 53

THE WEEK FOLLOWING THE FIRE WAS TORTURE. THERE WERE interviews with the police and Detective Mercier made his appearance again, as well as other gendarmes. It was definitely arson. Gasoline had been poured around the kitchen, then the gas burners lit, until eventually it all exploded in flames. The kitchen was completely gutted and smoke had damaged every other part of the hotel.

I didn't know if the insurance would cover it, but because it was arson they were stalling my claim anyway, I guessed until it could be proven I was not the culprit. There were no clues, no witnesses, no evidence. I was already under suspicion for murdering my husband, and now I was a suspected arsonist. Who would believe me if I told them I thought Solis's wife had set fire to my hotel because she wanted me out of there? Or that maybe Giselle Castille had done it, because she wanted Patrick? Or that Jeb Falcon had done it, acting on Laurent Solis's instructions?

After the first shock of the fire was over, Miss Nightingale dropped her bombshell and told me that she had seen Patrick. "It was him, all right, my dear," she said, "so now you can stop worrying about the murder rap, it'll never stick. Patrick is alive and well and driving a very expensive motorbike."

At first, I felt relief that Patrick was alive after all. Then came the anger, that same *futile* anger. And then the big question. *Why?*

"It's a woman of course," Miss N said, smoothing her blue and white linen dress over her knees. "With men like Patrick, it's always a woman. And since Giselle seems not to know his whereabouts my best guess is Evgenia Solis."

"But Patrick doesn't know her," I said, astonished.

"How do you know he doesn't?" Miss N said.

She was right, I didn't know. It seems I didn't know much about anything.

"If it is Evgenia," Miss N said, "then Patrick's playing a very dangerous game."

Miss N gave Jack all the details about the Ducati, apologizing for not getting the number. "I'm afraid I'm just not as quick off the mark as I used to be," she said, "but perhaps you can check out the Ducati dealers on the coast, see which one of them sold a 748S recently, matte dark gray paint job, red magnesium wheels. A beauty if there ever was one; my Tom would have loved it.

"Speaking of Tom," she said, "it's time I went home. I spoke with Mrs. Wormesly at the pub last night and she tells me Little Nell is getting quite out of hand. Spoiled rotten, I fear. Anyhow, my dears"—she included both Jack and myself in her warm glance—"I'm sure you can manage without me for a while, and you can always reach me by telephone."

"Must you go?" I said, then realized how selfish I sounded.

"Yes, of course you must," I added firmly. "You've got your home and your little dog needs you, and before you know it, it will be Christmas."

"Why not come with me, child?" she said suddenly, looking at me as though I were one of her former pupils, a lost soul in need of care. "Come stay at the cottage. I'd love the company, and you can help spoil Little Nell some more. Besides, they offer a very nice lager and lime at the Blakelys Arms, and Mrs. Wormesly's steak-and-kidney pie is excellent."

I laughed, imagining myself for an instant in the Blakelys village pub, but I shook my head. "Can't do it," I said, "I've got to stay here and take care of business."

"Why can't you?" Jack said. I turned to look at him. "Work can't start on the hotel until you get the insurance check," he added, "and besides, you need a break."

"What about Patrick?"

"I'll check on Patrick. I'll call you to let you know as soon as I find out anything. Besides, I'm gonna be busy for the next few weeks, back and forth to the States, working on the boat."

I glanced at them, my good friend and my lover, torn between the two. Then, "Of course, you'll come," Miss N said firmly. And so I went to Blakelys.

CHAPTER 54

Evgenia

EVGENIA SOLIS WAS AT THE WHEEL OF THE SQUAT ARMY-green Hummer, driving east on the A8 to Menton. Jeb Falcon, his bulk crammed into the expensive low-roofed vehicle, was in the passenger seat next to her. She put her foot down and swerved past a lumbering eighteen-wheeler that was going too slow for her, swerving back in front of it, causing Falcon to grip the edges of his seat and curse.

"Coward," she said, throwing him an icy glance from her sunglassed eyes.

"For chrissake, Evgenia," he said, sweating profusely as she whizzed past the traffic, "what's the fuckin' hurry, anyways?"

"Better safe than dead's your motto, eh, Falcon," she said, laughing. "Don't you know you're gonna end up dead one of these days? Pity it didn't happen in the fire at the Hotel Riviera. You botched that up, all right, didn't you?"

He was silent, staring at the road ahead. It was all Patrick's fault . . . He hadn't taken care of his part of the deal, he hadn't even shown up—and anyhow Lola was nowhere around, even though he'd scouted the place and knew she should have been home alone that afternoon.

He hated Evgenia Solis with every fiber of his being. He wished he'd never met her, never become her fuckin' bodyguard. The woman was a disaster in the making. Already she'd changed his life around. Goddammit, he'd been making good money from Laurent Solis. Why had he succumbed to her bribery, anyway? He'd caught her with Patrick in Menton, and she'd offered him more money than he could refuse. He was a double-spy now, working for Solis and for Evgenia, and hating them both.

As if reading his thoughts, Evgenia said, "You're a whore, Falcon, always available for the right kind of money. That's why you're here now, with me. That's why you can't go to my husband and tell him what you know, because if you do, both you and I are as good as dead. We're in this together, Falcon. Better not forget that."

"Fuck you," Falcon said, and heard her sigh.

"You're a man with a very limited vocabulary, y'know that," Evgenia said, exiting the autoroute at Menton. She took the familiar road up into the hills and parked outside a modest villa. She climbed out and without looking at Falcon said, "Pick me up at three. And don't be late."

Falcon glared at her. He hesitated just for a second, then he called her name. She looked impatiently over her shoulder. "What?"

"There's something you should know," he said.

Something in the way he said it stopped her in her tracks. "What?" she asked again, only this time she walked back to the car. Falcon got out of the passenger seat, walked around and climbed into the driver's seat.

"About the boyfriend," he said. "He's doing pretty well at the casino in San Remo. He wins some, he loses some. And it's all your money, Evgenia."

She stared at him, silenced for a minute. Then, "Liar," she said.

Falcon shrugged. "So why don't you ask him?"

Evgenia looked at her feet, uncertain. "If you are lying, I'll kill you myself," she said in a tone of quiet menace.

Falcon grinned. He had the upper hand again in this battle of wits and violence. "Oh, no you won't, Evgenia," he said. "You *need* me. Who else are you gonna get to burn down hotels and to lie to your husband for you and to help you carry out the rest of your plans? Only me, little Evgenia, that's who. And only if you pay me enough. Remember that, why don't you." He slammed the door and put the Hummer in gear. "See you at three," he said, swinging the car around and driving back down the hill.

"And Patrick," she yelled after him. "I've got Patrick for all the rest. I don't need you anymore." But Falcon did not hear her.

Patrick stuck his head out of the front door. "What's happening?" he said. "What's all the shouting about?"

Evgenia shrugged as she stalked past him into the tiny villa, her heels ringing on the terra-cotta–tiled floors. She stopped and glanced around her; a look of distaste crossed her face. "I hate this place," she said. "I've had it with sneaking around. I can't take this any longer. It's time to get on with things."

Patrick sighed. It was going to be one of those Evgenia days. "Let's go to bed, *chérie,*" he said, taking her by the hand and leading her toward the only bedroom.

"Did you hear about the fire?" Evgenia asked.

"What fire, sweetheart?" His arms were around her now, he was dropping hot kisses onto her neck, her hair, her upturned face, edging her backward toward the bed.

"The one at the Hotel Riviera," she said, sitting on the edge of the bed.

Patrick came suddenly to his senses. *"What did you say?"*

"There was a fire at the Riviera. It burned down."

For a minute, he stared at her, shocked. Then he gave her such a look of fury she shrank back, afraid. He gripped her shoulders. *"Lola,"* he hissed through gritted teeth. *"What did you do to Lola?"*

Evgenia tossed her long blond hair, glaring back at him. "I might have known it. All you think about is *Lola*. You never think about what *I'm* doing for you, all you think about is *Lola*. And gambling away my money."

Patrick pushed her away. He walked to the window and stood looking out onto the scrubby patch of dying garden. "Did you harm Lola?" he said again, quietly—but Evgenia caught the violence in his tone.

"Oh no, *dear* Patrick, *dear* Lola is very much alive and kicking. But she's gonna have to get out of that *dear* little hotel now, because there's not much of it left."

Patrick continued to look out the window, his back to her. He didn't want her to see the look of relief on his face.

"But it's got to happen sometime," Evgenia carried on, pushing him, always pushing him. "It's me or Lola, Patrick. You've always known that. And it's me and the money, Patrick, you've always known that too. And after all, a gambler always needs money. Right?"

He turned to look at her, spread-eagled on the bed in their shoddy little love nest.

"We can't go on like this, Patrick, darling," she purred in that throaty, creamy, Russian-accented voice. "We are destined for better things, my love, much better things than stolen afternoons in this awful place. We'll live the high life together, anywhere and everywhere. It'll be you and me against the world, Patrick." Her sea-green eyes met his, held his gaze, "You and me and the whole world to play with."

Evgenia held out her hand and Patrick took it. He lay next to her on the bed. They faced each other, their glances still locked. Minutes ticked by. Then, "Oh God, Evgenia," he groaned, taking her in his arms.

Evgenia sighed with pleasure. It had been a tricky moment, but she had won.

CHAPTER 55

Lola

THE SKIES WERE GRAY WITH A MISTY RAIN FALLING WHEN the train from Paddington pulled into Oxford.

"Typical," was Miss Nightingale's sighing comment as we stepped out onto the platform, along with about a hundred other people, all obviously in a rush to get somewhere. I hauled out Miss Nightingale's boxy brown suitcase that was almost an antique, and my own little Samsonite on wheels, then we walked along the windy platform and out into the street.

"There you are, Miss Nightingale," somebody said, and we swung round to see a burly, bearded man in a blue anorak, wiping the rain off his glasses and smiling at us. "Good to see you back again, though I'm sorry about the weather," he added.

"Par for the course, Fred," Miss Nightingale said, shaking his hand. "It always rains when I return from holiday. This is Lola March Laforêt, my friend from France, via California. Lola, this is Fred Wormesly, keeper of my Little Nell and the

Blakelys Arms, as well as many of the village secrets."

Fred's laughter boomed over us as he grabbed our suitcases and led the way to the dark blue Volvo wagon parked in the lot. "Not too many secrets in Blakelys anymore, Miss Nightingale," he said. "All's peace and quiet here lately."

"Well, thank heavens for that," she said, climbing into the passenger seat. "Lola and I have had quite enough excitement to last us a while."

Fred Wormesly drove us through Oxford, the city of "dreaming spires," though it was hard to make out the lovely ancient stone colleges through what had now turned into a downpour. However, Miss N promised to bring me back and show me around "when the weather picks up," she said, and Fred said the forecast wasn't looking too good and maybe I'd have been better off staying in the south of France.

We circled a roundabout and suddenly we were out in the countryside, driving past thick hedgerows and fields filled with woolly black-faced sheep, past gas stations whose high prices startled me, with shops selling crisps and "cigs" and cold drinks. Little side roads led off to villages with names like Witney, Eynsham, and Widford.

We turned into the lovely village of Burford, bowling down the high street lined with quaint bow-windowed shops and tearooms and pubs, across a little stone bridge over the Windrush River, then we turned off once more and we were in Blakelys.

"Home at last," Miss Nightingale murmured, as we curved along the village street, sheltered with big old plane trees, past a store that sold bread and eggs and milk and small everyday supplies. We drove through a little stream, fording it like the stagecoaches of old must have done, swung a right, and ended up in front of the Blakelys Arms, all honey-colored stone, low roofed, and with a jolly crested sign swinging in the wind. A blackboard outside said:

PUB FOOD—TODAY'S SPECIALS: MACARONI AND CHEESE, PLOUGHMAN'S WITH STILTON AND HOME-BAKED BREAD, AND THE BEST STEAK AND KIDNEY PUD IN OXFORDSHIRE.

"We'll have a bit of that for our supper," Miss Nightingale said, climbing stiffly out of the car. "It's good to be home." She lifted her face happily to the soft, cold rain. "And my Little Nell will be waiting for me."

"That she is, Miss Nightingale," Fred said, holding open the car door for me. "And welcome to Blakelys, Ms. March."

The "saloon" bar was low ceilinged with ancient black beams and lath-and-plaster walls, crisscrossed with more beams. A fire burned in the huge stone grate and a couple of old codgers in cords and tweed jackets and flat tweed caps sat in front of it, quaffing pint mugs of dark brown ale. They glanced our way, lifting their caps as they recognized Miss N, saying, good to see you home again, ma'am.

Little Nell, the Yorkie of the lusty yelps, had already bounced up into Miss N's arms and was busy licking her face. A stately blond woman emerged from behind the bar, a smile of welcome on her face. "Well, there you are at last, Miss Nightingale," she said. "It's lovely to see you again."

"And you too, Mary," Miss N replied, returning Mrs. Wormesly's embrace. "And thank you for taking such good care of my Little Nell. Though you've spoiled her rotten of course, as you always do. Just look at her, she's quite the little porker."

Mary Wormesly laughed and tickled Little Nell under the chin. "She's a right one for the beer, Miss Nightingale, better get her home and sobered up. But how about something to eat first? You must be starving after that journey."

Miss N introduced me and said we would love two steak-and-kidneys, please, and two lager and limes, nice and cold if she had it.

We made ourselves comfortable in a high-backed pine settle with red velvet cushions that looked as though it might once have been in a church. Little Nell was tucked between us. Miss N made the formal introductions and told the terrier she had better behave and make me welcome or she was for it. Little Nell gave my hand an exploratory sniff, then a lick, then sat back smiling at me. And yes, dogs do smile, you know that.

"This is so nice," I said, sipping my cold lager and lime, relaxing as the logs crackled in the hearth and the old boys settled into a game of dominoes.

"It's early yet though," Miss N said. "It'll fill up later, especially on a night like this."

A night like this, I thought, with a little shiver of apprehension. A gray, cold, rainy night, so far away from "home" and from the sunshine. And from Patrick. But I pushed away those thoughts and tackled my steak-and-kidney pie, hot and aromatic with a thick gravy and a buttery crust. It was very good, even to my critical chef's taste buds.

"Exactly what we needed," Miss Nightingale said, feeding a bit of gravy-soaked crust to Little Nell, who for a miniature

Yorkshire terrier was certainly looking a bit "porky." "I know it's wrong," she admitted, "but Nell's been ruined here, and I don't want to look like the ogre all at once. I'll have to wean her off all this and back onto dog food—and no beer. It all takes time, it does every year," she added with a mischievous grin. "I believe Little Nell looks forward to her vacation at Blakelys Arms as much as I look forward to mine at the Hotel Riviera."

Our stomachs full, warm and tired, it was time to go. Miss N collected Little Nell, we said our good-nights, then Fred drove us back through the village, to Miss N's cottage. Across the river and through the woods to Grandmother's house we go, I thought, smiling.

Gardener's Cottage was typically Cotswolds, built of the local golden stone with sloping roof lines, set in a riotous cottage garden surrounded by a low dry-stone wall. Dormer windows peeked from under the eaves, and on the ground floor were diamond-paned arched windows. The door was planked wood with massive iron hinges, and the last of the yellow roses draped the lean-to garage. With the sweep of treed hillside in back of it, and the little brook we had forded earlier bubbling in front of it, it was the perfect calendar cottage.

"It's just a hodgepodge, really," Miss Nightingale explained as she unlocked the front door and ushered me inside. "Part Elizabethan, part Gothic Victorian, and anything in between."

I found myself in a small, beamed sitting room, crammed with tables of knickknacks: silver polo trophies and sepia photos of rather grand-looking people in tweeds holding shotguns, standing on the steps of the manor house, with an array of slaughtered pheasant displayed at their feet. Dozens more photos in lovely old silver frames; a Chinese tea service of exquisite design and fragility arranged in a beautiful antique glass-fronted cabinet; a square of scarlet silk embroidered with dragons framed in ebony, and oil paintings of horses and dogs on the walls. There were two deep sofas in rose-patterned chintz arranged in front of the stone fireplace. Some kind person, probably Mary Wormesly, had lit the kindling, so there was a bright fire crackling in the grate to greet us. An Oriental rug in reds and blues warmed the wide-planked dark wood floor, which Miss N told me was chestnut.

Books were everywhere, books, books, and more books, crammed into the built-in shelves, in piles on the floor, tumbling from chairs, propping up lamps.

"My little library," Miss N said, taking modest credit for the accumulation of a lifetime of reading. "I do like a good book on a long winter's night."

There were baskets too, filled with bright wools and knitting needles, and doggie toys and chew bones scattered around. This was a true home, with all the love and chaos that went into creating it.

In the kitchen a bright-red Aga stove murmured softly, sending out wafts of heat, and next to it was Little Nell's bed, a soft blue cushion that she instantly climbed on. She circled three times, then curled up in a tight little ball, head on her paws, watching us with bright dark eyes.

The kitchen was softly lit and cozy with a long pine table that could seat eight comfortably, a couple of old leather armchairs that Miss N said had come from the manor, and red and white checked curtains at the Gothic-arched windows.

A small hallway divided the living room from the kitchen and a central staircase, carpeted in red, obviously Miss N's favorite color, ran up from it. The staircase walls were lined with school photos, and Miss Nightingale told me they were her Queen Wilhelmina's girls, a photo for every year she had been headmistress.

Miss Nightingale's room had a surprising red-lacquered Chinese marriage bed in an ornate cupboard, which was almost like a little room in itself, and Miss N told me she had slept in it as a child in Shanghai, where, she astonished me by saying, she had been born.

She lifted the lid of an old leather trunk and showed me silken cheongsams and old fans, and tiny little shoes worn by the bound-foot women, and which looked suitable only for dolls. There was a splendid Queen Anne chest with the luster of generations of careful polishing, soft Persian rugs, and heavy linen curtains patterned with more roses, which matched the sofa next to the Victorian iron fire grate. Leading off was a comfortable modern bathroom, and down the hall and up another couple of steps was my sweet little room, tucked under the eaves with a sloping ceiling and a pair of those dormer windows, diamond paned and looking like something from a fairy tale.

There was a regular bed, not a Chinese one, covered in a green and white patterned quilt and piled with pillows. A shaggy white rug on dark chestnut boards, a lovely old dresser in blond burled walnut with an oval mirror, a comfortable chair, a reading lamp, a small table by the bed, piled with books. I checked the titles: Lawrence Durrell's *Justine;* the poems of Edna St. Vincent Millay; *Steps in Time,* Fred Astaire's 1960 biography, a first edition at that, signed by the man himself; a leather-bound memoir of the Blakely Nightingales; *The Leopard Hat,* the story of a daughter's relationship with her mother and their Park Avenue life in the sixties, written by Valerie Steiker; and a couple of the latest novels by Anita Shreve and Nora Roberts.

"Plenty to choose from," I said, smiling.

"Sometimes the nights can be very long, my dear," Miss N said.

"And here's your own little bathroom." She showed me the tiny room where the ceiling sloped so steeply no man could have ever stood up in it without cracking his head on the massive oak beam that ran through it.

"Everything a girl could need," I said, smiling at my friend. "It's like a cottage in a fairy tale."

And she laughed and said, well, maybe not quite, then she led me back downstairs where she made us both a cup of tea. The fire crackled and spit and flared up nicely, settling into a delightful orange-red glow that warmed our feet, while the tea warmed the rest of us. It was time to say good night. "How can I ever thank you?" I said, hugging Miss N. "This is so lovely, so different . . ."

"It's always good to get away when things are a little difficult," Miss N said, throwing another log on the fire. "A little distance between you and your problems can put a different perspective on things."

Curled up in that comfortable bed, my head on the soft pillows covered in lavender-scented linen pillowcases so old and soft they felt like silk, I thought about my life and my worries, and about Patrick who was alive after all.

I wondered whether it was he who had set fire to the hotel. Did he have something to do with Scramble's death? Was he still involved with Giselle, or with Evgenia Solis? I could think of no answers, only that now I was afraid of him. I did not know what he might do. But here, in my cozy room, curtains drawn, rain spattering on the windows, with the duvet pulled up to my chin, I felt safe.

CHAPTER 56

Miss N

MOLLIE NIGHTINGALE SAT ON THE ROSE-PATTERNED SOFA in front of the fire, gazing into the flames and thinking about the past. Returning home always brought back memories of the old days, when Mr. Hemstridge, the head gardener of Blakelys Manor, had lived in this very cottage and where she, the daughter of the manor and the granddaughter of Sir Blakely Nightingale, would come by to visit on her pony. She would stop for a chat with Mrs. Hemstridge, and a glass of milk, fresh from the cow, still warm and smelling almost as good as the fresh lemon cake Mrs. Hemstridge somehow always had tucked away in her pantry, and which Mollie doted on.

"Ah, how times have changed," Miss Nightingale said to Little Nell, who shook her long bronze hair out of her sharp little dark eyes and cocked one ear, listening. "You never knew Blakelys Manor, Nell, but it was a fairly grand house," Miss Nightingale said, and the little terrier climbed onto her knee and settled down, anticipating perhaps a long night of reminiscences. "Though it wasn't by any means a stately home," Miss Nightingale added, "just a rambling seventeenth-century stone pile surrounded by acres of parkland."

THERE USED TO BE MORE LAND, OF COURSE, BUT THAT WAS IN the old days when Mollie's grandfather, Sir Blakely Nightingale, whom she never knew, had received his baronetcy for services rendered to his country. In fact, his "services" meant the lavish party he had thrown for Queen Alexandra, who'd been visiting nearby and who had consented to open the annual Blakelys Village Fête. But with four deaths in quick succession, inheritance taxes had taken care of the family fortune.

Miss Nightingale's father became assistant to the British Commissioner in Shanghai, and Mollie, as she was named, grew up in the British sector of the international concessions, where all the foreigners then lived, under the warm and loving care of Chinese servants who doted on her. Which was perhaps as well because her parents lived the Shanghai high life and traveled a great deal, leaving her alone with the gentle cheongsam-clad nannies while they attended balls at Government House in Hong Kong, or sailed with friends down the big yellow Yangtze River, or partied in Shanghai's sophisticated nightclubs.

Even when they were home, sometimes Mollie wouldn't see her parents for days; her father would be "too busy" and her mother would be shopping in the smart boutiques that lined the Nanking Road, or taking afternoon tea with friends in the lobbies of the grand skyscraper hotels, or dancing the night away, because Shanghai then was one of the most swinging cities in the world. A couple of times her parents even returned to England, leaving her alone with the nannies she had come to believe were really her "mothers."

And that's how it was that Mollie's first words were Mandarin. In fact for several years that was all she spoke, learning from the scary ghost stories the servants would tell her at bedtime, and which she still remembered with a *frisson* of fear today. The Chinese servants also taught her to respect her elders and to kowtow, touching her forehead respectfully to the floor, something her parents found hilarious. They showed her off to party guests—"our little Chinese daughter" they called her, and Mollie blushed, wondering what she had done wrong.

Anyhow, it all came to an end with the death of her father and her return to live at Blakelys.

Parting with her "little mothers" at the age of six broke Mollie's heart and she never did become accustomed to the dampness of an English summer, or the bitter cold of an English winter. Especially in that by-now crumbling pile called Blakelys, where the few radiators managed only to melt the frost from the inside of the great oriel windows, and where the many coal fires tended by an ancient retainer who went by the name of Fire Bob left a layer of black dust on everything, including the scones you were eating for afternoon tea.

Lady Teresa was as vague as ever about bringing up her daughter, drifting through her days in a miasma of needlepoint and tea parties and local "good works." A lonely child, Mollie passed the long days (and sometimes half the night too, with the help of a flashlight) reading anything and everything in the manor's library, or else rowing her boat alone on Blakelys' lake. She named her boat *Li Po* after the master poet of the Tang dynasty, whom she was studying in her spare time, of which she seemed to have an endless amount.

She rowed across the lake to the small island she called home, where she'd built a treehouse furnished with cushions stolen from the drawing room sofas, and a table made from a wooden kitchen tray balanced on four bricks. She'd discovered a Chinese tea set in a glass-fronted china cabinet in the dining room, brought back, she supposed, by her father and probably horribly valuable. It had never been used, except now by her when she drank her homemade brews of tea or lemonade and munched on gingersnap biscuits, with her nose in the latest book from Blakelys' extensive library.

It was only through the intervention of a friend that matters changed. Lady Teresa was told in no uncertain terms, in fact, she was told *forcefully,* that she had better do something or the child would be completely socially unacceptable. So Lady Teresa, in the one helpful thing she ever did for her daughter, enrolled her in boarding school.

Mollie did well; she relished the companionship of the other girls and she enjoyed her lessons, particularly Latin. From there, it seemed but a short journey to Oxford and then to teaching and her progress to head of a small girls' school, and then to the "jewel in her crown," head of Queen Wilhelmina's.

She'd been an agreeable girl, plain and sturdy, who'd grown into a plain sturdy woman, though there was something commanding about her presence. It must be the blue blood, her mother had said, puzzled.

When Lady Teresa died, the manor was sold for taxes and Mollie was left with her great-grandmother's pearls and just enough to buy the tiniest flat off Sloane Square in London, as well as the rundown former gardener's cottage in Blakelys village.

And then, of course, came Tom. "Her" Tom, as she always thought of him, affectionately, oh so affectionately. *Tom.* A big man with strong opinions and a working-class north-country reserve that was hard to penetrate and distinctly off-putting, until she'd realized that the trouble was he was Shy with a capital *S.* Shy with women, that is. She herself had never been the backward sort, having quite a strong personality, and somehow after she'd discovered this, their temperaments had meshed.

They'd met in the bar of the Royal Court Theatre in Sloane Square, just around the corner from where she'd lived. It was a fine performance of Noel Coward's *Private Lives,* a perennial favorite of hers. And, so it turned out, surprisingly, of Tom's.

She'd been alone, sipping a small gin and tonic, when he'd bumped into her. The drink had spilled; he'd insisted on buying her another; they'd chatted about this and that. At least she had—Tom had mostly listened. But he'd been waiting outside for her after the show. He'd asked if she fancied a coffee and it had taken off—rather slowly—from there. It was four years before he'd asked her to marry him and six weeks later she'd said "I do" in the small church at Blakelys, where she'd been brought up.

The village had turned out in full force for the "daughter of the manor." They manned the old pine pews in their Sunday suits, best frocks, and "wedding" hats, their faces happy with memories of the way life used to be when the Blakely

Nightingales still lived at the manor, instead of the car-sales mogul who owned it now, pleased that Mollie had finally caught herself a husband.

The tiny gray-stone Norman church was piled with bouquets of iris and daffodil. It was spring and of course still chilly, and the flowers looked frozen in their perfection, too cold to be able to drop so much as a leaf. Miss N wore a silvery-gray silk dress with her inherited pearls (thank heavens the tax man hadn't taken them away; they were all she had of real jewelry) and carried a bouquet of horribly expensive out-of-season lilies that smelled divine and whose scent she would remember to her dying day.

"So that's that, darling Tom," she said after, and Tom beamed back at her, smart in his dark suit and gray silk tie (the one she'd bought for him). He said, "That's that, my love, now you are Mrs. Tom Knight." Of course she'd put him straight about that little matter later, and she remained Miss Nightingale, as she would for the rest of her days.

And they had lived happily ever after, the two of them from their different worlds, enjoying each other, caring for each other, loving each other with a love so true Miss Nightingale knew it would last forever.

Then Tom, so full of life, had died. She'd buried him here, in Blakelys' churchyard and planted the primroses and daffodils he liked so much on his grave. Eventually, because life had to go on, she'd come to terms with it, and that's when she'd taken to traveling.

But it was her remembered loving childhood in Shanghai's sun and heat and her hatred of those bleak, lonely English winters when she'd shivered in her frosty room that had first brought her to the Mediterranean. Now, of course, she went because she'd found the Hotel Riviera. And because she loved Lola like a daughter.

And that was it. Mollie Nightingale's life story. From China to the Cotswolds, to the south of France. And to the unsolved mystery of Patrick Laforêt's disappearance. And his equally mysterious reappearance.

How she could have used her Tom now, used his experience, his shrewd knowledge of people, to find out the truth.

Ah well. It was up to her to solve this one.

CHAPTER 57

Jack

JACK WAS IN SAINT-TROPEZ, SITTING IN THE SHADE OF THE chestnut trees at the Café des Arts, as usual, sipping his morning *café au lait* and eating croissants. The Place des Lices had a deserted air. A cool north wind, the tail end of a blustery mistral, rattled the leaves on the chestnut trees and sent the paper napkins fluttering across the cobbles. The season was definitely over and life was for the locals again, except for hangers-on like himself who just didn't know when to go home.

Of course, he should have stayed home in the U.S. when the *In a Minute* sank, and at no other time in his life would he even have thought twice about that. Except now, and all because of Lola March Laforêt. How had she gotten herself into this kind of trouble? And why did he feel compelled to help get her out of it?

He called for a double espresso, deciding it might clear his head, sharpen his thoughts in this matter, because all he was working on right now was emotion, pure gut reaction to a woman who had gotten under his skin the way no other woman had since the beautiful Mexican, Luisa. That relationship had lasted exactly three months, and he wondered if it would be the same with Lola. Three months and he would be back in his own world, back cranking the *In a Minute* into tip-top shape, assembling his crew, sailing halfway round the world in search of adventure. That was the kind of guy he was. Right? So why would he change? He heaved a big sigh as he downed the espresso. There was no answer.

He dialed his boatyard on his world phone and spoke to Carlos. The *In a Minute* had been raised the day after it sank from fifty feet of water, using heavy-duty cranes. Repairs were progressing slowly. "But you'll be back soon, right?" Carlos said. "Yeah, right," Jack replied, one more time.

He ended the call and studied the yellow legal pad in front of him on the table. A long list of automobile and bike dealers scrawled the length of the page. All were crossed out with the exception of two that his detective friend in Marseilles had just provided him with. He thought the one in Paris was a long shot, but then you never knew, Patrick might be moving around, one place to the other, hiding out. The other was in Genoa, the port city up the coast on the Ligurian Sea. He'd give it one last chance.

He dialed the number, asked to speak to the manager or anyone who could speak English, waited endlessly with Italian rock blasting in his ear, then somebody came on and said, "*Pronto,* I can help you?" Jack asked about the Ducati. Yes, the Italian said, he sold Ducatis, the 748S was a lovely machine, the best in the world and not always available, one had to order, then wait.

"How long a wait?"

Jack could almost feel his shrug. "Three, six months."

"Sold many lately?" Jack asked, feeling him out.

"Sold many? Hah, I wish, but my allocation was only two."

"Sell any to foreigners?" Jack asked.

The Italian laughed and said, "Signore, there is no foreigner's discount, if that's what you are asking."

"You know what," Jack said, "I'll be there tomorrow and you can show me what you have."

"But I have only one, signore, and it is already sold."

"So, I'll order one like it," Jack said, "and the name is Jack Farrar. Expect me tomorrow, in the afternoon."

He finished his coffee, fed the rest of the croissant to Bad Dog, who was lounging under the table, walked back to the quai, and took the dinghy back to the sloop. Within half an hour, Bad Dog was in his life jacket and running excitedly back and forth on deck, barking, and Jack was chugging out of Lola's cove, rigging his sails and heading west to Genoa.

GENOA IS A BIG CITY THAT HAS GROWN ALONG THE COAST, encompassing many of the old fishing towns and villages into its urban sprawl. It was not exactly where Jack wanted to be on a breezy sunny afternoon, but he moored the sloop and took the dinghy into the old port. Bad Dog panted next to him as they walked up the unprepossessing street in search of a taxi. It took a while, and when they did, the driver wasn't too happy about having the dog in his cab, but consented for an extra few euros to let him ride along.

Muttering darkly in Italian, the driver wound through a series of narrow streets, into a busy area crowded with traffic. The fumes were killing and Jack thought longingly of the sea and the fresh wind behind him, sails billowing. He only hoped it wasn't a wild-goose chase, but he had a gut feeling about this one, and he always trusted that. Or at least he had, until the gut feeling he had about Lola March and exactly what he felt about her.

Hands shoved in the pockets of his shorts, in a blue T-shirt bleached gray by the sun and the salt water, wearing his comfortable old Tod's, Jack tied Bad Dog to a convenient lamppost and strolled into the glossy premises of the automobile dealer. He got a couple of sharp looks from the young salesmen hanging about, who decided he didn't warrant their efforts and left him alone. He headed for the manager's office, pausing to admire a shiny black Fiat Barchetta en route, smiling at the young woman assistant, who looked at him twice and decided he was definitely worth the effort.

"Hi," Jack said, "I'm looking for Signor Mosconi, he's expecting me."

"He is?" She gave him a dazzled look, then remembered to ask his name.

Signor Mosconi came bustling from his office, a middle-aged man in a pin-striped suit and polished wing tips, a thin mustache and rimless glasses.

"Signor Farrar," he said, offering his hand. "*Buona sera.* But I'm afraid your visit is in vain. I warned you there are no Ducatis. The last one has gone. We must await our shipment, and those are already pre-ordered."

He ushered Jack into his office, offered him a seat, an espresso, and a large brochure showing the Ducati motorcycles.

"So, what is the one that interests you?" he asked, struggling with his English.

"As a matter of fact, it's this one here." Jack pointed to the picture of the 748S. Then said, "Sell many of these lately?"

"Of course, signore, we sold two just a month ago. A magnificent machine, a *magnifico* design, and the *power*. Ahh, forget the Harley, there is nothing to match a Ducati."

"Any chance one of the new owners might want to sell? At a substantial profit, of course?"

Signor Mosconi assessed him in a quick up-and-down glance. "You are talking a great deal of money, Signor Farrar."

Jack nodded conspiratorially. "I guess so. But a man's gotta do what he's gotta do to get a Ducati these days. And with a little help from you, Signor Mosconi, I can guarantee I'm a very generous man."

The Italian sat silently for a moment, thinking, then he got to his feet. "Why don't we discuss this over an *aperitivo,* Signor Farrar," he suggested. "There is a very nice bar not too far from here."

TWO HOURS LATER, JACK AND THE MUTT WERE BACK ON BOARD the sloop, munching on a slab of still-hot-from-the-oven focaccia sprinkled with salt and olive oil, a local specialty picked up in a pizza joint in the greasy-spoon quarter near the docks. The wind had dropped and Jack started up the engine and headed out to sea, then, hugging the coast, headed west to the dowager queen of the Ligurian resorts. San Remo.

In his pocket was the name of the Ducati owner, Cosmo March, and the address of the Hotel Rossi.

CHAPTER 58

Lola

I'VE BEEN HERE THREE WEEKS AND I'M ONLY JUST GETTING used to *(a)* the weather, *(b)* more weather, and *(c)* the Englishness of it all. I just love it, apart from the weather that is, and apart from the fact that I'm missing Jack Farrar more than any woman has a right to, especially since he is definitely not in my future.

He'd given me his phone number, but of course I haven't called him. To say what? I ask myself when I'm tempted. Hi, how are you? How're things? *I miss you.* No, if there were important news Jack would call me. Meanwhile, I guessed he was checking out the Ducatis, plus getting on with his own life, back and forth to the U.S Maybe there was even a new Sugar around by now.

When I thought about Patrick, alive and hiding out, I felt afraid of him. I was suspended in space and time, living in a dream world, here in the heart of the English countryside. I was hiding out too, like the scared little rabbit I was. But we were on Miss N's turf now, far from the south of France, and

I was getting to know a side of her I'd only glimpsed at the Hotel Riviera. The woman I didn't know.

Days flickered past in the gray mist, a week, then two. I sent postcards to Jack of High Street, Burford, and Christchurch, Oxford, and Bourton-on-the-Water, with hasty messages saying only things like, "You wouldn't believe it, but the village looks exactly like this, it's like stepping back in time." And, "Food good at this pub, you would have enjoyed it. Hope the Ducati search is progressing." Only once did I say, "Miss you," and then I wished I hadn't because, after all, he wasn't writing any postcards to me and I obviously was not on his mind.

When he finally called one afternoon, I was out, and Miss Nightingale took the message. He was back in the States on urgent business, his friend the Marseilles ex-detective was checking the Ducati dealers, he would be back soon, love to us both.

"Love to us both." I dreamed about that phrase that night, in my soft-pillowed bed.

The weather turned cold and crisp and one morning I woke to find a shiny white frost covering the grass. Muffled up in scarves and heavy sweaters we walked the country lanes with Little Nell trotting at our heels, and Miss Nightingale pointed out the first scarlet berries in the hedgerows and said they were early, which the farmers always said meant a hard winter ahead.

We went shopping together in Cheltenham, a gracious little town with fine Regency buildings that somehow reminded me of New Orleans without the razzmatazz and the humidity, and I bought a pink cashmere sweater, on sale of course, that clashed with my ginger hair but was soft as a kitten's fur and twice as warm.

We walked everywhere, Miss N and I, talking about her past, and her interesting life, and about my past and my problems with Patrick. But we didn't talk about Jack.

We tramped the leafy lanes in the rain, with Miss N in a green Barbour oilskin jacket and green wellies and a flat tweed cap like the ones the old codgers wore in the pub, and me in Tom's old Burberry trench coat, wrapped around me twice and trailing over the tops of my clompy old wellies, with an olive-green oilskin bucket hat clamped on my head. We looked like nothing more than a couple of country spinsters, hiking around, picking up branches filled with berries, hair straggling in the rain, red-nosed and healthy.

"If only Jack could see me now," I said, looking at the pair of us and laughing.

Miss N's glance from behind her rain-swiped specs was shrewd. "Do you want him to?"

"Oh," I said, surprised. Then, "Oh yes, I'm rather afraid I do." I sounded so English, we both shrieked with laughter and ran back through the rain, followed by Little Nell looking like a bedraggled wet mop. Back to the cozy kitchen and the Aga puffing warm air and the bubbling kettle on the hob, and the hot cup of tea. Darjeeling, of course, none of that fancy Earl Grey for Miss N, with a ginger biscuit hard enough to rock your teeth, as we pulled off our wellies and flung off our wet rain gear, and toasted our toes companionably in front of the fire.

It couldn't go on like this, of course. Idylls are not meant to last.

CHAPTER 59

GLOOM SETTLED OVER ME AS I SAT WITH MISS N IN BROWNS Café in Oxford, devouring scones with strawberry jam and thick dollops of Devonshire cream, because as you know it's my belief that there's nothing like food in a crisis. It's comfort of the most "comforting" sort, except perhaps being in the arms of a man who loves you. I don't mean to sound wistful, but I am, just a little.

Anyhow, Miss N has just shown me the treasures of Oxford, the beautiful college of Christchurch, where her own father and her grandfather were once students, and where she herself graduated, too many years ago to admit to, she'd said with a roguish smile. We had seen the Radcliffe and Blackwells bookstore and peeked into courtyards and admired the architecture. We had also shopped at Waitrose, the supermarket on our way into Oxford, and I was planning on cooking a fine supper for Miss Nightingale tonight, with a bottle of good Côtes du Rhône, a hearty red to warm our fingers and toes on these sharp nights.

We were indulging ourselves, sipping tea and eating our scones, when quite suddenly, Miss N put down the scone piled with jam and cream that she was just about to bite into. "Oh my dear," she said. "Of course. That's it!"

"Are you all right?"

"Oh yes, I am very much all right. My dear, I think I've just solved the question of Patrick's whereabouts."

I put down my scone too. Her eyes were dancing with delight behind the pale plastic spectacles. "You have?"

"Where else would a gambler go in Europe," she said, "when he can no longer hit Monte Carlo?"

"Where?" I couldn't imagine.

"The next casino along the coast, and a jolly good one it is too. My grandparents used to go there in the good old days."

"So? *Where?*" I could hardly wait.

"Why, San Remo, of course. Hence the Italian number plate on the Ducati. It all fits, you see."

She was so excited I smiled, admitting that it made sense, so we finished our scones in record time and headed back to the flashy red Mini Cooper, and she drove as fast as she could along the Oxford Road without getting a ticket, back to Blakelys, to call Jack.

Miss N parked the Mini Cooper with a flourish next to Tom's turquoise Harley, which she personally kept polished to a showroom shine, treasuring her man's memories as she did so. I grabbed the plastic bags of groceries from the back and followed her inside.

Little Nell bounded up into Miss N's arms, the way she always did, like a little rubber ball, but this time Miss N was too excited to give her much time. "Wait there," she said sternly, dropping her back onto her cushion next to the Aga, and Little Nell tucked her tail under and stared mournfully back at her. "We have to make a phone call," Miss N explained, and I swear the dog understood.

Miss N did the dialing while I hovered nearby, trying to look casual, but when she said, "Jack, is that you?" my knees went weak at the thought that he was on the other end of the line. I sank into the leather armchair from the old manor, curling up like Little Nell, and gazing in exactly the same beseeching way at Miss N.

"Listen to me, Jack," Miss N was saying, "where else would a gambler with Italian number plates be? Why, San Remo, of course." She was grinning like a Cheshire cat, excited and looking most unqueenly, as she imparted this information, then she said, astonished, "What? You're already in San Remo?" She listened and said, "Ah, I see, the Ducati. Yes, of course." She glanced at me, listening. "Yes, she's right here, I'll put her on," she said, and handed me the phone.

"Hi, there," Jack said.

The sound of his voice made me melt all over again. I was behaving like a teenager, I told myself sternly, as I said a hearty, "Hello, Jack, how are you?"

"Missing you," he said, surprising me.

"Oh yes, well, good. I guess the food isn't so great when I'm away."

Miss N glanced at me, brows raised and a look of exasperation on her face. "Sorry," I said, "it was just a joke."

"Are you okay, there in England?" Jack said.

"It's so beautiful, and Miss Nightingale is the perfect host," I said. "You must come and visit, her cottage is like something from a fairy tale."

"I will," he promised. Then sounding serious he said,

"Lola, I have some news, but first I want you to tell me if you know a Cosmo March."

"Cosmo March . . . but that's my father. *Michael Cosmo March.*"

"Yeah, well, Patrick took his name as his alias. He's been staying here, at the Hotel Rossi in San Remo. He was Mr. Rich Guy with a fancy suite and playing the big shot at the casino. In fact, I missed him by a couple of days. He packed up and left, just like that. And no forwarding address."

I took a deep breath. "You're sure it's him?"

"He fits the description, and besides, who else would know the name Cosmo March?"

"It's him," I said, feeling sure now. A tremor of fear rippled down my spine. "We have to track him down, Jack. I have to come back right away. I'll be on a flight tomorrow. Where shall I meet you?"

"I'm sailing out of San Remo now. Call and let me know your flight, I'll pick you up."

"Thank you," I said, my voice a grateful whisper.

"I told you I missed you, honey," he said, and I could tell he was smiling.

I put down the phone and said, "I'm sorry, Miss N, but I must go back."

"Well, of course I shall come with you," she said. "We can't let Patrick get away from us now." And with that, she picked up the phone and called Mary Wormesly to tell her Little Nell would be back, and that she was off on urgent business back to France.

CHAPTER 60

IT WAS MORE THAN JUST THE FEELING OF "COMING HOME" when Jack put his arms around me at Nice Airport the following evening; it was more like I "belonged." I buried my head in his chest, feeling the muscles in his arms tighten as he held me close, and for a few seconds we clung together. Miss N busied herself discreetly with the luggage while Jack whispered in my ear.

"You look like strawberries and cream, very English," he said, perhaps because I had my new English pink cashmere sweater tossed around my shoulders and my hair pulled back, preppy style, and neat for once.

"And you look good enough to eat too," I said, with a goofy grin on my face. Then he went to help Miss N with the luggage, giving her a kiss too, on the cheek, and hefting the bags as though they were feathers.

Miss N gave a pleased little sigh, and said it was so good to have a man around to take care of these things, then we walked together out into the sunshine to find the car. Only it wasn't a car. Instead we took a taxi to the port where the dinghy was waiting, then sailed home on the sloop, with Bad Dog the mutt taking the place of the aristocratic Little Nell. With his head in Miss N's lap and the wind in our sails as we headed for Saint-Tropez.

I was almost beginning to like boats.

JACK AND I WERE SITTING ON THE DECK OF THE SLOOP, LOOKing across the water at the ruin of my hotel. The entire right side where the kitchen had been was a mass of charred beams and twisted steel. What had been left of the roof on that side had been demolished because it was dangerous. The terrace was piled with debris and the rose-colored walls were blackened with smoke. But the bougainvillea struggled bravely on, even though it was the end of November, and the garden still rampaged, wild as ever under the autumn sun.

The hotel had been my reason for living. Without it I was nobody. I had no guests to take care of, no one to cook for, no one to complain to at the end of a long day that my feet ached and what was I going to do about Jean-Paul who hadn't showed up for work. How I longed to have it all back again, every grumble, every complaint, every bit of the hard work I loved.

"It looks sad," I said, "so neglected and gray. Where did all the charm go?"

"It's still here," Jack said. "You made the Hotel Riviera what it was. You did it once, you can do it again. All it needs is a little TLC."

"Hah, and money. A *lot* of money."

"The insurance company will pay up. Mr. Honeymoon's father in Avignon is onto them every day. You'll see, you'll be getting a check soon."

I thought about all the time that had gone into the creating of the hotel. I remembered the construction workers tramping in and out for months; the struggle to get the plans approved by the local authorities; the bureaucracy I'd battled; all the love and pleasure that had gone into putting together rooms from the miscellaneous grab bag of auction finds that somehow had all fitted together like a pretty jigsaw puzzle. I thought about my lovely kitchen and how it could never be re-created. I remembered the love that had gone into the Hotel Riviera, and the "love" it had given back to me, and I despaired. Something that was "me" had gone up in the flames, and I doubted I could ever find it again.

"I can't do it," I said. "I just can't do it, all over again."

I felt Jack's eyes on me in a long assessing look. He said, "I'm sorry that's the way you feel. The hotel was so much a part of your life."

"I don't even know if I own it anymore," I said bitterly.

"You own it until the courts say you don't, if they ever do, which I doubt now we're on Patrick's trail. And anyhow that process could take years."

"And I'll just build it up again so Evgenia can live here happily ever after."

I turned to look at him, sitting on the deck next to me, knees hunched, arms folded across his chest. He looked like the salt of the earth, strong, reliable, too darn good to be true . . . but not for me, that was for sure.

"I'm afraid," I said. "I'm scared to go back to my own house. I'm scared of Patrick."

"You don't have to go back, you can stay here on the boat."

He wasn't coming on to me, he was just being nice. "Thank you," I muttered, "but I hate boats. Anyhow, I guess I'll be okay. Miss Nightingale is staying with me." I laughed. "We've become like a couple of old maids, we know each other so well now, with our cups of tea before bed and 'good night, sleep tight.' " I looked at him. "I do love her. She's the kind of friend every woman should have." I reached out and took his hand. "And so are you, Jack Farrar. A good friend, zipping back and forth from the U.S. to help me, when I know you should be home fixing up your boat and making plans for your next trip."

"I came back because I wanted to see you again," he said, gripping my hand tightly. "And because I want to help you get out of this mess. I'm also afraid of what Patrick might do."

I was wondering which of those reasons I liked best, but I didn't have much time to think, because he put his arms around me, and I was breathing the familiar male scent of him. The stubble on his chin roughed my cheek. "I missed you, Lola," he said, and I smiled as I kissed him. Even though he hadn't said he *loved* me, missing me would do for now.

We made love in that hard little bed tucked under the bow, with the squall of the seabirds overhead and the soft rustle of the sea in our ears. "You look different," Jack said, sliding my arms out of my pink cashmere sweater. "Your hair is longer, your eyes are the color of good whisky, your skin is paler."

"But don't I feel the same?" My arms and legs were wrapped around him.

"Oh yes," he said, "I remember the way you feel, I

dreamed about it on those transatlantic flights, didn't I tell you that?"

"Not exactly," I murmured, nibbling on his earlobe while his hand did magical things to my inner thigh. He sat back, stroking my body, admiring me, linking his eyes with mine, linking our bodies together in a soft sensuous dance of love.

I'd never been loved like this before, never been with a man so gentle, so intense, so caring of me, so sure of what he was doing to my body and the pleasure I would take in it. When Jack entered me, it was the stars and the planets all over again. I shouted out my happiness and he gripped me to his chest so I could feel his heart thundering next to mine, as we lay slippery and still entwined. "Lost in France in Love," as the old song goes.

CHAPTER 61

FALLING IN LOVE. THE WORDS RIPPLED THROUGH MY SLEEPing brain like a neon-colored Slinky, crashing in cascades of pink and orange spirals. There was no getting away from it, even my subconscious was telling me I was in love.

I awoke to the dawn light coming in my French windows. I was on my own living room sofa covered with a blanket, while Miss Nightingale slept in my gold lamé bed; she said she had never seen anything quite like it, except at the cinema.

We hadn't wanted to leave Miss N alone, and besides, Jack said he wanted to keep an eye on things. So he kept guard outside the front door, sleeping on the white wicker sofa with his legs hanging over the end, with Bad Dog next to him.

I heard voices and jolted upright, clutching the blanket to my T-shirted chest. A glance at my watch told me it was ten o'clock. I'd overslept.

I ran to the window. Jack was talking to a small man in a brown suit, carrying a briefcase and looking very official. At least he didn't look like a cop, I thought, pulling on my sweat pants.

"Good morning," I said, trying to look as though I'd been up for hours. I caught Jack's grin and bit my lip to stop from smiling. "Can I help you?"

The man was sizing me up, shifting uneasily from foot to foot. I guess I looked as though I'd just stepped out of bed. "Madame Laforêt?"

"That's me." I smiled at him. He seemed harmless enough, but he might be another of Solis's minions here to slap me with another claim.

"I represent the insurance company, madame. I'm here to tell you that we are pleased to finally settle your claim in full. I have here the necessary papers for you to sign."

My jaw dropped, then my eyes lit up. Grabbing his hand I led him inside. Embarrassed, he removed his hand and sat stiffly opposite me at the table.

"Please read through the papers, Madame Laforêt. I will need your signature, here and also here."

I read them through, signed here and there, and he handed me a check. *A big fat Hotel Riviera check.* A check that meant a new roof and rose-pink walls and shutters that would hang evenly. It meant more auctions and old rugs and silver jugs and gilded beds, and Provençal fabrics fresh from the market. It meant apple logs in baskets again, it meant flowers blooming and windows flung open to the sunshine, the sound of happy voices on the terrace and small children running in and out of lacy wavelets. It meant a new kitchen with a rosemary hedge outside the door. It meant the smell of good things cooking and cold rosé wine on a warm summer night. It meant everything. It meant freedom. It meant "home."

TO CELEBRATE, WE DINED THAT NIGHT AT THE MOULIN DE Mougins, a favorite of mine for many years, and where, though he was no longer the chef, Roger Vergé's touch was still to be felt in every dish.

Dressed to kill and looking good, we sailed into the restaurant. I ordered champagne and told my guests they must have whatever they wanted.

Miss N looked delightful and very queenly in navy silk with her beautiful pearls, which I now knew were the real thing. She said she was sure the food wasn't going to be as good as mine, but she did fancy the wild mushroom soup, and the dorade sounded awfully good.

And Jack, *my* Jack, I thought fondly, squeezing his hand under the table, because he was mine. For tonight at least. *My* Jack was wearing cream linen pants, wrinkled it's true, but at least they weren't shorts; a nice blue shirt he'd bought specially that morning in Saint-Tropez; and a dark linen jacket that, though it had seen better days, somehow on him looked elegant.

As for me, I'd splurged on a raspberry-colored dress, simple as only good money can buy. It clashed wonderfully with my ginger hair, which I wore flowing round my shoulders in a long shiny fall. I'd tucked back my bangs and put on dangly amber earrings, adding to the color mix, plus I wore three-inch heels with pointy toes that would kill me but what did I care. I wore mascara and blusher and lip gloss and a big smile, and the insurance check was already doing wonders for my morale.

"You look different," Jack said, checking me out.

"Hope so," I said smugly. "It cost enough."

He laughed. "Money talks, honey, you can always tell."

"Yeah, well, let it talk some more. Tonight we'll wine and dine like kings," I said, enjoying myself more than I had in months. Except for the times when I was making love to Jack, that is.

The night was memorable, three friends, two lovers. We forgot Patrick and all the fears and problems, and just had a good time. Tomorrow would be soon enough for reality, and the rebuilding of the Hotel Riviera and my life.

PATRICK SEEMED TO HAVE DISAPPEARED FROM THE FACE OF THE earth, or at least the parts of it that Jack searched. Meanwhile, I got on with the work. It was back to long discussions with the contractor, back to cranes and containers full of debris; back to the sound of walls being demolished and the screech of drills and the thump of a jackhammer. Rebuilding must be almost as painful as giving birth, but like childbirth, it was worth it.

The part of the hotel that fronted onto the parking lot was intact, so Miss Nightingale was able to move back into the Marie-Antoinette, while Jack pretty much moved into my own house. He'd hired a security guard who patrolled the property from dusk to dawn, and Bad Dog was around to growl and snap at any stranger. I felt safe again.

Days slid by in a frenzy of activity; constant decisions to be made, always something going wrong, workmen not showing up, materials not delivered. When finally the roof went on, we celebrated with the traditional French party, setting up a table in the garden laden with goodies for the workmen and their wives and families. Many beers were drunk and many toasts were made to the success of the new Hotel

Riviera. Then it began to rain. The cheering stopped and we stared dismayed at the lowering gray sky, and at each other. Then I remembered. "I have a roof," I said, and we began to laugh. Oh, what a difference a roof can make.

I was so happy that night. Everything was going right. Who knew, I might even get to keep my hotel after all. I was up, optimistic, happy.

But this was just the lull before the storm.

CHAPTER 62

Patrick

PATRICK LAFORÊT WAS BROKE. HE HAD EXACTLY ENOUGH IN his pocket to buy a cup of coffee for his breakfast, a sandwich for his lunch, and a drink and a bite in the evening. Evgenia had cut off the funds, angry at his gambling. He'd lost most of the money she had ferried to him, via the FedEx in Menton, including the pearl and diamond earrings, the sum total of which Patrick didn't even like to think about. It was far more than he'd thought, that was certain.

Now Evgenia was keeping him on a tight rein. He lived alone in the sordid little villa in the hills that had been their love nest, though Evgenia would no longer visit him there. She hadn't let him near her in weeks and he was going crazy. His metallic-blue Mercedes was gone; his grand hotel life in San Remo was gone; only the Ducati remained. He was not a happy man.

And neither was Evgenia Solis a happy woman. She was angry, bitter, driven, and dangerous. They had spent the afternoon together, lunching at a small place in the village of

La Turbie, high in the mountains above Monte Carlo.

She'd sat opposite him, calm and cool in a yellow sweater, because it was chilly up there, and a string of diamonds threaded along a platinum chain that dangled on her breast, picking at a plate of ravioli and barely looking at him.

He reached for her hand and she pushed him away. "Don't bother me, Patrick. I'm thinking," she said.

He took another gulp of red wine and said, "So what are you thinking about this time?" Wondering if she were going to tell him goodbye, and if she were he didn't know what he would do. He couldn't live without this woman. She was like a virus you couldn't shake, bad for you but you didn't want to take the medicine because you loved the way the illness made you feel.

"We can't go on like this," Evgenia said, and he nodded humbly, for he knew they could not. "It's time for action," she said briskly. "Our plan is ready, now all we have to do is carry it out."

He poured more wine, looked at her across the table: so beautiful, so malignant . . . he no longer knew whether he loved her or hated her.

"Falcon will make the calls," she said. "The man, Farrar, will be out of the way. Lola will come alone."

"You really think she'll come?"

Evgenia smiled. "I know she will, Patrick," she said, "after all, she's coming to see you."

Patrick stared sadly into his glass. It had all gone too far, there was no way out. Except he couldn't do it. "I will not drive the car," he said, staring stubbornly into his glass.

Evgenia sighed. Patrick was weak, she had always known it. "Don't worry, it will be taken care of," she said. "This time tomorrow, you will be a free man."

CHAPTER 63

Jack

JACK WAS SHOVELING SAND FOR THE CONCRETE MIXER, OUTside what used to be the kitchen. Helping out and supplying the workmen with a cold beer every now and then, sending out for big wheels of pizza piled with sausage and peppers, and generally coddling them got them working faster.

His phone rang, and he downed tools and answered it. "Jack Farrar," he said.

"Mr. Farrar," a man's voice answered, speaking in a low whisper, "if you wish to know where Patrick Laforêt is, then meet me in Nice, in the Place Garibaldi, tomorrow at five A.M."

The line went dead. Jack clicked the caller ID, got a number, and dialed it. It was a public phone. He might have guessed it.

He thought about the voice, trying to identify it, but it was no one he knew. He thought of telling Lola about the call, then decided it would frighten her.

He called the car rental company and hired a car to be ready and waiting for him in Saint-Tropez, early the following morning.

CHAPTER 64

Lola

I WAS ALONE WITH MISS NIGHTINGALE. JACK HAD GONE FOR A sail on *Bad Dog,* and the security guard had retreated to the comfortable undamaged front hall of the hotel, where he was warming his toes and eating his supper while watching a portable TV.

The phone rang. I picked up and said hello wearily, thinking it was going to be the contractor again calling to say the tiles had failed to arrive and there would be a three-week delay.

"Listen to what I have to say," a man said. "If you wish to see your husband alive, be in the village of La Turbie at six tomorrow morning. Let me make it clear, madame, if you wish Patrick to remain alive, you will be there. Do not go to the police, do not speak to anyone. If you do . . ." There was a long silence. "If you do, you know the consequences."

I dropped the phone and stared, saucer-eyed, at Miss Nightingale. I repeated the message.

"He said I wasn't to tell anyone," I added, shocked.

"Well, of course that doesn't include me," Miss Nightingale said. "Of course you'd tell me."

"What about Jack?"

"We should tell him too." Miss N sounded very firm.

"But I can't tell him, they'll kill Patrick."

"What if you don't show up?"

"I can't take that chance."

Miss Nightingale heaved a sigh. "I still think we should tell Jack," she said, "but if you insist on going, then of course I'm going with you."

"Don't you see," I said, "it's my only chance to find Patrick. I have to do it, Miss N. I just have to."

CHAPTER 65

Jack

JACK WASTED EXACTLY FIFTEEN MINUTES LOITERING IN THE Place Garibaldi in Nice before realizing he had made a mistake. It was still early but he called Lola anyway. There was no reply. He frowned, worried. Why wasn't she answering? On an impulse, he called his own number. There was a message from Miss Nightingale.

"I'm breaking a confidence telling you this," she said in the clipped British accent that always made him smile, "but Lola got this weird telephone call last night. The man made her promise not to tell, but of course she told *me,* and now I'm telling *you.* We're on our way to La Turbie to meet Patrick—at least, that's what the man said. He also told Lola that if she didn't show up, she knew what the consequences would be. And that made me think about my Tom, and what he would have done. So now, dear Jack, I'm telling you because I don't like the sound of this one little bit. Anyhow, we're to meet in the village square at La Turbie at six A.M. I'd be so pleased if you could join us," she added, just as though she were inviting him to a party.

Jack clicked off the phone. He'd been duped, gotten out of the way. He was back in the rented Peugeot and on the road to La Turbie before Miss Nightingale could have said Jack Robinson.

THE VEHICLE IN FRONT OF JACK WAS A CAMOUFLAGE-GREEN Hummer, wide and squat. In front of that was the little silver Fiat with Miss N at the wheel, belting along hell-for-leather, as though there were no hairpin bends and no hundred-foot drop. The Hummer was a shade behind and edging closer. Too close, Jack thought with a twinge of alarm. It looked as if the Hummer driver wanted to pass the Fiat, though how he hoped to manage that maneuver on this road and with the width of his vehicle, he had no idea.

He dropped back a bit, giving the Hummer room to fall back and stop pressing the Fiat so hard, but all he succeeded in doing was lengthening the gap between them. What the hell was wrong with them anyway? He peered through the windshield trying to catch a glimpse of the driver, but the windows were dark and all he could see was a silhouetted head.

"Idiot," he yelled, leaning on the horn, but the driver took no notice.

CHAPTER 66

Miss N

MY DEAR," MISS NIGHTINGALE SAID TO LOLA, PEERING through the rearview mirror, "don't you think that army vehicle is too close to our tail?"

Lola checked. "That's no army vehicle, it's a customized Hummer, very expensive and murder on gas."

"Hmmm," Miss N said, pressing her foot to the metal. The little Fiat gave a hiccuping jolt, then surged forward, making Lola gasp.

"Oh my God," she said, with a quick check of the sheer drop to the right. "Oh my God, *slow down,* Miss N. When we get to a turnabout just let him pass if he's in such a hurry."

"Question is, *why* is he in such a hurry?" Miss N negotiated an S-bend with nonchalant flair, though in truth she was starting to get a little worried. The Hummer was still tailgating, forcing her to go even faster, and now she was afraid to slow down for fear it would hit them. There had been another car behind the Hummer earlier, but it was no longer there. There were no other cars on the road. They were, so to speak, on their own.

CHAPTER 67

Jack

STEAM HISSED FROM THE PEUGEOT'S RADIATOR AND A CLUNKing sound came from the engine as the car slid to a stop.

Jack slammed the steering wheel with both hands. He got out and surveyed the steam coming out of the radiator. What a fuckin' time to overheat. Now what? Miss N must be a mile away by now and that Hummer was right behind her. He dragged out the red warning flares, ran back a few yards, put them on the road and lit them. He stopped and stared into the rocky chasm below the road.

"Oh no," he said, "oh no . . ." Grabbing his cell phone, he dialed the emergency number, told the police in execrable French/American that there was a dangerous driver on the Moyenne Corniche, he was afraid there was going to be an accident, it might even be a murder . . . Better get a helicopter out there *right now. Before it was too late.*

He hoped they'd taken him seriously as he jogged back up the road, heart pounding, praying as he'd never needed to pray in his life before. He heard a car behind him, spun round thumbing it. It slowed and he climbed in behind a startled German couple.

"Hurry," he told them, "there's trouble ahead, people need help." The German didn't stop to ask questions, he just put his foot down and went.

CHAPTER 68

Miss N

MY DEAR," MISS N SAID TO LOLA AGAIN, "I THINK WE'VE got trouble. This Hummer is trying to edge me over."

Lola peered out the back window. She waved at the Hummer to back off, but instead it surged forward. "Omigod," she screamed as the Hummer's front bumper nudged them. "Oh my God, Miss N, he's trying to kill us!"

Miss N swallowed hard; the Fiat couldn't go any faster, they were trapped with a crazy murderous driver. All she could do was pray to Tom, to tell her what to do.

Zigzag! The answer came like a bolt from the blue and Miss N swerved obediently into the oncoming lane, praying again that nothing was heading her way. The Hummer swerved with her.

"Pull to the side, just stop," Lola yelled. "Oh God, I shouldn't have gotten you into this, Miss N, I'm just so sorry, so sorry." She screamed as the Hummer bumped them again and sent them skidding out of control.

CHAPTER 69

Jack

JACK HEARD THE SOUND OF A MOTORCYCLE BEHIND, JUST AS the German got the Hummer in his sights. It was halfway across the road, its nose on the tail of the Fiat that was skidding out of control. "Dear God, no, no . . . ," he yelled, and the Fiat somehow righted itself and took off up the road again.

The Hummer's engine revved into top gear just as a gray Ducati shot past them. The German woman tourist screamed and her husband slammed on his brakes, cursing the Ducati driver who wasn't stopping for anything, not even the two cars battling it out in the middle of the road.

CHAPTER 70

Lola

I PUT MY HANDS OVER MY EYES. WE WERE AS GOOD AS DEAD; my whole life should be passing before me and all I could think about was Jack and that I would never see him again. And Miss Nightingale, the innocent I'd involved in my troubled life. "I'm sorry, Miss Nightingale, I'm so sorry," I said, through chattering teeth as the Hummer driver put his foot to the metal one more time.

"Oh, my dear," Miss Nightingale said, knowing it was the end and the enemy had won. She was thinking of Tom as she clung to the wheel, still striving for control.

CHAPTER 71

Jack

JACK SAW THE DUCATI SWING PAST THE HUMMER, SO CLOSE the bike's wheels almost scraped the car's hubs. His mind registered that it was Patrick Laforêt's Ducati and that he was trying to cut off the Hummer but the driver wasn't letting him. In the seat in front of him the German woman was still screaming, and there was the sudden clatter of a helicopter overhead. It swooped in low alongside the road, just as the Ducati swung in front of the Hummer. There was a screeching of brakes as the Hummer hit it, then the Ducati arced slowly into the air, losing its driver at the top of the arc. He seemed to hang in the air for a split second, then he and the bike plunged into the canyon.

The Hummer did a full spin, balanced on the edge of the sheer drop for a moment, then plunged after the Ducati.

CHAPTER 72

Patrick

THEY SAY A MAN'S LIFE PASSES BEFORE HIS EYES IN THOSE split seconds before he meets his maker. What Patrick Laforêt saw, like a film unrolling, was Evgenia's beautiful face hovering over his as she made love to him. Her fingernails are digging into his shoulders, her eyes are wide open, locked onto his. *"You must kill Lola,"* she is saying to him. *"This has to come first."*

He pushes her off him, slapping her hard, snapping her head back with the force of the blow. She doesn't make a sound, just looks balefully at him with those translucent green eyes. He can see her now, as the Ducati spins out of control, and then he's flying through the air . . .

"You will kill Lola first," she's saying as though it were the most normal thing in the world, and to a sociopath like Evgenia, it was. "Then we'll be equals. You can never tell on me, and I can never tell on you. All's fair," she reminds him, lighting up another cigarette.

"I'll just divorce Lola, then I'll marry you," Patrick says fiercely.

She shakes her silken head. "It will take years, Lola will contest it, she'll claim half of your land, you'll have to sell it to pay her off. Remember, I got your property back. It's for us. We'll build *my* house there." And Patrick, full of sympathy, knows this is Evgenia, the poor Russian child who'd never had a real home, speaking. "I want to live there with you, Patrick," she says, "with Laurent's money. There's no room for ghosts from our past."

"I'll divorce Lola," he says stubbornly.

"And what happens to me in the meantime, while you are going through all these procedures in the courts? Am I supposed to wait around for you to be free? To be ready to marry me, when she lets you? After all I will have done for you?"

Patrick didn't accept her plan, he never agreed to it. He thought she was just playing the James Bond girl or something. He hadn't realized this was for real, that she had the heart and soul of a ruthless killer. And so, when he stalled her, then refused point-blank, Evgenia decided to take matters into her own hands. *She* would kill Lola.

By the time Patrick realized this, it was almost too late. But he was no killer, he couldn't let her kill Lola, he just couldn't. Whatever Evgenia wanted, she went after. And she got it. Now she had got him. Forever and ever, amen.

CHAPTER 73

Lola

THE FIAT SHUDDERED TO A STOP ON THE WRONG SIDE OF the road, slamming me against the dash with a terrific thump. My head hurt as I turned to look at Miss N. She was looking at me and seemed okay. I flung my arms around her, weeping into her neck, still murmuring, "Oh my God, I'm so sorry, I'm so sorry . . ."

"It's all right, my dear," she said, adjusting her glasses and patting her hair into place. I guessed like me she was waiting for her heart to stop racing. "Everything will be all right now," she added confidently. I wished I could believe her.

A PARAMILITARY HELICOPTER LANDED TWENTY YARDS DOWN the road and men with guns came running after Jack who was running toward us. He wrenched open the car door and grabbed me; he was saying, "Thank God, sweetheart, oh thank God, you're all right," over and over again.

Troops and medics and fire trucks were arriving at the gallop. Jack pulled me out of the car and sat me down on the side of the road, frowning at the blood trickling down my forehead into my eyes. I was shivering and my teeth were chattering with shock. He took off his shirt and wrapped it around me, then ran back to check on Miss N.

He helped her out of the car, and took her hands in his. He stared down at her blue-veined hands, the hands of an old woman. A *brave* old woman. He bent his head and kissed them. "How can I ever thank you?" he said.

"No need, young man, I rather enjoyed it," Miss N said, but her voice was shaky.

"You've got some cool head on those shoulders," Jack said, just as a paramilitary grabbed him. "Bet you're gonna tell me next who that was driving the Hummer."

"When I get a minute," Miss N said, dusting herself off and adjusting her pearls. She fished her linen hankie out of her bag and mopped the sweat and dust from her face, then came to sit next to me on the side of the road.

Fire trucks and ambulances and police cars screeched down the hill and troopers lined the cliff edge, peering at the wreckage far below. We heard a boom and I knew the Hummer's fuel tank had exploded. Whoever was driving it, if he wasn't dead already, was surely dead now.

The Germans were still sitting, stunned, in their car. Jack said he was sorry for involving them but, as they could see, it was a matter of life and death. He gave them the hotel telephone number and asked them to come by so we could all thank them properly. Then he was grabbed by the police, handcuffed, and stuffed into the back of the cop car, alongside me and Miss N.

"Never thought I'd get to sit in the back of one of these," she said, smiling, though I knew she was uncomfortable with her hands cuffed behind her. The cops began asking questions, treating Miss N respectfully because she was an old lady, even though right now, as the Fiat driver, she seemed to be responsible for the deaths of at least two people.

She answered their questions clearly, telling them exactly what had happened. Jack verified her story and the German couple backed him up. Out from under suspicion for the time being, our handcuffs were removed. Not knowing quite what to do, we went back to sit by the side of the road.

By now all traffic had ground to a halt, unable to turn back or go forward. Drivers paced, staring at the disaster below, looking at their watches and cursing. These deaths were not part of their lives and they were late. Yet another rescue truck arrived, then the helicopter clattered off over the edge of the ravine, surveying the trail of debris. The brush caught fire, it was spreading rapidly, and more *pompiers* were needed.

The cop taking notes asked Jack if they knew who the victims were. "I don't know who the driver of the Hummer was," Jack said, looking at me. "But the motorcycle driver was Patrick Laforêt."

I tried to speak, to say how could it be, but no sound came out. I just stared at him. Later, stuffed between him and Miss N again, on the way to the hospital to check out our injuries, I asked him, "Why did Patrick do it?"

"Patrick realized just in time what was going to happen. He saved your life," Jack said, squeezing my hand tighter.

"It's very simple, my dear," Miss Nightingale added. "Patrick loved you after all. In his own way."

CHAPTER 74

WE WERE HOME, DRINKING BRANDY AND NOT SAYING much. We'd showered, cleaned ourselves up, tried to clean the horror out of our heads and the memory from our souls. It wasn't over yet but somehow it was more bearable now we were "home."

The sun was down and there was a nip in the air. Jack went to fetch Miss N's cardigan and a shawl for me—I was still shivering—and then Nadine bustled in with mugs of hot soup.

I stared at it. "How can I eat when Patrick just died?"

"Patrick died saving you, Lola, but he was the one who put you in danger in the first place." Jack was blunt.

"But he redeemed himself . . ."

"Yes, he did redeem himself, though it doesn't absolve what he did to you," Miss N said.

I took a tentative sip of the soup. Its warmth seemed to untangle part of the knot in my stomach and I sipped again, then held the mug to my face, breathing its fragrant warmth, still guilty that I was alive and drinking soup and Patrick was dead. *Really* dead this time. "Didn't I always tell you," I said, "Patrick was a bad husband, but he wasn't a bad man." I shrugged wearily. "Now you know I was right."

"It's time to get on with your own life," Miss Nightingale said briskly. "Because you do have a life, you know. An independent life, to do with as you will."

"Thanks to Patrick." I pressed my lips against the mug to stop them trembling.

"Not only thanks to Patrick. You're your own woman, Lola. You've created your own life, here, your own place in the world." Miss N had never sounded so firm, so assertive.

"Now I want to tell you about the woman driving the Hummer," she said. "And her companion. The police haven't identified the remains yet, but I am certain of their identities."

Jack nodded. "I think I know too, but I'm not sure why."

Miss Nightingale gave me a searching look. "This may be painful, my dear," she said, "but it's better you know exactly what happened."

And then she told us about Evgenia and Patrick, and about the spell she must have had, not only over my husband, but also over her own. A spell to inspire a man to murder.

CHAPTER 75

THE REPORT ON TV, AND IN THE NEWSPAPERS, SAID THAT Evgenia Solis had died in a car accident on the Corniche road. On the same day, it was reported that the "missing" man, Patrick Laforêt, had been "discovered," and killed riding his motorcycle.

The Solis yacht slipped quietly out of Monte Carlo that same night, without the body of Evgenia Solis, or what was left of it, on board. Instructions had been given to Maître Dumas for Evgenia to be interred in a convenient cemetery. No headstone, other than a plain marker with her name and the dates of her birth and death, was planned. There would be no memorial service and no questions asked. Laurent Solis donated a large sum of money to the fund for the restoration of ancient artifacts and went quickly back to living the high life. If he had any wounds, he certainly didn't lick them in public.

That night too an envelope was hand-delivered to my door. In it was Patrick's note assigning the hotel to Solis. It was torn into little pieces. Solis had given up his claim to the Hotel Riviera. He had given me a gift, instead of giving the hotel to his wife.

If there was anyone, besides poor Patrick, I felt sorry for in this whole tragic affair, it was Laurent Solis. That is, if it's possible to feel sorry for a billionaire. I believed his story of how Patrick's grandmother had saved him. Solis wasn't a wicked man; he was a good businessman in the spell of a beautiful, powerful, crazy woman.

The police came round, asking questions about Jeb Falcon, who had died in the crash, alongside Evgenia, but we claimed to know nothing. And as for Giselle Castille, she'd slunk back to Paris and her villa was now up for sale.

"Good riddance to bad rubbish," Miss Nightingale said, satisfied, though whether she meant Patrick as well was unclear.

However, I gave Patrick a bang-up memorial service, attended by all his "friends," including quite a few attractive women. Plus the Shoups came down from the Dordogne to lend support and the Honeymooners sent a bountiful bouquet, though it was for me, not Patrick. Even Budgie Lampson sent a note of condolence, though I got the impression that, all things considered, she felt Patrick's death was a relief.

I hosted the "wake" on the Riviera's terrace, shaking hands with Patrick's friends and being kissed on both cheeks by women who had been his lovers. They drank champagne and reminisced in hushed voices while wolfing down excellent hors d'oeuvres prepared by Nadine and served by Jean-Paul, returned for the occasion and somberly suited in a black T-shirt and black pants.

Jack kept watch and his distance, because after all, this was my husband's funeral. But Miss Nightingale stood squarely at my side, sizing up the mourners and occasionally patting my arm for comfort.

I'd gotten myself properly together for my last goodbye to Patrick, in a sleeveless black linen shift and my highest heels. A big-brimmed hat of black straw hid my eyes, which anyway were already hidden behind the darkest sunglasses I could find. Jack seemed surprised by my new look and Miss Nightingale said I made a very beautiful widow, which made me laugh. At that moment, with the sound of my own laughter in my ears, I realized that I really was my own woman. That Patrick had chosen his path, and now I was free to choose mine.

And what would I choose? I stole a glance over my shoulder at Jack, standing behind me. He looked solemn and a bit wary, and so incredibly strong and handsome that my heart turned over. The only question now was, would *he* choose *me*? I doubted it. After all, he was a sailor, and anyhow, I was far too shy to ask.

The mourners were gone, drifting off like a flock of crows in their funeral black, laughing and chattering and making plans for the evening. It was goodbye, Patrick, and on with their lives. And I supposed there was nothing wrong with that.

We dined out that night, with Red and Jerry Shoup to lighten our hearts and "take us out of ourselves," as Miss Nightingale put it. I chose the Auberge des Maures, off the Place des Lices in Saint-Tropez, where, wrapped in sweaters and in sneakers and jeans, we dined with other locals under the grape arbor on barbecued loup de mer and platters of tiny green lentils, and quite a few bottles of rosé.

We drank a toast to the Hotel Riviera, which was now mine to "have and to hold" forever, and I vowed to make it as beautiful as it was before. Then we drank a toast to Patrick, and I remembered that he had loved me, after all.

Back at the hotel, the Shoups had their old room, now fully restored; Miss Nightingale was in her Marie-Antoinette, and Jack and I were in my cottage.

"Isn't this wrong?" I asked nervously as he closed the door and slid his arms around me. "I feel like a wicked woman. After all, I've just buried my husband."

"Sweetheart, you buried him a long time ago." He nuzzled my ear, sending shivers through me. "Today was just a formality."

Though the night was warm, I lit the fire and we snuggled together on the sofa, watching the flames, listening to Bad Dog snoring at our feet and the soothing sound of Antonio Carlos Jobim, singing of love in Portuguese, backed by the even softer sound of the sea. In my heart, I thanked Patrick again, and I thanked God for sending me Miss Nightingale and for Jack Farrar. Oddly, at the end of this terrible week of tragedy I felt comforted. At that moment I was a contented woman.

CHAPTER 76

I DROVE MISS NIGHTINGALE TO THE NICE AIRPORT AND PUT her on the flight to London. I would miss her more than anyone could know; there was so much more to her than discussions about the weather and how the drought was affecting her roses this year. Miss N was as deep and mysterious as Pandora's box, and the truth was I loved her and I hated to see her go.

"Stay, please, why don't you?" I'd begged. I wanted to say "I love you" but understood that Miss Nightingale would disapprove of such a show of emotion: in Miss Nightingale's view it went without saying that we cared about each other.

"Well, dear," she replied, as we sipped a final after-dinner brandy together. "I have my garden to look after, you know. The wisteria needs cutting back, and the roses, and Little Nell is still boarding with the Wormeslys at the Blakelys Arms and no doubt missing me, though I sometimes wonder, because the Wormeslys spoil her so—all those pork sausages and the spilled beer."

"Then come for Christmas?" I eyed her hopefully, already planning our Christmas feast and wondering in the back of my mind if I could persuade Jack to stay too. Oh, Jack, I thought with a sudden drop of my heart . . . The sailor, the wanderer, a nomad just like Patrick . . .

"That's sweet of you"—Miss Nightingale was genuinely pleased with her invitation—"but you see, I'm always so busy with my church activities at Christmas. There's the carol singing Christmas Eve, though it does seem a little odd to go and stand on the doorstep of what was once my home and sing 'God Bless Ye Merry Gentlemen' to the total stranger who now owns it. And then there's the annual pantomime at the village hall. It's *Cinderella* this year, the children always like that, and my Little Nell has a walk-on as Cinder's faithful little doggie, dressed in a tutu, which always brings a round of applause. Then, of course, the vicar and his wife are sure to invite me for Christmas lunch and I couldn't disappoint them. So you see, my dear, how busy I am?"

"Of course, I understand," I said, thinking of my own lonesome Christmas.

"But perhaps in the New Year?" Miss Nightingale suggested.

And I said I hoped so, oh I hoped so.

AFTER I'D PUT MISS N ON THE PLANE, ON AN IMPULSE I TURNED east out of Nice, heading for Cap-Ferrat, and the old villa she had told me about. The one that had belonged to a woman called Leonie, and where Miss Nightingale had said I would find a true peace. I needed to be alone with my thoughts.

I remembered the directions only hazily, but somehow I

found my way there. As though it were destined, I thought, looking at the name La Vieille Auberge inscribed in faded script across the two huge white stones that marked the entrance to the overgrown driveway.

I pushed open the creaking iron gate, and walked under the tall, shadowy trees, along the rutted gravel path to the house. And there it was, a dilapidated white house set amid green-black cypresses and silvery olives. A series of paths and little terraces led to a spit of white sand, and a flight of rather rickety-looking steps led down to the sea.

It was, I thought, wandering slowly along the overgrown paths, not a million miles from my own place, though this had more grandeur than the Hotel Riviera. And yet it had about it the feel of a family home. There were memories in this place, you could feel them in the air around you, breathe them in with the scent of wild thyme and rosemary and the salty sea.

I came to a stone bench beneath a jacaranda, the perfect place to sit and dream away a warm afternoon, watching the sea change color from turquoise to ink-blue as evening approached. The perfect place to dream about life, and about love. The perfect place to come to terms with my true self, and with my own life, just as I somehow knew the woman known as Leonie must have done, many years before.

I sank onto the bench, gazing out at the magical view, and I remembered Patrick, and the good times and that, in the end, he had loved me. I thought about the Hotel Riviera, and how now I would work even harder to make it a success, and how much I enjoyed pampering my guests, and sharing their days. I even planned a couple of new menus, just sitting there, staring into that blue space.

I thought about my friend Mollie Nightingale, and how I would never be able to call her Mollie, even though I loved her.

And of course, I thought about Jack. Just a jumble of thoughts . . . how I loved his body and the touch of his hands and how blue his eyes were, narrowed in that smile that knocked me for a loop. I remembered his voice with that faint New England twang, telling me how much he loved his boat. Soon, he too would be gone, sailing halfway around the world in search of adventure, because that's the kind of man he was.

And I would be alone again, at the Hotel Riviera, waiting for the summer when I would bloom again like the bougainvillea.

Loneliness wrapped itself around me like a damp blanket and I shivered, though the day was warm. "Lonely" was not a good place to be. I heard a faint rustling noise and turned to look.

A little chocolate-brown cat with golden eyes looked back at me. It was small and dainty, with a sweet pink-tipped nose, a little triangular face and pointed ears.

"Well, hello," I said, "and who are you?"

The cat arched its back in a long stretch, then it slinked over to me, and rubbed against my legs, purring throatily. I held out my hand. The cat sniffed it, then sat on its elegant haunches, looking at me. I picked it up and held it on my lap, stroking its fur, the softest fur I had ever touched. It licked my hand with its rough pink tongue.

Suddenly I began to cry, finally letting out the emotion of the past months. And the little cat sat quietly in my lap, not purring now, just comforting me with her presence.

When the tears finally stopped, I mopped my face on the edge of my T-shirt, because I had no Kleenex handy. I looked down at the little brown cat in my lap. She had no collar, no identification . . . she was just a little lost cat. And now she was mine. She would be my guardian angel, she would fit into my life as though it were always meant to be.

Picking her up, I took her into my life, which, had I known it, was exactly what Leonie Bahri had done, many years ago.

There was only one name for her. Chocolate, of course. It suited her soft brown color and my culinary career. I think Scramble would have liked her. I hoped so, because from now on, Chocolate would be sleeping on my pillow at night, and I would no longer be alone.

CHAPTER 77

THE WEATHER HAS CHANGED. THE PINES RUSTLE IN THE brisk breezes and the brilliant summer light has softened, touching the countryside with ochre and rose. I light the fire early and the resiny aroma of pine and wood smoke scents the air.

At the Saturday market it's just us locals, wrapped in sweaters and jackets, rubbing our cold hands, the men knocking back a hearty glass of brandy with breakfast to ward off the early morning chill.

Sometimes I think this is my favorite time of the year, quieter, more gentle, with the fresh breeze and satiny scents and the sea sparkling under the lowering gray horizon.

I wondered what I was going to do with the rest of the long winter. Saint-Tropez is the only town on the Côte d'Azur that faces north; it can be cold and blustery, and most hotels close from mid-October to March, though not us. The Hotel Riviera stays open all year to rescue those diehards, the waifs and strays, the true romantics escaping real life for their dream of the south of France.

I stared out my window at the waves frothed with white foam. The black sloop no longer danced in the bay and it looked lonely. Jack had been gone for several days; a meeting, he'd said, with a boat builder in Marseilles.

We'd had dinner the night before he left, at the Auberge des Maures. He'd held my hand under the table and the sexy look in his eyes had left me, for once, unable to concentrate on my food.

After, we strolled the almost empty streets, stopping to look in a shop window here and there, stumbling occasionally on the cobblestones, wandering down darkened winter alleys toward the port. As we turned the corner a snatch of music drifted from the Quai Suffren. We looked at each other surprised. Most of the big yachts were gone, heading for warmer winter climes, and the shops selling postcards and T-shirts were shuttered.

The music came from a CD in a smoothly tiled area in front of the stores. Tango music. Five or six couples, oblivious to us watching, solemnly danced a perfect Argentinean tango.

We caught our breaths at the strange beauty of the moment, then hands clasped, we left them to their music. But I'll never forget that moment of magic, on a cold Saint-Tropez winter night. And neither, I believe, will Jack.

I sighed, remembering, then I pulled another sweater over my head and wrapped Miss N's striped muffler several times around my neck. It trailed past my knees, and if she'd stayed any longer, I knew it would have grown another couple of feet. Calling Chocolate, I walked across the empty terrace, through the windswept garden to the cove.

Shivering, I contemplated the waves. Chocolate gave me a miserable glare, then streaked, tail down, back to the comfort of the sofa in front of the fire.

I paced the beach, head down, waves splashing over my sandals. My eyes stung from the wind and my nose glowed red from the cold.

I heard a whistle and lifted my head. Jack was jogging toward me with Bad Dog, as always, circling wildly around him.

I turned to stone. Oh God, I thought, this is it. He's coming to say goodbye.

Bad Dog got to me first, jumping and barking, wondering why I wasn't patting him and ruffling his scruffy fur. Oh, Bad Dog, I thought, you are the most beautiful dog in the whole world. I just can't say goodbye to you. Turn now and go away, go back to your master.

"Lola," Jack said.

I stared down at my frozen sandaled feet.

"Lola," he said again, coming closer but not touching. "The sloop's sprung a leak. She'll have to go into dry dock for repairs."

"Oh? Does that mean you'll be staying here for a while?" I didn't know if I wanted him to stay. I didn't know whether I could bear to go through this misery again in a few months' time when he would leave for good.

"As a matter of fact I'm having her completely overhauled. I thought she might make a nice little pleasure boat for our guests. Y'know, sunset cruises, fishing excursions, sort of like that."

I lifted my head. *"Sunset cruises?"*

"Sure. After all, they won't get a better skipper than me."

"That they won't," I said, thoughtfully.

He jogged on the spot, trying to keep warm, grinning at me. In his faded jeans and old sweatshirt he looked better than anybody's apple pie, including my own.

"Come on then, what d'you say?" He stopped jogging and grabbed my frozen hands. Pulling me toward him he held them to his cheek. "What do you say, Lola?" he whispered.

"About what?" My eyes were tearing from the wind, or at least I pretended that was the reason. He laughed and dropped onto one knee.

"About marrying me?"

"Oh . . . that," I said airily. Then I stared at him. *"What?"*

"Please, Lola, will you marry me?"

Another wave splashed over my feet but I hardly noticed. "You want *me* to marry *you*?"

"That's it. Only please hurry and say yes before we both freeze to death."

"Are you serious?"

"Never more, sweetheart."

"But your boat, your long-haul trip, your sailor's life . . . Can you really stay in one place?"

"We'll work it out together," he said, giving me that long lingering look that turned me to jelly. My heart did a little jump. *I* did a little jump. My feet actually lifted off the ground!

"Tell me again."

"Damn it, woman, you're marrying me," he said. "Sunset cruises and all." And he lifted me off my feet—*really* this time. We were hugging and laughing in between kisses and Bad

Dog was jumping up at us, barking his head off.

Jack held me close, murmuring did I know how much he loved me, and other things I don't think I should confess to right here and now. I was lost in his words when he suddenly pushed me away. He held me at arm's length, gazing heavenward.

"Lola, look what the gods have sent us as a celebration," he said.

I saw the icy white flakes drifting gently to earth. "It's *snow*!" I yelled. "It's *snowing* on the Riviera." And like a big kid I stuck out my tongue to catch them.

Then we were hugging again and laughing until Jack stopped my laughter by kissing those snowflakes right out of my mouth. When we finally came up for air I had to blow my nose and wipe away the tears, but they were tears of laughter this time.

"By the way, I will," I said.

"Will what?" he answered, putting on a pretend-bemused face.

"Think about marrying you," I answered, sighing, as he nuzzled my neck, holding me close so the warmth of his body thawed my frozen heart.

"Darn right you'll marry me," he said.

EPILOGUE

It's early morning on the Côte d'Azur and the May sky is a limpid pearly-pink, like the inside of an oyster shell. On my way to the kitchen I stopped to watch the sun drifting lazily above the horizon, touching the sea and treetops and tiled roofs with gold until the whole world glowed as it must have at the dawn of creation.

Lucky me, I thought, to get to see this every morning. Lucky me, heading for the early market again. Lucky me, with the Hotel Riviera back in business, already with six guests who'll soon be stirring and looking for croissants and coffee to begin their leisurely day.

And lucky, oh so lucky me, to have slept the carefree night away in the arms of the man I love, the sexy, wonderful captain of the sloop *Bad Dog,* and now captain and owner of my heart. "You're too much," you might be saying, "you're too romantic, too over the top." Of course I am, but then I've never felt like this before. I'm head over dizzy heels in love, and this time he loves me too. *Really* loves me.

How do I know? Why, because Jack Farrar, the nomad, the roamer of the sea, the man's man whose usual hangouts are the fishing ports of the world, told me so. And to prove it, he married me on New Year's Day in the little nineteenth-century church of Saint Torpes, conveniently overlooking Saint-Tropez yacht harbor.

The locals have finally taken us to their French bosoms and many attended, including the firemen who saved the Hotel Riviera from the flames, and even a couple of the local gendarmes who came to show their support.

Jack looked so to-die-for handsome in a nautical dark blue blazer, his eyes linked reassuringly with mine, as I walked toward him like a woman in a dream. Bad Dog trotted down the aisle behind me wearing a scarlet bow tie that matched his master's and minding his manners for once, though he did give a quick exploratory sniff to the priest's shoes. Of course, Chocolate, my little love, had to be left at the hotel as we were not sure of her "wedding manners." She had a special bowl of fresh fish to compensate her for missing the banquet.

I wore a vintage lace dress that I feel sure must have belonged to Rita Hayworth when she was married to Aly Khan, here on the Côte d'Azur all those years ago. It was glamorous and low-cut and ruched up the rear like old-time cinema curtains. Very sexy. Which, to tell the truth, is exactly the way I was feeling. I wore dangly pearl earrings and carried a bouquet of pinky-red roses, and as usual, my pointy red shoes were killing me.

A small retinue of children threw rose petals and waved banners as we left the church, laughing and greeting people, and I swear our happiness was contagious.

Afterward, we dined and drank champagne at a bistro in

the Place des Lices, with Bad Dog sneaking every morsel he could from the plates. Jack wore a permanent smile and, clutching his hand, I fizzed like the champagne with delight. Everyone was laughing, the band played under the plane trees, and lovers kissed in the shadows.

Later, we sailed off in the old sloop for our three-day honeymoon, floating happily around the Mediterranean. Did I mention earlier that I hated boats? I've changed my mind. Making love rocked by the waves can do that for you.

Bad Dog went with us, of course. He goes everywhere with us. He sleeps at the foot of our bed and Chocolate sleeps on my pillow. (By the way, the gold lamé has been replaced with white linen.) At least, Bad Dog starts out at the foot of the bed and Chocolate at the top. Come morning, though, Bad Dog's cute little black nose is usually propped on my chin. I open my eyes and find both he and Chocolate staring intently at me, willing me to wake up. I know Bad Dog wants me to take him to the market where he'll find food. Like me, this dog is food obsessed, while Chocolate (also like me) wants love and attention.

Jack still has his boatbuilding business in Rhode Island which he visits regularly, but he's put Carlos in charge there. Now he's opening a local branch, and, of course, he still plans on doing those sunset cruises around the bay for our guests.

And as for me, the nester-in-chief, this time my "nest" is complete. I have a special person to love and to cherish, to laugh with, to make love with—and I have to say that making love with Jack Farrar makes my toes curl.

I sigh with happiness as I walk up the steps and along the terrace to the kitchen. Nadine gives me a welcoming good-morning grin. The new assistant, a replica of last year's Marit, is rolling out the croissant dough and singing along to the radio, and as usual our new "youth of all work" is late. *C'est la même vie,* here at the Hotel Riviera. Everything's the same.

After a quick cup of coffee and a consultation, I decide we'll go for the spiny Mediterranean lobsters as our special tonight, with a mustardy aioli sauce, and a salad of mesclun greens topped with wild mushrooms and shavings of Parmesan in a light vinaigrette. Then the lamb from Sisteron, of course, and how about that lavender crème brûlée?

I snatch up my list, whistle for Bad Dog, and amble toward the car. The dog's in it almost before I have the door open. He sits there panting, glancing impatiently at me, as though I'm holding him up from some important meeting. I'm not sure if it's that, like his master, he can't bear to leave my side, or simply the allure of those gleanings from the marketplace. The vendors all know him by now and most of them feed him. In fact, he's getting quite portly. "Hmm, might be a diet for you, Bad Dog," I say, just as Jack comes tearing around the corner, hitching up his shorts and waving madly at me.

"What's up?" I ask, rolling down the window with that soppy madly-in-love smile on my face.

"Don't ever leave without saying goodbye," he says, snaking his arms around me through the open window and pressing my head against his chest.

His heart beats in my ear and I clutch him even closer. "But you were sleeping."

"Then wake me up. Just don't leave me. Ever."

"I won't," I say, linking my eyes with his in a promise, as we disentwine ourselves.

I wave goodbye and chug up the lane in my trusty old Deux Chevaux, stopping at the junction with the road to admire our new "Welcome to the Hotel Riviera" sign, grinning as I read "Under New Management." And, of course, as the sign promises, our welcome will always be bigger than our small but perfect hotel.

So, Jack and I, and, of course, Miss Nightingale, are looking forward to seeing you again, and to sharing those long summer days on the beach. We look forward to the sunset cruises and to perfect evenings dining on the flowery terrace, where the wine is cool and hopefully the men are hot, and the food is as delicious as I can make it, with, of course, the perfect brownie to top it off. Which, as always, will be made with love.

À bientôt, mes amis. Until then.